WINGS AND TEETH

CYBORG SHIFTERS #9

NAOMI LUCAS

Once a wartime hero, Keir was famous for a Cyborg, his face plastered on military banners on every side of the galaxy.

But he wasn't a hero, not really.

He was a hunter, Nightheart's free agent for the most classified missions. No one knew Keir worked for the EPED. He was beholden to no one. Stalking the most dangerous monsters across the universe.

So, when he encounters a beautiful, intriguing woman in the alien wilds on his latest assignment, he's immediately taken aback. She's smart, capable, and completely unafraid of her surroundings, no matter how brutal. But she's scared of *him*.

She has a past, one she refuses to share, and it's connected to everything he's been searching for.

Luckily, there's no one more determined than Keir... Now that he has his mate to capture.

For everyone who wanted Keir to be a bat. Guess what!
He's not.

ONE

Echo scanned the trees, waiting for the leaves to shift. As quietly as she could, she hunkered farther into the bushy foliage around her.

She'd been tracking the ashtrax across the plains all morning, stalking behind the herd. Lumbering, indifferent creatures, the ashtrax traveled in massive packs, spanning thousands. Normally uncaring of the wilds around them, they only attacked when approached, swarming around their target and crushing them under their hooves.

Echo wiped her brow across the sleeve of her jacket. There was a group of adolescent ashtrax forming on the edge of the herd that she had her eyes on.

Their jaws were large and strong, and if one got ahold of her—even a young bull—she'd be obliterated, flung back and forth until her limbs snapped and her body broke, only then to be dropped and trampled upon by the others.

The ashtrax were grazers, not meat eaters, yet had no

problem killing in defense, even actively doing so with premeditation.

Because on Utha's moon, Volun, everything else here was even more vicious. And that viciousness skyrocketed the days before a burnout.

The change in the air made Volun's natural inhabitants restless.

Her earpiece blipped, startling Echo, almost alerting the ashtrax of her presence. Inhaling, she reached up and adjusted the device, ending the noise. It would be Jonah or Gregory—she'd see them soon enough. Frequently, she received comms from them from within the compound. They were always needing something.

Everyone always needed something. As the compound's primary hunter and tech support, her tasks were endless.

But food—fresh meat—was in low supply. So it was either bring in a kill now, or wait several weeks after the burnout.

Echo glimpsed the sky.

Fat storm clouds streaked across it, blending seamlessly into the constant gloomy ambience of Volun's landscape. The sun partially hid behind the giant planet, Utha, casting across the moon with a miasma of blustery twilight. The sun was too close and too large for a world like Volun, but with Utha blocking most of it, and the near-constant cloud cover rolling in from the oceans west of the mountains, it was habitable.

Yet with each of Utha's rotations, there came burnouts

—times when the planets were not aligned, leaving Volun briefly in the direct path of the sun.

Something flashed, drawing Echo's gaze to her right, and she dropped her hand from her ear. She focused on the anomaly; it twinkled as it flew over the mountain peaks.

Not a razorbeak queen.

A ship?

Her brows furrowed.

There were no ships scheduled for landing—at least none that she was aware of. Deliveries from offworld happened several times a standard year. Everyone in the compound was notified about deliveries weeks in advance so they had time to prepare their wares for bartering, their messages to be sent out to family, and medical visits, if the corresponding delivery ship also had doctors.

Echo hunkered farther into the bushes. The ship soared above one peak and toward the next, barely more than a speck in the distance.

Was it someone from the south? Echo squinted.

No... The ship couldn't be from the southern colony. No one there had a working vessel anymore, nor had access to one. And those from the south wouldn't be caught dead using a ship anyway.

Jonah? No. Greg? No.

She'd know if one of them was out scouting the area because it was her job to do so. They wouldn't send another without telling her first.

Unless...

Echo closed her eyes as her guesses turned a dark corner.

An offworlder.

A trespasser.

Old worries surged to the forefront of her thoughts. She fisted her hands and loosened them, allowing the emotions to take their course, letting the immediate flare of anxiety flood her only for her to exhale it out. She gave in to it, knowing she was alone and no one was around to see her.

She was safe.

The blipping went off in her ear again, and Echo cursed under her breath. This time, she checked who was trying to reach out, seeing Jonah's name appear on her wristcon.

She cursed again, sitting back on her haunches. The timing of his calls couldn't be a coincidence. If she saw a ship, he'd know there was one within the vicinity too. Jonah monitored the sky whereas she monitored the land.

Despite the wind, clouds, and general bleak atmosphere here, the compound still used and maintained the old security systems the military had installed long ago. Though generations out of date, it was better than what most outer world colony security measures had. Immensely better.

Echo rose and headed for her bike to answer the call when one of the adolescent ashtrax wandered away from the herd. She paused to see if it would return to the fold, but the ashtrax wandered deeper into the brush instead.

She unsheathed her knife and crouched.

With her focus back on the hunt, Jonah's call and the ship slipped from her thoughts.

The ashtrax grunted, huffed the air while long threads of dried-up grain swayed around its thick brown legs, and headed for a patch of rockflower growing out from a boulder to her right.

Some luck was on her side today after all.

She checked her net and readied a sleeping dart, sticking it in her mouth as she left her hiding spot. Keeping low, she followed the young ashtrax to where it snuffed at the flowers. She had waited hours for this opportunity. One adolescent ashtrax had enough meat to feed the entire compound several times over.

Shuffling closer, she unlocked the mechanism on her net and placed it aside. Afterward, she positioned the blowpipe of the dart in her mouth, making sure it was clear and the toxins hadn't congealed.

Echo dug her teeth into the blowpipe's indents. The ashtrax was grazing the flowers, completely unaware. She glanced at her net one last time. Despite mastering the process, the moments before a kill were always the most stressful. She inhaled deeply and aimed her blowpipe.

Her earpiece buzzed.

Echo blew the dart.

It connected directly with the ashtrax's neck. The beast jerked. Snapping its head side to side, the ashtrax tried to swipe the dart off with one of its long ears. But the cartilage wasn't strong enough to knock it out. Echo counted down from one hundred, praying the dart's paralytic agents took hold before the beast returned to the herd.

The ashtrax took a single step and limped forward,

crashing to the ground when it tried to take another right after. It huffed, tried to rise, and grunted once, dropping again. Then its ears drooped and its eyes closed. The body settled into the grasses with a final snort.

Echo grabbed her net and approached the beast.

One deep slash across the ashtrax's neck and it was dead.

Blood spilled over her hand as she pulled her knife back. She unleashed her net. The cords cinched around its large frame, tightening until the net locked back together fully around the corpse. Two drones detached from the net's clutch, hauling the body off of the ground.

After wiping her hands on the grass, she took hold of the clutch and made her way back to her bike.

The compound would have fresh meat.

She smiled and imagined Gregory's face when she delivered the ashtrax to him to clean and butcher this evening. He was a hunter like her—had even taught her much of what she knew—but Greg was getting old and tired like everyone else and now remained behind the compound's walls most of the time. He had eased into retirement over the past decade, and Echo couldn't blame him.

Hunting, cleaning, and butchering took a lot of physical work. She'd had to step in more and more over the years.

Glimpsing her bike, Echo jogged the rest of the way toward it. She latched her net and stretched before hooking her leg over the seat and tearing out her earpiece.

There were three calls and one message waiting for her.

Her fingers strained across her wristcon as she played the message.

"Call me back, Echo. It's an emergency."

She dragged her eyes back to the mountains, searching the sky. She couldn't avoid Jonah and the ship she spied earlier for much longer. Powering up her bike, she commed Jonah back. He answered on the first ring.

"Echo, why haven't you been picking up?" His tone was full of accusation and worry. It slammed all her misgivings right back into the forefront of her mind.

"I was on a hunt, kinda still am," she answered evenly. "What's the matter?"

"Ah, hell. I should've known."

Echo rubbed her eyes. "I took down what I was after. I'll be heading into the compound soon, and with fresh meat. What's the emergency?"

Jonah was paranoid but loyal, a worrier who was more stubborn than most. Being the compound's overseer to a bunch of elderly veterans, one had to be. He was a lot of effort to deal with but worth the time in doing so because underneath his often blustery exterior was a man who'd fight to the bitter end for those he cared about.

And he cared about the compound and those within it more than anything, except perhaps her.

When her father left, Jonah had stepped in, even though she didn't need nor want him to, and because of that, she'd handled him with more patience and caring than the others. How could she not? Unlike her parents, Jonah was a constant in her life.

"Oh, good. That's good," Jonah said. "We'll need the extra protein in the days to come. We have a problem, and I was going to have you come into the compound anyway. Not only don't I have time to check the weather data from the outposts, but there's also been a breach in our airspace. I thought at first it was an error, but—"

"I spotted a ship." Her eyes drifted to the mountain peaks again.

A long, grunt-like sigh filled her ear—Echo had her answer. The dread building in her chest morphed right into exhaustion. Prepping for a burnout was already stressful enough, but to now have to deal with a trespasser on top of it?

Thoughts tumbled through her head... Iron, bars, fire, restraints, and the scent of burning flesh and heated metal. Piercing, furious eyes staring at her, promising death, promising torture. Eyes that permeated retribution for the murder she committed...

Her mind drifted to the poignant silence that followed those memories when none of it had come to pass.

Because she had won.

Echo loosened up her hands; her palms were clammy.

"Well, hell." Jonah sighed. "That settles that then."

She stared at the peaks and inhaled, filling her lungs to the max and holding the air there, letting the pressure expand uncomfortably. Jonah sighed again. Because unlike everyone else in the compound, he knew more of her secrets than most.

"Do you know anything more than that yet?" she asked, exhaling a giant breath. "Who they might be?"

"Not yet. I've only been aware of the breach for a couple of hours. No contact has been made yet on their end. I've tried to reach out but am unable to connect. I think it's the weather."

"Maybe they'll move on."

One could hope.

"And go where?" He grunted. "If my readings here are accurate, the ship's been scouting the plains around the compound, the mountains beyond. And it only appeared after it had already entered the atmosphere. Who knows how long it's been here before we caught it?"

"So, whoever they are, they're getting a lay of the land," she whispered, looking down at her bike.

"It seems so."

"All right," Echo said, straightening. "I'm coming in. I'll see you soon at Greg's garage. We'll talk more then. Out."

She thrust her earpiece into her pocket, unlocking her bike's break at the same time.

Heading toward the compound, she prayed whoever was flying the ship wasn't a Cyborg.

Because only two types of people trespassed on Volun: criminals and Cyborgs. And out of the two, criminals were far, far easier to kill.

TWO

THE WIND WHIPPED Keir's hair.

Fields of high, sharp grasses danced for miles. Trees like long sticks and giant fan-like leaves were scattered throughout the grass, catching the wind, and ballooning outward. Boulders and large rocks were amongst the plains, and with the random tree groupings between them, it seemed as if they had at some point rained down from the sky.

Surrounding the plains on nearly all sides were mountains. They, and the plains, framed an old military space base far south of him in one giant ring. A nearly deserted compound.

It took him half the night to fly around the space base's periphery and get a lay of the land to figure out what he was dealing with; to create a blueprint in his mind. But it was the landscape's harrowing beauty that had him investigate further afield.

Streams and rivers came down from the mountains to end in deep springs, and beyond the mountains to the west, there laid an ocean. Large and gray and bleak.

And the mountains...

Jagged peaks like spiraling needles jutted up into the sky, piercing the heavy cloud coverage above. He'd never seen mountains like the ones here. Volun was covered in them, decorated with massive ranges framing even larger swathes of plains across the whole moon. Against the planet Utha and the gray skies in the background, Volun was a staggering sight at first glance.

The landmass before him appeared wounded as if it had been beaten upon by giants for thousands of years. Which it had been, at least for a few generations, by the military.

There were two human colonies left on Volun, one to the south of him within the confines of the base, and a smaller one even further south. The larger colony was established nearly two hundred years ago and had once thrived with thousands of humans, brought here by expansion and new-age *manifest destiny*, and then war.

Now, nearly six decades after the Intergalactic War against the Trentians, and two hundred years later, there were maybe a hundred and fifty colonists left, and the space base had long been shut down.

All that remained were some humans and outdated infrastructure.

Volun was no longer open to travel; it wasn't even listed as a colony on the network. For a colony that used to thrive and be funded by the military, there was almost no information about Utha's moon anywhere.

The only concrete information Keir had on the subject was that it had been shut down due to inhospitable weather and a lack of resources, not only for the colonists to conduct trade but also to sustain the base. During the war, Volun's space base would have been a waypoint for the army, but now that the war was over, it was near useless being so far from Earth.

He shifted on his feet. The freedom of the moon called to him. It was a habitable world that mainstream humanity had abandoned. An *open* world. The plates in his back urged him to release his wings and to master it, take control, make it his own.

Keir's eyes shot across the landscape a hundred times over, taking in every detail.

And as for a mission, being sent to an open world, with little to no humans on it, was as good as it could get for him. The less time he spent in the company of humans, the happier he was.

The two things Volun had going for it were that it had an atmosphere close to Earth, and it was central to four major spaceports—just barely keeping the moon connected to the rest of civilization. There were still several commercial goods deliveries to Volun each standard year.

Keir palmed his mouth and turned away from the land.

Animals remembered. Instinctually, they remembered. Why couldn't he?

No part of him—machine, beast, or man—recollected

anything about Volun except for what he'd read. He scoured through his earliest memories, and there wasn't even a glimmer.

Yet he always knew there wouldn't be.

He only recalled the final conversation he had with his cybernetic engineers before they plugged him in and erased the location of his birth, and all other damaging information the Trentians could use against him and humanity as a whole if her were ever captured, before they were allowed to 'release' him.

Only, Keir thought there would at least be a feeling... A sense of déjà vu.

Something.

Keir looked down at the dust swirling around his boots. Each singular piece of dirt was a detail he noted. Nightheart believed Volun had the answers he was searching for: the birth of real, functioning Cyborgs. Their beginning. At least for those who belonged to the shifter class.

Keir frowned and turned in the direction where the old space base was.

Finish the mission and get paid. Get paid and return to Titan.

Each thread, each rumor, each whisper was important enough to Nightheart to be investigated, and that was what Keir did for the Swarm. It was the only thing Keir did for him. During the times between new leads, Keir resided among the war-ravaged lands on Titan, a planet much like Earth, but bigger, and far less inhabited now, devastated by Trentian Knights and *their* ships.

Titan had once been the second biggest human colonized world in the known universe. New Mecca. Humanity's future.

Now, it was still reeling from an ecological disaster on par with modern-day Earth.

With the payment Nightheart promised him—billions, including the EPED's complete support—Keir could finally jumpstart Titan's revival. Until now, he'd been buying up all the land he could on the ravaged planet, ensuring no human or Trentian could touch it.

Then Nightheart promised him billions in relief. The EPED had already donated much to Titan's restoration, but nowhere near the amount Nightheart was offering now. *To shift recovery funds from Earth to Titan...* Keir palmed his mouth.

Whatever Nightheart wanted from their old cybernetics laboratory was worth enough to him to consider political warfare.

It wasn't what Keir's hawk *wanted*—returning to civilization—but it was what he needed. What their home needed. And until his bird had all the freedom it wanted and *he* was left alone, Keir would never know true peace. There had been none after the war ended, not for him. Because, no matter where he went, people still fucking recognized him. Even after generations, people still knew who he was.

His lips twisted.

He wanted to be left alone, in an environment that agreed with him, and forgotten.

Keir released his wings, strode off the ledge, and dove to the plains below where he had landed his planetary ship. He touched down gently beside it and brought his wings back inside of him.

The small planetary craft wasn't his main ship. It was only deployed to bring bartering goods with him and to not frighten the locals. Arriving at the space base in a war vessel would give the people here the wrong message.

Keeping low to the ground, Keir headed for the compound, catching every last detail and pitfall. Nothing got past him and his eyes, not even the old hoverbike hidden in the shadows of a large boulder he'd spotted hours earlier. As he passed the boulder again, the bike was gone.

He slowed his skiff.

The bike had been the only human activity he'd seen outside the base's walls since his arrival. With one glance at the hunting supplies sticking out of a pack attached to the vehicle, he'd decided to move on and come back later.

Now, in the bike's place was a splattering of blood and several small creatures around it. Stopping his skiff, he got out and approached the blood, bringing forth his talons. Kneeling down, one whiff told him it wasn't human.

Good for them.

Whoever was out hunting today bagged their prey.

Keir walked back to his ship and wondered if he'd beat them to the compound.

THREE

RETURNING to the old military base was easy. No map was needed. The plains the base resided in had been partially leveled out and cleared for miles outside it in every direction. Apparently, the plains were still clear decades later, due to the ground having been churned up and destroyed by the thousands of spacecrafts that had once landed and been stored here. Decades later, only small shrubs had returned.

He'd seen it all before on other worlds, on other space bases. Humans destroyed as much as they created. He was beginning to think life and death had a balance in the universe much like energy. For everything a human created, something, somewhere was destroyed.

By the time the base came into his view, the clouds were darkening overhead. Utha's sun was descending behind them.

It was time for him to officially announce his arrival.

Connecting to the only signal his ship could find around the base, Keir sent a request for landing.

His request was answered immediately.

Keir slowed his ship. It had been a possibility. He hadn't tried all that hard to remain hidden. He hadn't shielded his electrical signature in any way and would easily be picked up by any standard satellite reading.

The colony's knowledge of his arrival told him the space base's security measures were still somewhat intact. He wasn't dealing with anti-tech cultists. *Thank the devil.*

As he neared the landing field, several people came out of nearby buildings to watch his descent.

Even from a distance, at speed, and through glass, he saw every detail of them; every wrinkle, every patched up stitch to their clothes, every shift of their features. He caught everything. The few below were old, grizzled people, remnants of a life he and his kind put to rest many years ago. One of the humans, the one that headed directly for the airfield, had a gun resting on his hip and a scowl on his face.

Some people never moved on.

At least Keir understood these people, probably better than most. Humans only chose to live a remote life if they valued their privacy and their freedoms above everything else. It was either that, or fear. Fear kept humans from wanting to be a part of a community. He was the former, though, as a Cyborg, he had no need for community.

The man coming out to greet him with the gun sported a bulging stomach. With a frame smoothed over by layers of fat, he stood as if the extra weight was a shield, defying the mass. For some reason, Keir was reminded of Cypher. If Cypher were old and had eaten enough food that even his own cybernetic metabolism couldn't keep up.

The human wore a thick, faded flannel shirt that had seen better days, sported salt and pepper facial hair, and had deep wrinkles across his brow. He had a worn-down, no-nonsense air about him, and appeared eager to put Keir in his place for invading his dominion.

Keir hadn't expected anything different. There would be no warm welcome for him. Not on a secluded base with a potentially-segmented, and feudal caste system. Solely based on the crumbs of information Nightheart gave him about Volun in its current state, the colony didn't get many visitors. In fact, it wasn't growing at all.

Landing his skiff in the open spot of the field, Keir surveyed the land once more before ducking out to greet his surly welcomer.

The man came to a stop a short distance away and scanned Keir over. One of his bushy eyebrows twitched when their eyes met, narrowing upon him. He then saluted. "Welcome to Volun, Commander Keir," he rumbled, his whiskers cinching, his voice filled with disdain.

Keir halted. "You know me."

"There's a large portrait of you collecting dust in one of the old warehouses. If that's what you're here for, you can take it. We have no use for art here. You commanded, were on the frontlines, battled several Knights of Xanteaus during the war, and had survived it all. Of course I know who you are. I served my time. I served under your brethren. I thank you for your service," the man ended with a spat. "But it's time for you to turn around and leave."

Keir cocked his head, annoyed. He was still recognized, it seemed, even on a forgotten moon like Volun.

Great.

"I thank you for your service too," Keir lied right back. "And no, I'm not here for the picture. When I was put into the field, the military wanted a face, someone to rally the troops and to protect them. Many people saw me, knew me, and from there I became a beacon of salvation. At the time, I had little choice in the matter. I would prefer you burn it."

His time as a glorified mascot was an embarrassment to him.

He didn't want to be known or recognized. He didn't want the whole fucking universe after him, his services, and the priceless technology under his skin. If there was a portrait of him, the man depicted upon it wasn't a hero. Yes, he was a commander. But he had never battled any Knights of Xanteaus, nor had he ever once been at any real risk. Those were all lies.

No, it had been his brethren who had warred, not Keir. He'd been too busy behind cameras, shaking hands and convincing young men and women to sacrifice their lives and join the fight. All while knowing he'd be the one better off fighting.

"I don't care about your face, Cyborg," the man barked.

"Neither do I."

They eyed each other, and the longer his welcomer scowled, the more Keir's jaw locked up.

The overseer didn't trust him.

Interesting.

Keir ran his tongue across his teeth, recalculating his approach to the situation.

The man broke the silence first. "If it isn't the picture you want, you won't find whatever else you're looking for. We don't want you or your kind here."

"Why would you say that?" Keir was intrigued by the turn of events. There were many humans who despised his kind. But this man was clearly a veteran and had served with or under other Cyborgs, fighting for the same cause, the same side, willing to die for it. Usually, it was civilians who didn't like his kind, not soldiers. The military had always been pro-mecha. "I haven't told you why I'm here. Or are you just assuming?"

"Because you're here for the same reason every Cyborg that ends up here is for."

Keir stilled at the man's words. There had been other Cyborgs here before him? "And tell me," he said carefully, "what reason is that?"

The man smiled, and it wasn't a pleasant one. "You won't get information out of me that easily. You best do what the others have done and leave. Now, before I notify the space guard and make your presence known. You are trespassing."

Keir shifted on his feet, glancing at the several other colonists at the edge of the landing field watching them.

The wind gusted, making dust streak across the rough pavement around his boots.

It was true, Keir *was* trespassing.

"I don't plan on staying long. No more than a few days at most," he reassured them. "I'm here to simply tour the base and learn about its history. Perhaps we can make a trade?" He turned back to his welcomer.

The man's eyes narrowed. "No. No trades. There's nothing we want or need from you. You'd do best to turn around and leave." His voice rose as he placed his hand on the gun at his side. "Before I'm forced to make you."

"I have liquor, beer." Keir indicated the skiff behind him. "Medical supplies. Screws, nails, and bullets. Chocolate for the children—"

"You're all the same."

"We are?"

"You come here, for whatever godforsaken reason, only to find after several days, weeks, months of being here, you've wasted your damned time. And in that damned time, you ingratiate yourself with my people, messing up our way of life, creating chaos, and causing grief. You show up right before a burnout knowing we'll be distracted, probably hoping we'll need your help—"

"Jonah, did he say chocolate?" a woman's voice called out.

Keir looked up to see an older woman approaching them from behind Jonah.

"Linda, let me handle this," Jonah growled over his shoulder. The woman ignored him and continued onward anyway. He sighed when she neared. "Best go back to Madeline, Linda. I've got this handled."

Linda stopped and met Keir's eyes. "You're a handsome one. Let me get an eyeful of you, young man. Did I hear you commanded?"

Keir straightened under her blatant perusal. He'd been called worse. Much worse. Men and women had always found his features intriguing, but for as many who thought him attractive, there were just as many who found his hawkish appearance unsettling.

The woman, who couldn't be much younger than Jonah —now that he had a name for his welcomer—had sharp, analytical eyes.

"Thank you, ma'am. And yes, I commanded." The words tasted sour on Keir's tongue.

"Linda, you really should leave this to—" Jonah tried to interject again.

"You're welcome." Linda popped a brow at Keir. "You say you have chocolate?"

"Linda," Jonah hissed. "This is not the time or place."

She waved him away. "He's already here. Might as well see what he has to offer. And he couldn't arrive at a better time, right? We always need all the help we can get in the heat. Come with me...Keir, is it? And I'll set you up for a place for the night for some of that chocolate of yours. We still have an extra bed made up after Lenneth's passing that will suit you just fine. He was a tall man, just like you."

Finding his opening, Keir turned his full attention to Linda. "I do have chocolate."

Jonah's bearing diminished as Linda smiled.

Not everyone here had a prejudice against him. Which —*thank the devils*—would make his mission easier.

Because, at the end of the day, he didn't want to be here, with these humans, at all. He would love to hightail it home and make Jonah happy.

Linda grabbed his arm and began leading him toward the uniform industrial buildings before them. The others that had come out to watch them, scattered.

"You're wasting your time," Jonah warned, trudging behind. "Both of you. There isn't a type of chocolate in all the universe that could survive through the next two weeks, Linda, and there isn't anything here for you, Cyborg."

"Don't listen to him. He's our overseer, self-appointed sheriff, president, supreme ruler of Volun, and the orneriest fellow you'll ever have the pleasure of meeting. He takes the job far, far too seriously." Linda patted Keir's arm like he needed comforting. "Nobody likes him. But I'm afraid he's right, you won't find what you're looking for here. Everything that had been left here by the military has long since been recycled, scavenged, and sold off."

"I can hear you, woman," Jonah grumbled. "I'm not deaf. You try to do my job and keep everyone safe, nobody'll like you either."

Linda snorted.

"I'm not here to scavenge," Keir interjected. "You two seem to know why I'm here. Do you often have Cyborgs come visiting?"

Linda squeezed his arm. "Not in years, but we'll have

you talk to Echo soon enough. You already called her, Jonah?" Linda looked over her shoulder at the man. "She's coming into town? She's got a great deal of knowledge of the subject. She and Hanna housed the last one that came through here."

Jonah's face fell at Linda's words but then quickly recovered. "Yes. Echo's aware."

Keir's eyes narrowed upon him. "Echo?"

"See? Jonah's just giving you a hard time. We'll get you set up for the night, and Echo will answer all your questions in good time. She's the one to talk to if you're curious about our history. Though I'm afraid it's not that interesting. Once the military shut down the base, they transported out the enlisted soldiers and removed their machinery. We're all that's left." She pointed at the buildings before them. "We've been nothing but a small civilian colony since. But in the meantime, you and that chocolate, and any gossip you may have, are mine, young man. It's been months since I last caught a whiff of what's happening in the universe."

"And you shall have it," Keir agreed, his thoughts shifting to the woman named Echo.

If this Echo held answers and was willing to work with him, he'd be back on Titan by the end of the month. And if she also knew why others of his kind had ventured here, he needed to know. Keir glanced at the swirling torrent of clouds overhead and off into the distance where he could still see the jagged mountain peaks piercing them.

He frowned. He'd been here for a day. In that time, he had far, far more questions than answers since he'd arrived.

FOUR

THE COMPOUND's lights were on by the time she made it to the inner gates of the base.

"It's Echo. Open up," she called out, parking her bike off to the side of the road and looking up at the two lights flashing on the wall high above her.

"Hey, Echo," someone grumbled. "Give me a second."

Several minutes later she was through and walking her load to Gregory's garage. The garage used to be a ship bunker but was now sectioned off into smaller spaces for skinning and cleaning kills, storing local resources, and placing up shops or bartering wares between residents. The high-rafter ceilings, still holding old hangar equipment, gave the space an open, welcoming feel.

When Echo was younger, there used to be big celebrations here, except now, no one had the energy for them anymore. Now, it was just the center of their 'colony' and a place for everyone to gather and talk.

As she neared, she noticed the large garage was open and lit as residents prepared for the coming burnout. Extra cots were being set up, industrial fans were being pulled out of storage, and capsules of water were being filled. A gust of wind pulled some of her hair out from her hairband as she took in the progress being made. Echo hunkered against it and lowered her chin to her chest, swiping the strands from her face.

When she looked up again, she spotted Gregory standing with Jonah and several others deeper within the space. They were conversing in hushed voices, their heads tilted towards one another, with cigs in their hands.

The conversation dropped when they caught sight of her.

Gregory acknowledged her with a nod. "Hey, Echo's finally here."

Bypassing them, she lugged her kill to the weight in-take platform. Jonah and Gregory came striding toward her. "Hi."

Gregory eyed the dead ashtrax while Echo removed her netting, drawing it back within its rod with a huff. "Good kill. The cut could be a little better, but otherwise, I don't think this guy felt much pain." He patted the stiff hide.

"Thanks." Echo rose up with a huff. "I was distracted."

"Do you think you're well enough to take over the cleaning, Greg?" Jonah asked him, appreciating her kill with a nod of his own. "I need to catch Echo up."

"Hmm..." Gregory looked between them warily, making

Echo immediately suspicious. "I suppose I could," he said, though, not sounding happy about it.

"I can prepare it later." She side-eyed both men until Jonah turned and walked away. "But I'm not staying inside the walls tonight. It'll have to hang in the freezer for a bit before I can get to it."

Gregory waved his hand. "No, no, I'll take care of it. You're busy."

She narrowed her eyes. "You sure?"

Gregory kneeled beside the dead ashtrax and started saying a prayer, giving her his answer. Whatever he and Jonah had been discussing before she arrived, he didn't want to get further involved in it, at least not with her. Echo sighed and turned to Jonah, who was now waiting for her outside. Joining him, she braced herself.

"I thought the last one would be it." Jonah offered her a cig.

She waved it away. "Me too."

"I don't like this, Echo. We can't have a repeat of what happened last time. Not with this one. We were damned lucky it didn't turn out worse."

And there it was. Echo scrubbed her face. She'd hoped it wasn't a Cyborg's ship she'd spotted in the sky. She prayed all the way here and far more adamantly than Gregory's prayers over the ashtrax. "Have you corresponded with them yet?"

"Him. And yes, several hours ago he made his official arrival. He's with Linda and Madeline right now, doing something with chocolate."

"Chocolate?" She frowned. "I don't understand? At least they'll keep him preoccupied. Linda loves talking. What's this about chocolate?"

Jonah grunted a laugh. "Yeah, she does. Chocolate, you know? That brown sugary stuff people love?"

Echo shook her head slowly.

"Ah, never mind. Are we..." Jonah sobered and peered to her left, into the growing shadows of twilight. His eyes clouded.

"We'll handle it like we did the last one. *I'll* handle him," she corrected. The last thing she needed was Jonah to get too involved. It was safer that way.

"I can't let you do that. Hanna isn't here, and your father..." He shook his head. "What happened last time shouldn't have ever—"

"Did he tell you why he's here?" Jonah had a tendency to go on tirades, and she neither had the time nor the patience for one right now.

"To tour the place," Jonah spat. "Dumbest non-answer I've ever heard."

Her frown deepened. Non-answer it was. But an answer from a Cyborg nonetheless. "That's all he said? He made no mention that he was searching for someone or someplace?"

"He didn't know another had been here before him."

"Wait." Echo straightened. "What did you say? You told him?"

"Told him what?"

"That another of his kind has been here before him?"

"I didn't outright."

"But you still did?"

Jonah growled. "I didn't say one way or another. Linda butted in and took over."

Echo's stomach curled into a ball. "If he wasn't looking for someone before, he will be now!" She cursed, a thousand thoughts racing through her head all at once. And none of them were good. It was one thing if the Cyborg was here, searching for his 'past'. It was another thing entirely if he was searching for a missing person. A missing *Cyborg*. Her lips flattened. "It's too late now. That settles it then."

Jonah took a long drag from his cig. "Settles what exactly?" He blew out the smoke.

Echo watched the smoke take off with the breeze. "Jonah, I'm tired. It's been a long couple of days tracking the weather readings and hunting. Let's not hash this out again. Our plan, albeit as simple as it is, will work. It has to. I've got this. I'll convince him that whatever he's looking for, well, it's not here. It never was. It never will be. Just like we discussed. He'll realize this and leave. Let's hope he's telling the truth and just wants some historical tour. We could get lucky."

Could a Cyborg feel nostalgic? She didn't think so. Although they did have long memories which was even worse.

"It's not like I want him here any more than you do," Jonah growled.

The wind picked up, gusting into her side. Echo

steadied and took a step back towards the garage. "He'll be gone before the week's end, I guarantee it."

"You're a good liar, but not that good. You think you can convince him when you can't even convince me? Girl, I taught you better. You'll be better off throwing on a skirt and acting dumb."

She threw her hands up into the air. "I'm not lying!"

"And if he attacks you like how Ares attacked Hanna? Who will be there to watch your back?"

Echo hesitated, her eyes falling to the ground. "It will never come to that. And if it does, I know how to protect myself."

"I liked our plan a lot more when it didn't need to be used."

"What choice do we have?"

For the next few minutes, they sat in silence while Jonah finished his cig.

She tried not to let his worries burrow into her, but it was of no use. Jonah depended on her because there was no one else left but her for him to depend upon. She was the last one on Volun, besides him, who knew the truth. But even then, Jonah didn't know everything *she* did. Nor did he have nearly the same stakes.

She wasn't going to let him deal with the Cyborg. Not even if it meant she had to face the devil alone. She knew it might always have come to this.

And they did have a plan, not a great one, but a straightforward one.

"Tell me about him, what's he like?" she asked when Jonah stomped out his cig. "Anything I should know?"

"He brought supplies with him."

She arched a brow. "He did? Why?"

The Cyborg didn't need to bring bartering chips to take what he wanted. They had no way to stop him if he tried. The compound had few defenses. Why would he go through the effort of bringing things to barter unless he'd come here amicably?

Oh, how she hoped.

"It doesn't matter what he brought—"

Echo stopped her eyes from rolling. "Tell me his name at least?"

"Keir," Jonah scowled. "Commander Keir. We have a portrait of him in storage. I'd recognized his face anywhere. He's the one with that long hooked nose and those black eyes that follow you everywhere you go. It isn't right."

Echo startled, knowing the exact picture he was refer-ring to. When she was a kid, she used to walk around the painted portrait and see if those eyes would follow her. They always did. "Commander Keir?" She rubbed the back of her neck, feeling those eyes on her now. "Didn't he battle and win against several Trentian Knights?"

"The very same."

"Great," she grumbled. "He's famous."

"Yep. We should tell Auryn—"

"No!" she snapped before she could stop herself. "We are not telling Dad."

Silence fell between her and Jonah again as the last

minutes of the day came to an end and the compound's lights flickered on. Jonah shook his head in disappointment.

Every Cyborg had a military history, whether they commanded or not. But she didn't expect one that she knew, at least their face, to ever show up on Volun. Her father had warned her it could happen—that more might come—just because of what Volun once was, and what the moon could mean to them—if they ever discovered what it hid.

She'd hoped he'd been wrong.

Still, bothering her dad about it would only make things a thousand times worse. She didn't know what he would do in his current state... She didn't want any more death.

"Well, it's time I hit the sack," Jonah said with a frown, watching her closely. I suggest you do the same and get some sleep if you're not staying the night. I don't like you traveling after dark."

"I will," she said, her thoughts still on the Cyborg.

"Good. I don't like what this wind means. It's too soon for it to pick up like this. The garage will only be half-supplied if the weather shifts tomorrow." Jonah wiped his hands on his pants and turned, only to face her again. "You know what this means don't you, Echo?"

She looked up from the dust swirling around her legs. "What?"

"It means the weather is moving fast. It's going to be a real bitch of a week ahead of us. Cyborg or not."

"I'll head to the outposts tomorrow."

"While you're handling the Cyborg too?"

"Yes, Jonah." She sighed wearily. "While I handle him

too. Goodnight." She pushed from the wall and walked away.

Jonah was a man for action and quick solutions, which was why she couldn't hide and let him deal with their visitor. And he had too much on his plate already anyway, being the overseer. He was apt to make a mistake.

She hurried across the crumbling pavement between buildings. The garages, shipping containers, and storage facilities were a short distance from the nearest dormitory where most of the colony's residents lived. Usually there would be others around finishing up their day, but with a burnout storm so close and it getting dark earlier because of it, they were all probably back at the garage preparing or home asleep.

The wind surrounded her as she went, howling in her ears. She uncurled her fists and wiped them on her jacket, wishing they weren't so clammy. Despite the war never reaching Volun's surface, she had always felt surrounded by the ghosts within the compound. The compound made her uneasy. It always had.

Echo stopped and closed her eyes.

She was nervous. Would she admit it? No. Because no good came out of that. Jonah would use it as an excuse to try and take over the situation, and if his plan was to tell her dad, then she couldn't let that happen.

No, the best solution was to face the situation head on.

Seeing lights on in the windows of the dormitory ahead of her, she strode forward.

He's just an enhanced man.

He's not here for me. He doesn't know anything. If Keir asked about Ares—which she knew he would—she was going to be as honest as possible.

Determined to not waste another second with terrible weather on the horizon, and go to the Cyborg at Linda's now, Echo yanked open the front door of the building.

And came face-to-face with *Jeepers Creepers* himself.

FIVE

HELL ON VOLUN, she cursed, jerking away from the Cyborg.

"Are you all right?" He grabbed her arm to steady her.

Echo righted her balance and met Keir's—Commander Keir's—gaze. As she did, a forceful gust of wind blasted her from behind and pushed her forward. The hand on her arm tightened, and before she could yank her limb from his grasp, he tugged her inside the building. Air whistled as the door slammed closed at her back.

"I'm fine." She took a step back and righted her jacket. "I didn't mean to run into you. Sorry." Echo tilted her head back; she had to strain her neck to meet his eyes. "You must be Commander Keir."

He was tall. Very tall. The tallest Cyborg she'd ever met.

"I am." His expression darkened for a moment. He then cocked his head to study her. "Please just call me Keir."

Echo swallowed thickly, taking another small step back.

His head, when uncocked, nearly touched the ceiling, and his lithe frame seemed to go on forever, contoured in the dark shadows made from the weak light cast from a single bulb down the hall from them. Where the light didn't reach, the shadows bled over him, emphasizing his dark clothing and pale face.

Even in the dim light, he looked nothing like Ares.

Ares had been a *God*, giving the ancient name and its meaning justice. Keir didn't have the same impact, despite his height.

"Damn," she breathed out, her brow furrowing. His features, though striking in themselves, faded into the background as she tried to judge just how tall he was. The top of her head lined up with his shoulder. *Seven feet?*

He uncocked his head. "Damn?"

Echo winced. "You're so tall."

"I am." His lips curled into an amused smile. "I needed to be."

"Why?" she asked before she thought better of it.

It wasn't often that she ran into a complete stranger.

Keir was handsome like she knew he would be, but it wasn't because of his perfected genetic features that were given to him by scientists long dead; it was his demeanor that distracted her.

Though she couldn't see his eyes in the low light, they appeared dark. She expected rage, calamity, and death within them but instead only found curiosity and calm interest reflecting back at her. Keir had sharp yet tapered features. His eyes were thin, nearly taken over by his thick, arching eyebrows that framed them with sharpened slants.

His face was long, his nose longer still and slightly hooked, giving him a hawkish appearance. And with his dark hair messy around his ears, his face appeared longer than it was, only tempered by the five-o-clock shadow along his jaw.

Echo felt her blood rush, catching his scent in the air. Heavy with heat, he had a distinct smell that reminded her of the riotous clouds outside.

Wet metal, static electricity, and soap, she decided.

He canted his head in the opposite direction. "My internal frame is large."

Her brow furrowed deeper. "Oh, right..." Echo shook herself, remembering she'd asked him a question. She offered her hand. "That makes sense. My name is Echo. You must be Keir. I was coming to find you. Jonah told me you were with Linda."

"Nice to meet you, Echo. And I was." With his head still cocked, he peered down at her hand and took it before meeting her eyes again. "I just left."

His actions were beginning to make her uneasy.

He was acting strangely.

Why was he cocking his head so much?

With his fingers wrapped fully around her hand, she was snared in his bubble. His hand was hot but not clammy. It didn't feel human, his warmth; it felt mechanical—perfectly regulated across his flesh. Echo's elbows locked, realizing she could still feel the imprints of them on her forearms where his hands had steadied her a minute earlier.

They shook hands.

He didn't release her when she tried to free herself afterward, holding onto her for an extra long moment instead.

When he did finally let her go, she tugged her hand to her chest and held it there.

They stared at each other.

Awkwardness crept into her limbs as he continued to study her face with his head bending from side-to-side. She swallowed again, becoming increasingly confused by what he was doing.

Her fingers twitched. Her breath hitched. She parted her lips to speak.

"I've been looking for you too." He broke the silence first, straightening his neck.

And suddenly, just like that, the tension broke and she found it easier to breathe.

"You were?"

"I was told you would be able to tell me the history of this place. That you would be able to answer some questions for me and possibly help me with my mission."

"I—Yes. Yes," she stated clearer. "That's why I was coming to find you. You're here on a mission?"

"Yes. I am here on a mission."

"What mission is that?"

His lips slowly curved into a smile.

She waited for his answer, bothered by his smile. Her

cheeks reddened when it became apparent he was not going to say any more on the matter. She needed to relax.

If this Cyborg wanted to, he could hurt her, maybe even kill her without a second's thought. She needed to keep her questions inside before she offended him. He might be trespassing, but he was still the one with all the cards.

"Sorry, I didn't mean to interrogate you. What is it you need, exactly?" she amended. "And how can I help? We rarely get visitors."

His smile grew, flustering her further, making her feel even more like an idiot because she didn't know why he was smiling. "I'm here to discover what happened to Volun and uncover its secrets."

Her stomach churned.

Jonah had warned her of his non-answers. But if the Cyborg was going to be vague, while practically goading all the while, she could give him a taste of his medicine.

"I hate to break it to you," she said with a fabricated modicum of regret, "Volun doesn't have many of those, and what it does have, I wouldn't call secrets."

"Ah, but the very nature of this place is shrouded. What would you call them?"

"Rumors," she answered easily.

Keir crossed his arms over his chest, bunching the dark material of his suit over his biceps, making them appear huge. *He wouldn't need a hovernet to drag an ashtrax corpse...* Echo glanced away before he caught her checking them out.

"And that's intriguing in its own right," he said.

"Is it?" She looked back at him. "I think the truth is far more interesting. Volun was once a military stronghold for humanity during the Trentian invasion of the Milky Way Galaxy. Not only is it well hidden and shielded by Utha and its star, Volun's the only habitable location for billions of miles in every direction. Without it, we may have lost Kepler and Gliese."

Echo relaxed, finding comfort in talking about Volun's military history.

"After the Trentians were defeated and the war ended," she continued, "it didn't make sense for the government to keep transporting valuable resources and personnel here when they were needed elsewhere, when so many worlds and colonies had been devastated. Volun was ultimately shut down, stripped, and evacuated by the military. The only people still here are those that decided to remain. The only upset is that the government keeps our colony classified all the same."

"And tell me, Echo, why is that?"

The way he uttered her name made goosebumps rise on her arms.

"It's obvious, isn't it?" She lowered her voice and leaned in conspiratorially. "The government is keeping this place in reserve just in case war should ever break out again. Also, opening the colony up to the general public would be noticed by the Trentians. A failsafe. After the base here was shut down, the military systematically wiped all information about it from all public databases and network servers."

It wasn't a lie. But it wasn't entirely the whole truth. Either way, it was the truth to everyone who was concerned.

Keir's eyes finally left her to look around, and she nearly sagged from the staggering pressure of them having been on her for so long. She felt like a weight had been lifted. For as shaded in shadows they were at the moment, his eyes, black and centered, ringed by storm clouds, pierced like blades straight to the very center of her.

Does he have x-ray vision?

She crossed her arms over her chest.

"I think you're right," he agreed.

She startled. "You do?"

"Yes."

Why did that not make her feel better?

"It's getting late for a human," he said and cocked his head again, the weight of his eyes returning to her. "Your vitals, though stable, indicate fatigue. Do you live in this building as well, Echo?"

"You don't always have to say my name like that," she snapped.

His brow furrowed. "Like what?"

"Like I'm not the only one here."

"Hmm."

"'*Hmm*' is right. But you are correct, I am tired, though we don't have much time," she added, shifting on her feet and peering at the door behind her.

"Is it because of this burnout I keep hearing about?"

She sighed again. "Yeah. The weather is changing and for the worst. Your timing right now is... terrible, at best, because we're about to enter into one any day now. If you don't conclude your mission soon, you might find yourself stuck here for longer than you want to be. Burnouts tend to... burn out ships."

Though his face remained unreadable, she could sense he wasn't happy about the news.

Good.

Maybe she'd get lucky and he would decide to leave on his own.

"But it is getting late," she agreed, her shoulders slumping. "I'm sure you have more questions. Are you free tomorrow evening? I'll be busy helping with preparations during the day."

"I am."

"Great." *Damn.* "We'll meet here and I'll answer whatever it is you want to know if that sounds good?"

"I would like that."

"Good," she said, solidifying their plans, gritting her teeth, even though he continued to stare at her with his disconcerting eyes. She wished she had the courage to stare back at him the same way and take in every detail, but she didn't. It would only give him more allowance to do the same, to go even further. "Tomorrow evening, then."

"Can I walk you to your door?"

The question took her aback. "Door? No. I don't live here." She turned toward the exit and pushed it open. "But I'm walking by the landing field if you need help getting back to your ship."

Wind blasted her face. Echo headed into the darkness,

relieved to no longer have walls enclosed around the two of them. She sucked in the cooler air, not realizing how badly she'd needed space.

Echo heard him follow her outside.

"Where do you live?" he asked when she faced him after he closed the dormitory door. He looked around at the other non-descript, evenly spaced-out buildings around them.

"Outside."

"Outside?" His gaze honed in on her. "Outside... the compound?"

"Yes, outside the compound," she huffed, unable to keep the sarcasm from her voice. "I've spent most of my life there. Come." She walked away before he could ask any more questions about her living arrangements. She'd heard enough of it from Jonah over the years. "I can give you a little tour while we head to the field."

Echo pointed to the buildings around them as they went, telling him what they were once used for and what they were used for now, and who they had been named after, adding tidbits of history. He remained silent at her side for the short trip, practically glowering now, and she wondered if he even cared about anything she was saying. Swallowing against the tightness in her throat, she continued anyway, pretending he did.

He wasn't here for the base despite what he'd said. She slanted her gaze in his direction, wondering when, and if, Keir would drop the ruse.

He was here for the rumored cybernetics laboratory. She just wanted him to say it and be honest.

Before long, they were at the edge of the landing field.

"Tomorrow evening," she reminded him, moving away. She wrapped her arms around her middle, warding off the chill. "Goodnight."

He stared forward but cocked his head in her direction. "Goodnight."

She didn't wait for anything more, pivoting and picking up her pace, fleeing for the gates. When she passed through, she stopped, leaned against the outer wall, and closed her eyes. She counted to twenty and then she did it twice more.

He hadn't threatened her.

Instead, the Cyborg had been reserved, observant, and strange, like his social skills were just as terrible as hers. Like he'd been measuring his responses as much as she had. It made her... oddly sad. The whole exchange made her sad.

And why had he kept cocking his head at her? She peered down at her body, expecting to find her answer.

Did he have a problem with his neck? Her lips quirked. *If he's here hoping to find some pyrizian metal for cheap...* She'd hand him some and wash her hands of the whole charade.

If only handing him over some of the rarest metal in the universe was even an option. Echo wanted to laugh.

Maybe Keir was here for Volun's history and didn't want to be. Maybe she was getting worked up over nothing and reading into things that weren't there. Maybe Jonah's paranoia was catching. The darkness had a way of distorting things.

Whatever it was... She had until tomorrow evening to prepare.

A flash caught her eye followed by two strobing red lights. She pushed off the wall to see the lights flying high above her. *His ship*. When the lights vanished into the distance a minute later, she slumped again, happy he was gone. Wherever he was going, she had no idea, but as long as it was away from her, she didn't care.

She stepped from the wall and toward her bike, stopping in her tracks. Pressure bore down on her.

She frowned and peered at the sky, staggering from the sensation.

It was the gaze of someone powerful, recording her every movement, monitoring her vitals, and probably discerning more about her person than she'd ever want any stranger—or being—to ever know.

Keir hadn't left at all.

SIX

HE WAS OUTSIDE HER HOME.

The sun was cresting, and as she watched the shadows in her hallway brighten with sunlight, her mood remained the same. Only, she couldn't hide anymore.

After she returned home, she'd locked herself inside her bedroom and had waited, readying her weapons, seeing Ares's face everywhere, her mom's, her dad's, certain Keir had followed her.

People depended on her, and she had a job to do. She'd made promises. With the wind picking up rapidly, Echo was certain Jonah was already awake and anxious about the weather readings.

She forced herself from the corner of her room and showered quickly, towel-drying her hair and face, scrubbing the sleepless night from her face and the stress she was certain had left their marks there.

The gun on her bedside table had its safety off, there

was a knife under her pillow at the ready, and a cattle prod in the corner by her bathroom door, fully charged. None of it would kill a Cyborg, but she'd felt better having them near just in case.

The trapdoor under her bedroom rug was oiled and ready. She glanced at the hidden mechanism beside her bathroom door, having tested it a dozen times during the night to be certain it still worked. She hoped she wouldn't need to use it.

Her bedroom didn't have a window. It was a room at the back of the outpost she lived within. It had originally been a large, changing space that had been remodeled after the outpost had been abandoned. She'd chosen it, not only for its special modifications, but because it made her feel safe. It was her mother's, and Echo had taken it over when her mother left for Earth.

Heading for the living area at the front of the outpost, long-ago renovated into a den, she scanned the forest outside, expecting to see a tall, dark figure waiting for her outside. There was nothing but gray light and wind. With a quick glimpse around the front room, everything was exactly how it was the night before.

Keir hadn't invaded while she'd hidden in the back, while she waited quietly in her room, listening for any stray sounds or movements...

Don't turn into Jonah...

She decided to skip food and just go for coffee.

Wiping her cup down, she filled it and walked out onto her deck, acting like nothing was amiss.

Echo sipped her drink, feeling stormy eyes return to her flesh, sensing Keir's presence. Longbeaks flew in packs from one tree to the next, searching for fresh sap. The gravel road leading to her steps had no new track marks upon it. Leaves fanned out and ballooned with each gust of the morning breeze coming down from the mountains.

Where is he?

She took another sip. Was he planning to stalk her until this evening?

Booted feet sounded on the stairs to her left, and her hands clenched around her mug, tampering down the sudden fury at him for losing a night's sleep.

Keir's deep, unmistakable voice called out to her from below the deck. "Good morning."

Echo twisted in his direction and feigned surprise. "Hello? Gregory, is that you?" She waited for Keir to appear, hearing him walk up the steps, nostrils flaring.

There was a fluttering in her chest she tried to stamp out as he neared, and her throat began to constrict in the seconds it took for him to make the short ascent.

She held her breath. The stairs creaked, the joints groaned, assuring her single niggle of doubt that it was the Cyborg coming toward her and not just someone from the compound.

Her mug cracked, and she quickly hid the fissure with her palm just as he appeared. First his head, and then the rest of him.

"Not Gregory," he corrected as he paused at the top. Keir gave her a once over. Echo straightened under his perusal, unable to remain still. Stopping several steps away, he placed his hand on the deck railing beside her and cocked his head in her direction.

He doesn't want to frighten me. Echo realized. *He just wants me off guard.*

"How did you find me?" she asked dryly, trying not to break her mug further. "Did someone give you directions? If it was an emergency, a comm would have sufficed."

"Ah, you can do better than that," he said almost teasingly, genuinely surprising her now. "I'm a powerful Cyborg, after all. This outpost showed up on my scans. One glance at that bike below and I knew this had to be the place. It's giving off a heat signature."

She took another sip of her coffee before she said something that she'd regret. "There are others living outside the compound, too. Farther south."

"I made an educated guess."

Echo glowered, unsure whether to be annoyed, frightened, or something else entirely. The Cyborg was acting differently from the evening before. Dirt smudged his pale features, reminding her he'd been outside her home all night. Otherwise, he looked the same as yesterday: tall, uncanny, and fiercely observant.

He wasn't wearing a fancy uniform, but standard outdoor gear. A black vest, black cargo pants, and there was a pack on his back that she was certain had all the equipment a Cyborg needed for long outings away from civilization. The only difference—now that she could see him clearly in the light—was the sniper rifle strapped around his neck. It hung under his arm.

She swallowed down the lump in her throat, turning away.

He *was* prepared. Cyborgs didn't need a lot to survive. And when it came to 'surviving' for them, they brought weapons and bullets, not food and tools.

"Why do you look like you're ready for battle?" she asked carefully.

He uncocked his head. "I'm not, but if I am going deep into an alien world, I like to be prepared. And since that is where you live, I have dressed for the occasion."

"Are you stalking me, Keir? You're here, at the crack of dawn, at my home. There's nothing outside the base's walls when it comes to Volun's history, and you're aware I can't join you sooner..." She glanced at the sky and the coils in the clouds where tornados threatened to form, a frown forming on her lips. "Why are you here?" She looked back at him.

She was tired and she was mad about it.

He shifted. "If I were stalking you, you would never know, and we would not be having this conversation."

The gravity in his words made her frown. "I thought we weren't meeting up until this evening. I have work to do today that can't wait." She glanced at the sky again, seeing him do the same out of the corner of her eye. "I'd make it wait, if I could," she mumbled, not liking the look of the clouds.

"Well, I concluded that I could spend the day talking to

the other colonists, listening to them reminisce about the good ole days, interloping into people's activities and endearing myself to them or—"

"Or you could save yourself a lot of pain and just follow me around instead?" she deadpanned. "The problem is, I won't be working in the compound today. I'm heading out to check the weather readings at several outposts, and I don't have a vehicle that fits two."

He shrugged. "Yes."

Echo squinted at him. *Yes?* Yes to what exactly? Following her around all day?

Echo sighed, realizing he was just answering her question. Why try and argue? "You're lucky that I'm nothing like Jonah."

He cocked a brow. "I am?"

"Jonah hates people inserting themselves into his business. Especially unannounced, if you haven't noticed."

Keir hummed. "I can relate."

"Right..."

"Well, I'm here now." He reached out and pushed a strand of her hair out of her face.

Echo went still as he drew his hand back, closing his fingers into his palm. She stared at his hand.

"You can trust me," she snapped, annoyed, deciding the exchange just now had never happened. "You don't need to show up unannounced at my home, before it's even light out, to keep me on my toes. I have nothing to hide from you or anyone. I live out here because I prefer peace and privacy."

What she really wanted to say was that she knew he'd been outside her home all night. And because of that, she was getting by on fumes. It was going to make her careless.

"Is that what you think I'm doing?" His gaze clouded.

"Yes!"

"Is that what my brethren did? Intimidate you? Psychologically manipulate you?"

Echo frowned, taken aback again. It took her a second to realize what he was doing, what he was saying. He was bringing up Ares.

He was playing her.

She turned back to the railing, suddenly very aware that he'd just intimately pushed her hair out of her face. "It doesn't matter. You found me and you're here now. Let's just forget it. I have a lot on my mind."

"It matters to me," he growled.

Her lips parted from the sudden vehemence in his voice.

She faced him right as his features smoothed out, as if his show of emotion had never happened.

"It was a long time ago now," she said carefully. "Either way, I'd rather not talk about it." She took another sip of her coffee, plastering a smile onto her face. "But if you must know... we don't get a lot of visitors outside our yearly suppliers. Sometimes there are criminals who make their way here, but they never remain here long. Jonah won't let them stay. And with so few of us left, well, we're not the most welcoming bunch anymore. With our track record, misunderstandings have occurred."

He leaned his hip on the railing and crossed his arms. "Misunderstandings? Tell me about them."

She watched his biceps bunch from the movement, and she quickly averted her eyes. "Like I said, in the past, people usually only end up on Volun to either escape a crime, to scavenge, hoping the rumors of an old cybernetics laboratory were true, or to hunt. We've had the rare environmental researcher or two along the way. You can guess which of the reasons your brethren have journeyed here before you. You don't need me for that."

His expression went from keen to predatory interest in the blink of an eye.

Echo went silent, her throat constricting. She'd baited him, mentioning the laboratory, and it had worked.

"I see," he growled. "Well, I can assure you I am not a criminal, nor am I here to scavenge."

"No, you're clearly here for Volun's fiercest game," she drawled.

His lips twitched at her remark, taking away some of the tension radiating between them. A breeze blew her hair forward again and she reached up to tuck it behind her ear before he had a chance to reenact the interaction.

She continued, her own lips twitching in response, "Jonah worries deeply about the hunters who recklessly come here, after all. He's afraid they're all going to die. Perhaps we're just trying to save your life."

"Ah, yes. He does seem like the caring sort."

"He takes his job very seriously."

His smile grew. "Does it come with pay?"

Echo nearly spat and laughed instead. "No! Could you imagine if it did?"

Keir moved closer. Her laughter died as he settled his hip back on the railing, invading her personal space, sucking it up, and making it his own.

He rested his forearms on the railing beside her and looked out at the land leading away from the outpost. "I take my job very seriously too. Every Cyborg does, whether they are working for themselves or for another. Whatever happened to you, to Jonah and any others, I am sorry. I can tell it went down badly."

"You can tell?" Echo looked down at the remaining coffee in her mug, her throat tightening. A thread of hope slithered into her. She wanted to believe him. He sounded sincere. It confused her.

Heat drifted off of his frame, warming her side. She caught a whiff of his scent. *His* smell. It was different from the men in the compound, there was nothing unpleasant about it.

She breathed him in, familiarizing it—even liking it.

Keir bathed regularly.

"Jonah's the least of your worries," she murmured, deciding it was best to move on. "The burnout is what you should be worrying about. But he'll be a problem for you the entire time you're here. It will be easiest for you to avoid him. He..."

"Doesn't like my kind?" Keir finished for her.

Echo licked her lips. "Not anymore."

"Can I ask you—"

"You want his name."

"Yes. I want his name."

"What will you do with that information? Will you keep it close to you or will you give it away?"

"That would depend."

"Then I'd rather keep the name to myself, if you don't mind."

"I do mind." He lifted off the railing and faced her. "I'm going to want it. I will have it before I leave here."

"Why? It was years ago. As you can see, they're not here now, and everyone is fine. I'm sure if you research many of Earth's government spaceports and colonies, you'd find that Cyborgs have visited all of them at one time or another."

"For you, perhaps, but for a Cyborg? Time is different for us. I want to know why they were here."

"But why does it matter?" she asked again, determined to have an answer. She needed to know how worried she should be.

Keir didn't speak, and as the seconds dragged on in silence, she was certain he wouldn't. So when he did decide to answer, she was surprised.

"It matters because there has clearly been damage done, and when one Cyborg acts without honor, his or her actions reflect on the rest of us."

"I can... understand that. But I'm keeping the name. I'm not going to share someone else's business with you, even if it is out of honor. I'll answer any questions about Volun and the old military base, even any you might have about its history, the rumors surrounding it, and the answers I'm sure you're looking for, that are, sadly, not here, but I won't get personal with you. What happened in the past should stay there. And if it really had been all that bad, we wouldn't be talking right now, would we?" she finished, throwing his words back at him.

He cocked his head at her in answer.

She wondered why he kept doing it, and if there really was something wrong with his neck. It was a strange quirk, and it made him seem animalistic. He'd been strange the night before, but in the light, he'd seemed almost human— except for his height—until he bent his head and his eyes contracted and sharpened unnaturally.

Too bad her mother wasn't here. She'd be able to fix his neck.

"Whatever the reason *you're* here, you can rest assured, Commander Keir, I will not share it with anyone who comes here after you, Cyborg or otherwise," she finished.

He scowled. "I see…"

"Then we understand each other."

He glowered at her as she held her ground, but his sharp eyes flicked over her frame, and the blatant perusal made her stomach knot. "We're at an impasse for now."

"We are." Echo crossed her arms. "I have to leave soon for the other outposts if I want to make it to the compound before nightfall. If you have no more questions for now…"

"Actually, I have a lot," he quipped. "But they can wait. Lead the way."

"I—" she started, startled. "I don't have an extra bike." Echo scanned the vicinity below, looking for an excuse to get him to leave. "And I don't see your skiff?" Where was his ship? *Had he come here on foot?* She frowned.

"Don't worry about me. I'll keep up."

"Keep up?" Her eyes slid his way.

"With you."

"You're planning on joining me? Without a vehicle?"

Did he plan on riding with her?

Echo took in his long, muscled frame, and the gear strapped to it. Her breath snagged, imagining him sitting flushed to her back, with his arms and legs around her, the utter closeness of such a position, and how dangerous it could be for her with him being so near, so pressed up against her...

She took a small step back.

Apart from the rare hug, sharing any type of physical contact with another wasn't something she was used to. And to be held by a strange man? A Cyborg at that? The idea sent fear straight into her soul.

"It's a long way and can be dangerous for those who don't know the terrain," she said, her voice lowering as she tried to figure out a way to lose him.

"I think I'll manage." He turned away, completely unaware of her rising horror. "Do you live alone?"

"Yes," she quipped.

He glanced at her then looked back at the outpost like he didn't believe her.

"My parents lived here before me."

"So you've lived on Volun your whole life?" he asked.

"I've never set a foot off of it."

"Perhaps I can change that."

Butterflies invaded her stomach only to shrivel up and die, their wings turning to ash.

Then, damnably, they resurrected.

She didn't know how to take his words or their meaning, and a blush rose to her cheeks. "I don't think so. I have no interest in leaving. So probably not."

Echo fled and grabbed her gear before he could see her face reddening. "We're wasting daylight," she called over her shoulder, pretending not to be fleeing from him.

No, Keir wasn't like Ares at all. He was going to be worse. He was going to make her like him. And that... that was bad.

Because, after all, she was a Cyborg's daughter.

And Keir could never, ever find out.

SEVEN

KEIR DIDN'T JOIN her on her bike.

And she was certain, if he had tried, she would have fought him.

Echo waited for him to reappear, searching for where he'd gone. Had he left without her noticing? Would that even be possible? She'd left abruptly, but had expected him to follow.

The sky was already thickening with storm clouds. The weather was changing swiftly, and she couldn't wait much longer unless she wanted to spend all day being rained upon. So after a quick check to see if he was still on her deck, she put her helmet on and drove off without him, relieved *and* disappointed.

She may not have any experience with men, but she'd always been curious. There were no men in the compound she'd readily say were both available, and a good match for someone like her. There was Jason, who was the closest in age, at forty-two. He would've made a great companion... If he weren't attracted to men.

Besides the idea of being with Jason, or one of the older, single veterans in the colony, Echo had never had any other real options, and the occasional captains and crew hands that came down in their shoddy commercial ships to help unload goods to be bought or bartered had always made her uncomfortable. If she were ever to pursue one, she was more likely to get her heart broken than to fall in love in the short time they were planetside. And most already had families they were providing for elsewhere.

When Ares first appeared, she'd been awestruck, infatuated, stupid, and so very naive. He had descended from the clouds with long, flaming hair and honeyed features. *A fire god*, she'd thought at the time. Echo had never seen another like him in all her life. She couldn't look away from him; his presence burned.

He scorched the universe in his wake.

Auryn, her father, had a much more normal appearance, which had made Ares all that more enticing. Unlike Ares, her dad had soft brown hair and eyes. His makeup resembled the other colonists, and he could easily fit in amongst them if it weren't for his unnaturally perfect features.

Ares had been one of the original class of Cyborgs, like The Great Lysander and Braco, and like those first ones, was harder, stricter, meaner—built by the hands of a desperate military, or so her mom had reassured her—to save them. She'd known he'd been one of the originals even without her mom telling her.

It hadn't taken Echo long after his arrival to realize how awful Ares would be as a partner.

Where Keir fell in the creation scheme, and how sociopathic he was, she had yet to figure out. She didn't have her mom's knowledge in the matter, and sending a comm out to her wasn't feasible considering the circumstances.

Echo sped toward the northern plains, leaving the road, and cutting through the woods. She couldn't sense Keir's gaze, nor hear or see him, but that didn't mean he wasn't there.

Madeline, the only other woman around the same age as Echo at the compound, had also fallen for Ares upon his arrival. He'd been a sight to behold.

Echo's hands tightened on her handlebars. She'd pitied Ares and what had happened to him after he'd attacked her mom—and what Echo did out of guilt afterwards.

Knowing what she was, and how she shouldn't technically exist, had been beaten into her. Mom feared her because of what her natural make up meant, and it could mean to humanity as a whole. It just didn't make Echo's choices—or her parent's choices—any easier for her to take. They'd made it clear that someone like herself, a human perfectly balanced with both organic cells and nanocells—without a lick of pyrzian metal inside her body—would be hurt if fallen into the wrong hands. She'd be tested and used, all while humans hailed evolutionary advancement.

And it wouldn't just be her, it would be her mom and dad too.

As well as everyone she so desperately tried to protect.

Echo tried to push out the disappointment from not having Keir join her all the while, annoyed that he had brought old fantasies and uncomfortable memories to the forefront of her thoughts. She didn't want to revisit them.

Even considering Keir—a Cyborg—as a potential partner was stupid and naive—and desperate. Echo's chest tightened. She'd been through this all before and she'd grown up. The idea was nice, having someone to share everything with, but in her situation, utterly unfeasible.

Following the mountain line until she hit the river, she kept the sky in her sights, avoiding the denser patches of the forest. The plains were vast, and many parts of them had grasses so tall it was impossible to see over them. Right now, they slashed and danced with the wind on the other side.

She followed the river to a small lake where the ashtrax often drank from. Searching for them, she noted that the pack's tracks had doubled back and towards the forest that lined the mountains she'd just turned from.

She frowned. If the ashtrax were seeking cover already, then the burnout was almost upon them, and the storm that was brewing was going to be much, much worse than she'd anticipated.

Extending her thrusters, she hunkered down and increased her speed, driving her bike over the water.

She slowed down at where the river turned into the lake, taking the risk of cutting through it to save time.

Several feet below her, the water chopped and whirled, turning tumultuous from the wind. It warned her not to come to a stop. Because if she did, she'd lose her bike and potentially, her life.

When the opposite shore appeared, her shoulders eased.

She stopped at the shore where the grasses had been trampled into the ground and inhaled sharply. Glancing behind her, she gave the waves on the lake's surface a frown, when she heard the telltale crush of dried grass being stepped upon behind her. Twisting back around, Keir walked toward her from the direction she was headed, completely unruffled except for his hair. Like a dark sliver amongst the washed out green, brown, and grey, he appeared entirely too confident for being out in the wilds of an alien world.

Echo straightened and their eyes caught. He kept her trapped like that as he approached. Stunned by his appearance, she tried to look away but couldn't. She'd momentarily forgotten about him.

She was way out of her depth. And for people *dealing* with his kind, she was better equipped than most. She wanted him to go back to being the strange creature he'd been the night before. At least then, she could view him as an oddity, like herself, and not someone who could be an enemy.

Her cheeks heated with each step he took.

Storm clouds brewed at his back, lightening his pupils to sharp dots as they seemed to bleed over his frame and directly into him. Like two little black holes, they had the power to not only snare their prey, but pull them inward, swallowing them whole.

His eyes looked past her flesh and directly into her soul. She shivered, frightened by what they might find there, what he might see.

And worst of all, how he would react to it.

Why she'd felt a twinge of disappointment earlier when she'd driven off without him baffled her. Echo frowned. He was attractive, but not like how Ares was. It was harder to figure Keir out. There was a stoicism about him. Whatever it was, unnerved her. She wanted to get up close and personal and study him, just so she could put these thoughts in a box and ship that box to the back of her mind.

Strands of her hair blew into her face again, and she quickly pushed them away, fearing he'd do it for her again.

She was not prepared for this and she made it a point to be prepared for *everything*.

Echo turned off her bike as he stopped at her side, hating that her neck had to bend just to keep his face in her view. Thankfully, he broke eye contact first and cocked his head, looking around them and at the lake.

Freedom had never tasted so bittersweet. Her frown deepened.

"That was dangerous," he muttered under his breath, glowering at the water.

"It saved us time." Echo used the reprieve to search for his transport and rub her neck. "How did you do that?" she asked, scanning the area behind him.

"Do what?"

"How were you able to keep up with me? Get ahead of me, even? I don't see a vehicle... Are you running? Is that what you do? Run fast? Do you have motors in your legs?"

Being the progeny of a Cyborg wasn't the same as being a *Cyborg*. She had no special powers or talents. She was a human, through and through. To other humans, she was physically superior, but to Cyborgs, she was just a human. Her mom, privy to a lot more information about Cyborgs than most, prepped her in on some of the basics of creating the war machines.

The rest, she learned from her dad.

Keir gave her a twitchy smile, clearly clued in on her knowledge of this secret. "I flew."

Echo squinted. "How?"

"Now that's a question that could take me several days to answer. Do you get bored easily?" His eyes slanted towards her.

She leaned away and checked out Keir's backside. When he realized what she was doing, he turned full-circle for her. His vest and long-sleeved dark undershirt were completely undisturbed except for some wrinkles. Her eyes dropped to his heavy black boots.

They were made of a dark leather material and had rubber soles.

He's not flying or hovering. Echo deadpanned, meeting his gaze with a frown. His face was amused and taunting. *I almost believed him.*

"Fine, let's say you flew. You can clearly keep up." Echo

pointed ahead. "We're heading for the northern outpost first, and then will make our way southwest, then farther south to our final outpost."

His eyes narrowed. "Through the grass?"

"We don't have much choice. The clouds are funneling. If we keep to the roads, it will add hours. Hours don't have seem to have anymore. Can you handle that?"

He didn't look happy with the plan, and she couldn't blame him. Traveling through the plains wasn't easy. It was hard to see. And if he was running, it would be even rougher...

"Yes," he said.

"Good."

He grabbed her wrist before she could restart her bike. "Be careful." He held her for a moment before letting her go and stepping back.

Tensing all over, Echo nodded and held her hand to her chest. Her heart quickened.

The next several hours were spent speeding through the drier patches across the plains, avoiding the tallest grasses whenever possible. The weather continued to worsen.

Echo emerged from the plains to hit the old road on the other side. To her left, she saw the outpost in the distance. Behind it, a black mass of clouds were descending from the mountains, and with it, a veil of rain. Sprinkles hit her cheeks, and she stopped her bike. Thunder boomed.

Swiping the water off her face, she cursed.

"How much worse will it get?" Keir asked, his voice grave.

Echo started and cursed again, turning to find him standing right next to her. "How?" she snapped, annoyed. "Never mind." She wiped her hands down her face, her mood falling as she looked back at the clouds. "I don't know, but those clouds" —she pointed out where several large funnels were forming— "may end up being a real problem for us."

He nodded in understanding. "Let's go then."

Keir stepped back and she turned her bike on. Glancing over her shoulder, he had vanished once again.

Echo dropped her helmet back on and drove into the storm.

EIGHT

UNLIKE ECHO'S HOME, the outpost she had taken him to was a tower built off the side of a gravel road, fully gated by a broken chain-link electric fence. Around it were three relay towers, old and worn, and no longer operational.

The outpost, like much of Volun, had seen better eras.

Echo drove her bike through a hole in the fence and parked it under the shade of the outpost's outer stairs. She dashed up them and inside the building, only calling out that she'd be several minutes. She didn't even turn around to see if he was there.

She would've seen him in flight, if she had.

Lips quirking, Keir used the time to scout around the old tower.

When he made certain the area was clear, he turned his attention back to Echo, seeing her through the higher windows of the upper floor of the outpost. She was hovering over several screens, completely absorbed by whatever was on them. He dove closer as rain drizzled over the dirty glass, giving him a clearer view.

Taking in her wide brown eyes, and the frown that deepened over her features, pricked his curiosity.

She was stressed about the weather, and about him. But which she was more concerned about, eluded him.

Humans had never intrigued him. He'd been around crowds of them, excitable fans, sycophants, fellow soldiers, and even furious mobs. Not once had he found any of them compelling enough to try and understand their motivations, at least not for long. Even when humans tried to seduce him, to take him to their beds—or get an invitation to *his* —he had firmly turned them down. All of them.

Yet, after being with Echo for hours now, he wasn't annoyed by her presence. Her place in this dying colony was odd to him, and seeing as she was one of the youngest left here, he wondered why she stayed.

Was it out of some misguided responsibility, freedom, or fear? He understood the first two. And if it was fear that kept her from the rest of humanity, what had caused that fear?

She pivoted from the computers and moved toward the heavy machinery behind it, giving her back to him. Taking that as his cue, Keir landed beside her bike, and shook the water out of his hair and off his metal wings.

Once he knew how to handle her, he'd lose interest. He always did when it came to humans. Eventually he would find something in her nature that disappointed him.

She knew things he wanted to know, that was all. An obstacle—or a tool—to completing his mission. Scanning her bike, and loading the information into his systems, it held no evidence to help him. He unclipped the baggage compartment from it next and rummaged through the contents, discovering nothing out of the ordinary except for some darts.

Bringing them to his nose, he sniffed them. A bittersweet scent filled his nostrils, one he couldn't place, and with a quick dab of his tongue to the dart's top, his body immediately counteracted natural paralytic agents. He put the darts back where he found them and repackaged her belongings.

The rain picked up and his eyes shifted to the clouds. Dark and ominous, they were simultaneously bloated and riotous.

Keir cocked his head.

He hadn't given much thought to the weather, though the pressure in the air and the increasing volatility of the wind were quickly becoming alarming.

For the world he was supposedly created upon, he retained no instincts to its nature.

He recognized nothing, and it wasn't like the locals were exactly hiding that there was an old research facility here, a laboratory. If Echo was willing to take him straight through the facility's doors...

This had to be the place right?

Nightheart has been searching for generations... Keir hadn't expected the lab would have closed down, but could it have been? Was that why it had been so hard for them to locate?

And what if it wasn't here at all? What if this mission turned out to be another failure? It had been eight years since Nightheart last called on Keir's help.

Keir's lips twisted.

He was ready to be done with this hunt so he could finally retire in peace, far away from humans and Cyborgs alike.

"Hey Keir, are you out there?"

He jerked at Echo's voice, craning his neck in her direction. His wires seized, igniting his systems with electricity. His wings burst from his back in a rush. He fisted his hands against the sudden rush, numbing his body's reaction to her voice. He drew his wings back in, and they sliced through the wind as they did.

She... calls for me?

He looked down at his body. Why had he reacted to her call like that? Blood pooled straight to his cock, rising the mass between his thighs with uncomfortable tension.

Fuck.

Keir drew away from Echo's bike, grabbing his erection and adjusting it with another curse. With it barely contained, he bounded up the stairs, crashing through the door that led to the outpost's middle floor from where her voice had called out from. Echo was on her knees, her ass in the air, digging through an open panel on the side of one of the machines.

She startled and looked back at him, sighed with frustration when she realized it was him, then went back to digging through the panel.

"Flying my ass," she muttered. "Fix the door, please."

His jaw ticked as he tried to hide his smile. He readjusted his bulge, taking her words as a promise.

Keir thrust his hand away, clenching it at his side.

What was wrong with him?

He had more control than this. Cracking his neck, he gathered up screws, and reattached the door.

Trying hard not to stare at her ass, Echo didn't look up again as he strode to her side. When she continued to ignore him, Keir sighed.

"What's wrong?" he asked, kneeling to see what she was fiddling with.

"The wires are rusty," she gritted. "The server keeps dropping, and without the server, I can't get a clear reading. I need to warn Jonah and the others that a storm's coming through, if they aren't already aware. Hell," she muttered under her breath. "They're probably already aware. I need to shut everything down. We don't have a generator to spare."

He canted his head, trying to follow. "What about your wristcon? Just comm him."

"I forgot it at home," she huffed. "I was distracted."

His lips twitched again. "My apologies."

"Can you help me?" She sat back and glanced at him. "Since it's clearly your fault that I forgot it. I just need a connection for a couple of minutes. I thought we had more time. Can you juice it?"

"Here," he said, amused. He moved toward the panel as she backed away. Inside were circuits and wires that had noticeably been tampered with a dozen times over, all coated in varying degrees of rust and decay. Pulling back the skin on his fingers, he pinched a wire between them, seeding outward and into the system's electrical blueprint.

The rest of the machines around them began to hum.

Echo gasped. "It's working. I only need a minute."

She hurried to the computers, typing something in. He settled, letting the machines and their electrical waves use him as a conduit.

Thunder boomed, shuddering the outer walls, the wires, and the panel. Subtle waves of static washed over him. "Hurry," he growled. As much as he enjoyed pure energy, as long as he was a conduit, he was vulnerable. Plugging in during an active storm was idiotic, even for him.

"Got it," she said. "Thank you."

Keir pulled his hands out from the machine and resealed his fingers. "You're welcome."

"I can't believe I forgot my wristcon. I don't make mistakes like that," Echo whispered. He rose and faced her. She was staring mutely at the screen in front of her and the readings upon it, ignoring the lighting now streaking out from the sky across the landscape behind it.

Sharp rain abruptly slammed into the windows in waves, sounding like pebbles.

Echo continued to stare at the screens, completely unfazed.

Keir tilted his head from side-to-side, seeing thousands

of splashing water droplets burst simultaneously, each detail recorded. The visual threatened to overload his systems and he blinked, looking away. "I will take the blame," he offered, amused. "I did show up unexpectedly."

"Even so, I'm never so scattered," she mumbled, finally glancing away from the screens and at the storm. "Jonah and the others will have time to get everything and everyone inside now." She glanced back at him.

Lightning bolts shot from the sky by the dozens, stealing his attention. Keir curled his hands as his shoulders straightened. The weather was worsening, and swiftly. Larger funnels emerged from the clouds.

Echo didn't pay them any mind, looking back at the screens.

So she cares more about warning others than she does for her own safety.

"Explain to me," he began, any amusement he found from the situation dying, "what exactly occurs during a... burnout?"

"Once, sometimes twice during Utha's rotation, a massive bubble of pressure fills the atmosphere, bringing with it a storm. But the storm doesn't last, not for more than a day, it's what happens afterwards that's rough. The clouds temporarily clear, giving Utha's sun direct access to scorch our land, burning everything, and evaporating much of our water supply. That's where the name comes from. They can last for several weeks, even though the clouds return much quicker than that. They trap the heat, and Volun bakes.

Most of the wildlife head for the forests and mountains to hibernate during this time."

He stared at the violence brewing outside. "Sounds dangerous. Is it always preceded by a storm like this?"

"Yes, though normally at this point we're usually much more prepared." She rubbed her eyes. "I was just out hunting yesterday..."

"You hunt?"

She moved from the screen and powered down the control panel, turning it off. "Of course I do. I've been hunting since I could walk. Nearly everyone here learns how too, in some capacity. My father always took me with him when he went."

"Your father?" Keir canted his head. She was opening up to him. He didn't want to waste the opportunity to learn more. "Is he still around?"

"He's not dead if that's what you're asking. I need to finish turning everything off—" Lightning struck the building, making the walls shake. Echo flinched, and he moved between her and the windows, grabbing her arm. They waited until the building settled.

Echo pulled from his grasp, and he let her go. She strode to the exit. Keir scowled and followed her, slamming his hand on the door before she yanked it open.

"What are you doing? I need to shut everything off before—"

Lightning struck the building again, blasting their ears.

"Not right now," he ordered.

When the building settled again, she pleaded with him.

"If the machines short circuit, we won't be able to replace them. The compound will be completely blind to everything north of it."

"None of that will matter if you're struck down by lightning."

"I've been in worse storms than this," she argued, waving her hand. "This is nothing. I've even been struck by lightning before." She swiped her tongue across her lower lip. "I'll survive. I'm sure you will too."

His eyes dipped to her mouth, and his cock strained against his pants, locking his jaw. Echo's lips were a pale pink, symmetrical, and bowed when resting. But he hadn't seen them resting enough yet for his own pleasure. Keir leaned in, his hand sliding down the door.

Had anyone kissed those lips? Or would he be the first? Would it be a first for both of them?

She inhaled sharply, the stress in her eyes morphing to confusion. "Keir, what are you doing? T-take your hand off the door." Fear tinged her voice.

He was scaring her.

Keir jerked back, horrified. "Wait here," he rasped, hiding his own confusion. "I'll take care of it."

He was reacting to her, and he didn't know why.

With that, he fled outside. Even being beaten by wind and rain from every side, water blasting his face, the need to taste her remained. To look at her ass again. To touch her hair. Keir vaulted over the railing, landing heavily on the wet ground two floors below. The rain drenched him while he tried to regain control of his body.

What the fuck was wrong with him?

He'd never even considered a woman's lips or ass before. And to do so, during a mission? He wasn't so weak to make such a terrible mistake. He wasn't like the other shifters...

Unlike them, freedom was all he craved, and taking a mate, even if it was for the duration of a mission, would only complicate things. Especially someone he was trying to manipulate.

Keir focused on the signals around him. He followed them to their roots, heading for a power station in a cement building next to the outpost. Breaking the locks on the door, he found the breakers and switched them off.

Echo's lips returned to his mind and he scowled.

Keir made his way back to the tower and up the stairs, yanking the door open and almost breaking it again. He paused on the threshold.

Echo was gone.

Twisting around, he surged into the sky. Lightning cracked by the dozens all around him, teasing his wings, when he caught sight of her beside her bike, her jacket tucked over her head.

He was at her side within the next instant. "What are you doing?" he yelled over the storm.

"We need to head to the next outpost and shut it down!" She lifted her leg over her bike.

"Not in this weather we're not," he growled under his breath, grabbing hold of her bike handle. Was she trying to get herself killed?

She peered up at him. "We can't lose the tech!"

"It's too dangerous!"

"It's my job. We depend on the servers. Now you can come with me, or you can stay here."

"You've warned them. Let that be enough. I'm sure the other stations will survive if they've survived this long."

"You could say the same thing about me. Is that what you would do if our situation were reversed?"

His grip tightened on her bike. "It's not the same. You know it's not."

"I'm more than capable. This" —she indicated the storm— "would've happened if you were here or not!" A surge of wind lifted her damp hair to flutter wildly around her face.

"That might be true," he yelled. "But I *am* here. Remember? Get back inside. I'll see what I can do about shutting off your systems remotely."

Her face went from annoyed to curious. "You can do that?"

"I can try." Whether he could or not would wait to be seen, but convincing Echo to wait out the storm seemed like a better plan than to carry her inside and force her against her will. "But we need to go inside where it's dry for me to do so. I need to concentrate."

She watched him for a moment, deciding. Her gaze shifted behind him and to the storm. When her shoulders slumped and she sat back, he knew he'd won.

"How long will it take?" she asked, dismounting her bike.

He took his hands off the handlebars. "A few minutes, maybe an hour at most."

She nodded, threading her fingers through her wet hair and pushing it back, conceding. "An hour then."

Relieved, Keir stepped back. He followed her as she dashed through the rain and back up the stairs. Instead of the second floor, she led him through the door to the first level where there was some old furniture scattered about, several folded-up cots, and basic supplies. She pulled off her jacket and threw it over a crate, grabbing two worn towels at the same time. She handed him one as she dried her neck and hands.

"Thanks," he said, doing the same.

Heading to one of the chairs, she sat towel-dried her hair. "Let me know when you're done." She yawned.

He stared at her for a moment. She seemed to know exactly what he was about to do as if she'd seen it happen before. Which was odd...

He was going to partially shut down, splitting his consciousness so he could leave his body. It was risky and dangerous and not often something a Cyborg did unless it was out of necessity. Although, in a circumstance like this, it was worth trying rather than braving the storm.

Keir skipped the fragile folding chair across from her, and found a crate to sit on instead. He closed his eyes.

He breathed in and searched for Echo's scent amongst the petrichor, but she smelled like the rain, and he couldn't discern hers yet. Then everything faded into the background of his systems as he left the confines of his body and seeded into Volun's. It would have been much easier if he'd done this before he powered off the outpost's machines, but he wasn't about to stop now and turn them back on.

So instead, he pressed outward, searching for where the channels had been and where they led when powered on, picturing the moon's localized landscape. The storm outside fought him.

Keir glanced at Echo on resting on the chair, her eyes hooded while she watched him. Her hair was wet and, once again, tied tightly back, pulling at her features. His fingers twitched, wishing she'd let her hair back down. Lightning hit the tower, washing the windowed room in light, and Keir closed his eyes again.

He amplified the signal coming out from his planetary vessel first. From there, he spread outward from his ship, threading through the compound.

Sensing more signals, he sorted through them until he found one similar to the other two outposts. He snipped the electrical sources of both, and flooding the primitive circuitry with amplified power, he safely short circuited them. Stealing the electrical signals, he rerouted them, cutting off the outposts completely until someone manually started them back up.

He left Echo's outpost alone.

Keir pulled his consciousness back into his body but paused when he sensed another extremely weak signal, unattached to the rest. Coming out from Echo's home, it didn't follow any of the same grids.

Trying to tap into it to see if he missed something, the

signal attacked him the second he touched it, blasting him away.

Keir's eyes snapped open just as another bolt of lightning struck. He tensed, clenched his jaw, adjusting to the shock. He'd never been attacked by a signal before that wasn't a highly specialized security system or...

He frowned.

Another Cyborg's...

Rubbing his mouth, he wondered how that was possible. He'd know if there was another Cyborg here; it was impossible for Cyborgs to mask themselves from each other. Was the signal connected to the one who'd been here previously?

More lightning hit, and his gaze shifted to the tempest outside then back to Echo, who was now slumped in the chair, chin resting on her chest, snoring softly.

It isn't possible, he decided. He'd know if there was another Cyborg;their signals weren't faint, and they didn't naturally attack each other. It had to be the storm.

Keir quietly went to the cots and pulled one out, setting one of them up in the back corner, farthest away from the windows. When he was done, he went to Echo and kneeled by her side.

She'd fallen asleep.

He'd sensed her exhaustion from the moment he'd laid eyes on her this morning. His jaw ticked, annoyed that she wasn't taking care of her body, and further annoyed she was more than willing to risk her life taking care of a bunch of people who knew their way of life was no longer sustainable.

He didn't understand her and it was really beginning to bother him.

He had never understood why humans did what they did, especially if their choices would directly hurt those around them. And so often, humans made those choices, forcing others to make terrible sacrifices on their behalf.

He'd been built to be a sacrifice for humans. To win a war they couldn't. To claim defeat when they couldn't. To die and not be mourned, because that was the job. Humans had run out of their own martyrs and heroes long ago. No human left was willing to sacrifice everything just so Earth's government and its many corporations could keep control of all the worlds and colonies they'd conquered.

He'd been built for it, and yet, had never done any of the great deeds he was meant for. Instead, he'd been made into a puppet.

Keir reached up and whispered his fingers along Echo's cheek. *I was made to protect you.*

He curled his fingers into his palm. The war had been won generations ago. Why were its scars not healing?

He gently threaded his arms around her and lifted Echo in his arms, cradling her to his chest. Her head rested against him as he straightened and carried her to the cot. Firm yet lightweight in his embrace, she felt like she belonged there, pressed against him, where she slept soundly, deeply. Placing her carefully upon the cot, she curled onto her side, facing him. He covered her in several blankets and tucked them around her.

When he was done, Keir went back to his crate to keep watch, finally peeling off his own weapons and wet clothes for a moment of reprieve. He inhaled, and when he did, Echo's scent filled his nose.

Shuddering, he exhaled quickly.

Something had happened here, to Echo, and the other colonists, between the end of the war and now. They'd chosen to remain, despite the government having deserted them. Whether it had anything to do with his mission, he no longer cared.

He was going to find out.

NINE

Lightning cracked.

Echo curled deeper into her blanket, wishing the storm would stop so she could go back to sleep. Her limbs ached, her body felt heavy, and she was certain a little more rest would fix everything because it always did. Sleep was the best.

"You're awake."

Her eyes snapped open. She sprung upright, grabbing her blanket and looking around at the same time. She found Keir still sitting on his crate. He was staring at her, draped in gray shadows and random shafts of light. His hair had fallen into his face, giving him a devilish air. To his right, and outside the overlook, lightning flashed in quick succession.

"I fell asleep." Echo dug her fingers into her blanket. Keir reminded her of the stories she'd heard about gargoyles, and how humans created them to scare off demons. She threw the blankets off her legs and rose. She'd never seen a gargoyle before, but she bet Keir was one of them.

He just need wings. And maybe some sharp teeth.

"Yes. You did. While I was powering off the other outposts."

"Were you able to?"

"Yes."

Echo's heart hammered as she walked to the window, keeping him in her sights all the while. "Thank you. Thank you for your help... for *all* of your help today." Her cheeks heated. "I can't believe I fell asleep." She pressed her palms against her face. "I don't know what's come over me."

He stood, and she straightened in turn, dropping her hands as he approached the window to stand at her side. "It was no effort on my part."

With him so near, his body heat enveloped her. Her hands clenched against it. She strained her neck to watch his face as she sought to regain some control over the situation.

"It means a lot to me." Echo was stifled with his nearness. It did mean a lot to her. Living how she lived, being able to depend on others was paramount to survival, and it had been a long time since she had that kind of trust in anyone besides Jonah and Gregory. It was a boon and a nice surprise when someone did her a favor.

But for the help to come from a Cyborg?

He'll want something in exchange...

"How long was I out?" she asked, suspicious.

"A couple of hours."

"I wish you had woken me."

"You needed the sleep."

"I would have been fine." She licked her lips. "I'll be able to rest soon enough."

"Are you sure about that?" Keir crossed his arms, canted his head, drawing her gaze away from his face and to his chest. He'd taken off his weapons and his vest. Without them on, his muscles were outlined with his tight undershirt. His abs, chest, and arms were on display. Thick, corded, and she assumed tough-as-rocks.

Echo stopped from shuffling away from him.

Strong men made her feel weak in comparison, especially those of the cybernetic variety. She hated feeling weak. Her gaze moved up his chest as her back straightened.

Unlike hers, Keir's hair was dry now, though remained close to his head, slicked back and away from his sharp features, making his dark eyes beacons. They glinted with each lightning strike, giving him a wild look.

He unbent his neck, and Echo realized she was staring.

Finding it hard to breathe, she glanced at the exit over his shoulder.

Because he had done more than just shut down the others servers while she slept. He'd moved her to a cot in the back corner and covered her with blankets. Last she remembered, she'd passed out in the chair.

Which meant he had touched her, been close to her, and could have discovered her secret.

Echo swallowed the ball of tightness in her throat. "Yes, I'm sure. The storm doesn't look as bad. If we want to make it back to the compound before evening, we should head out now, otherwise our tour will have to wait until tomorrow." Only right as she said it, the wind shifted in the direction of the windows, and erupted the room with the sound of pounding water. Her mood dropped.

She didn't want to go out in the storm. She knew it was dangerous. But so was being caught in it overnight, and with a Cyborg to boot. A Cyborg who tucked her hair behind her ear and had a way of getting much too close to her for comfort? If he was trying to confuse her, it was working.

Shifting nervously the longer Keir stared at her, she strode to her jacket and shook the remaining rainwater off of it.

Keir followed her movements but didn't pursue her, giving her a clear path to the door. She itched to leave and brave the storm. He looked towards the window.

Echo lowered her jacket. "Did you not want that tour tonight?"

"You mentioned earlier." His voice lowered. "When we spoke about people journeying to Volun, people like me, that there was a secret military research laboratory here. What did you mean by that?"

Her confusion vanished, and suddenly she was back to being tired. Her jacket went limp at the ends of her fingers.

She was going to pay for the break, and his help, by answering questions.

"Exactly what I meant. There is a military base here," she chose her words carefully, "and the bones of an old laboratory. But, like the base, it was shut down and stripped clean."

Keir's eyes narrowed. "Is it hidden?"

"Hidden?"

His face hardened at her response.

"The research facility," he answered, and faced her. "Is it hidden? You're nervous, Echo. You're scared. I can see your pulse, calibrate the shifts of your breaths. You clearly don't want me here with me, in this space. You've had run-ins with another of my kind and are afraid to give me their name. Yet not once have I told you or anyone else the reason why I'm really here. But you, and everyone else, are absolutely certain you know why. I can't help but be curious—and suspicious—of these assumptions. Which can only lead me to believe that the other Cyborg who had journeyed here before me had come for similar reasons." His hawkish features sharpened into points.

"You've had a lot to dwell on while I slept," she responded dryly, trying not to flinch.

"Pretending to not understand my question and whether this research facility is hidden or not tells me everything I need to know. So, *Echo*, if you do have the spine I'm certain you have, why was another Cyborg here, what did they want, and what made them leave?"

Her hands clenched at her sides, knowing she'd made a mistake in being too nonchalant about Keir's motives.

"You're assuming I've already made the assumption that you're here for the same reasons they'd come, when that isn't true—it's inference," she snapped. Keir's eyes flared with something she couldn't place, but she held her ground against it.

But then his demeanor abruptly changed and he glanced back outside at the storm before leveling his eyes back on her. "I'm not letting you leave this outpost and risk both our hides so we can make it back to the compound tonight for some tour." He'd spoken so matter-of-factly that it was a warning for her not to fight him on it.

She gritted her teeth. "*You* said you were here on a mission."

"I am."

"Your own?"

"Does it matter?"

"Yes!"

"Why?" he growled. "I don't like being in the dark."

She glanced at the door with regret, wishing she had dashed out while she'd still had the chance. If she went for it now, he'd know she was hiding something. "I'm not joking about the reason why you're here, and no one else is either. You wouldn't have made the effort, if it wasn't important, mission or not."

"I have a right to know."

Echo draped her jacket over a nearby crate. "Then I have a right to know if it's the truth."

Her jaw clenched as Keir trapped her with furious eyes, demanding her submission in this. She held her ground. She submitted to no one.

Fuck if Keir's mission was classified. She wasn't going to be cowed into giving up anything unless she received clemency in return, clemency equal enough to keep Volun and everyone living upon it safe.

And that was never, ever going to happen. Keir was only one being.

"Fine."

Echo startled. "You'll tell me? Honestly?"

"Yes. You have my word."

She eyed him warily. A Cyborg didn't make a promise without meaning it. "I want you to swear that no one will come to any harm. Can you make that promise?"

"Deal."

Her lips parted, stunned by his quick omission.

She sat beside her jacket with a tired sigh. Echo didn't know if she believed him, but she was intrigued. "Fine. I'll tell you what I can. You came here because you or someone else, whoever you work for, caught wind of a rumor, or bad intel, that there's a cybernetic warfare research cell, a facility—or laboratory, if that's what you want to call it— where Cyborgs were tested, bred, and created. For some reason, this information about your creation place has been wiped from your head entirely. Snippets of memories—that you can't even tell whether they are real or fake—are all you have on the exact origins of where you came into existence. *How* you came into existence."

Keir's face morphed into rapt curiosity as she spoke, his gaze distancing like he was considering her theories. Some of it was theory, though the rest was all based on what her mother had told her.

"But you're not here for nostalgia," Echo continued, "or

even for the cybernetics laboratory itself. You're here for the sliver in your mind that's blank. You understand why these memories have been wiped, but it doesn't matter. Inside, your codes reassure you that nothing's wrong, that your first memories after awakening are naturally unclear. Except when you try to understand this, there's no information, no answers as to why, only that it was a fail safe measure to keep that knowledge from being given to our enemy—if you were ever caught and disassembled.

"Perhaps you even traveled to other 'known' facilities and still find the blanks in your head unclear, because you have no true memories of those facilities either, but for whatever reason, you're lost. You can't stand the feeling. You're not created to feel 'lost' or weak or whatever it is that you're experiencing. It's all entirely too human for you." Echo sighed again, her fingers unclenching. The windows rattled from a powerful gust of wind.

When he didn't agree or disagree with her, she pressed on. "You've tried everywhere else to fill in these gaps and nothing has helped. Now you're chasing unsubstantiated whispers because all the main trails have led to dead ends." Echo inhaled. "Which has led you to Volun, thinking there's a conspiracy, thinking there's just some big secret about why these memories were wiped from you and that Volun's people are in on it. But do you want to know what I think? What I really think?"

He nodded sharply, his gaze unyielding. "Yes," he urged. "Tell me what you think. Tell me everything."

"I think you're going to be very disappointed. Sorry. I

don't know the other Cyborg's exact motivation for coming here, only that, sometimes your kind struggle with memory wipes."

She watched as the intensity Keir had embodied scattered like dust. The shadows cast over his gaze lightened, and tension seeped from his shoulders. He looked disappointed, but she couldn't be certain...

The pit in her stomach eased now that everything was out in the open. Why he was here at all would now be revealed to her, as per his promise. If it were for lost memories, she'd pledge her soul to the space gods because it meant he really wasn't here searching for Ares, but for the dangerous facility.

Because Ares was dead. He'd never left Volun.

And if he was here for the facility, then she and Jonah had planned for that.

"It's clear you have spent a great deal of time with another like me," he responded easily, the side of his lips almost lifting into a smile, completely throwing her off-guard. "I am searching for the very same research base. You are right in that."

She slumped from his admittance.

"Though my reasoning isn't because of some deleted memories," he added.

"It's not?"

"No. I don't give a fuck about what happened to me between my creation and my release into the universe. In fact, I'd prefer those memories stay lost. I'm here for money. And only money."

She guffawed, taken aback. "You're here for... money?"

Had she heard him correctly?

Keir started to pace as he answered her. "There is a sliver where our memories have been erased, that is true. I can recall the conversations with my creators in why this is essential, classified knowledge—those memories have not been deleted. If that is why my brethren had journeyed here before me, I can understand their reasoning now. I do apologize if they hurt you in their pursuit."

He believed her.

When he strode to her. Echo pushed off the crate, snapping her parted lips closed. Money? He was here for money? On Volun? He was apologizing?

"Will you take me there, Echo?" He side-eyed her. "To this research base?"

Her lips pursed. "Who do you work for exactly? You're being paid to be here?"

He cocked a brow. "I'm not directly employed by anyone. I'm here—let's say—trading favors."

"Then what do you want with an old lab that's already been torn apart?" She didn't believe him. "There's no money in it."

"Even I don't know that... but perhaps it has something to do with why the last Cyborg was here."

"What? Is your partner... another Cyborg?"

"He is."

Her heart quickened and the pit in her stomach returned with a vengeance. "And if I say no? If I won't take you?"

Keir leveled with her, and she tried not to wince from his searching perusal. She didn't want to be read, or studied, or focused on. Especially not by someone as dangerous as him. The fact that he was working with another Cyborg, one with his own unknown motives, was worse than she hoped. Keir might not hurt her, but the other...

"I can make you," he stated, drawing back.

Dread seeped into her chest.

The threat was always there. She just hadn't expected him to be upfront about it. Not after his teasing. Not after the promise... But the truth was that he *could* force her. He could force her, murder everyone in the compound, and be gone before anyone arrived to stop him. It would be so easy for him.

"You don't have to threaten me," she whispered. "I'll take you. I planned to take you. When Jonah called me yesterday saying you had arrived, I was sad."

Surprise crossed his features. "Sad? Why?"

"I knew you would leave as disappointed as the rest, and that I'd be the one to give you the bad news. It's a shitty position to be in."

"We'll see about that."

She looked away because he wouldn't. He couldn't see her deceit if he couldn't see her face. "I don't know you, Keir, and we don't like outsiders here, but you seem... like an honorable being." She looked down at her hands.

He strode to her side. "What's wrong?" he asked, sounding genuinely concerned. "I would never make you do anything you don't want to do. I didn't mean to frighten you. My words were in jest."

Except he had just done all of that and more. She shook her head. "When your partner realizes there's nothing here, can you promise me *he* won't—"

"What happened with the other Cyborg, Echo?" Anger and vehemence etched his question. He leaned down to capture her gaze, but she averted her eyes. "Who were they? What did they do?"

"Can you still promise us safety? Even from him?"

She wasn't joking around, not with this.

He growled. "I have no interest in hurting anyone, anymore. I had enough of that long ago. When my mission is done, I will leave this moon graciously and without issue. No one will come to any harm by my hand. Do you think you can believe me?" He caught her chin and forced her to face him.

His face was right before her own, mere inches apart. Her heart jumped into her throat from the proximity. She pushed his hand away and leaned back, discovering that she was trapped against the crate, and with walls on the other side of her, she had no easy escape that would make it appear like she wasn't trying to run.

Echo's cheeks heated as he waited for her answer. His closeness sent her nerves dancing and she could barely part her lips to breathe.

The imprints of his fingers, and their heat, remained on her chin. She reached up and rubbed it.

His eyes dropped to her hand.

Keir could also kiss her if he desired, and do it before she had a chance to resist.

She jerked back and he snapped forward as if by instinct. The small amount of space between them stifled her. She hitched as notes of wet leather and metal filled her nose.

"What are you doing?" she breathed.

She'd also never been this close to a strange man. Let alone one she found attractive, even if dangerous. Her blood quickened as rain, wind, thunder, and lightning wreaked havoc all around them. He leaned into her.

"I'm trying to figure you out." His breath fanned her face.

"Stop."

He pulled back. "I will if you do."

She frowned at him.

"I see," he mused, irritating her as she got up and moved away. If he was trying to make her uneasy, he was doing a great job at it. He walked to the door. "Get some rest."

Bristling, feeling manipulated, she quipped. "You're leaving?"

He stopped and cocked his head but didn't look back at her. His back and shoulders were bunched and tense. "I was going to give you privacy and spend the night upstairs. Did you want me to stay?"

"I, uh... Oh."

The night?

Her eyes slid to the windows.

What had just happened between them wasn't good.

But she didn't want him to leave, not if she was being honest. It was growing darker and darker outside. Even if night was hours away, the storm was going to make it arrive much sooner.

Her shoulders slumped. "Yes," she said, wishing it was a lie. "Stay. It'll be a long night to spend alone." Echo looked around, found a lantern and turned it on, hoping she didn't come across as something she wasn't.

And yet... the idea of it... if their situations were different, had her toes curling.

It was better that she knew where he was rather than not. Right?

Keir nodded slowly and went to the window, turning his back on her. The tension in his demeanor remained.

She watched him for a time, waiting for him to say more, but when it became apparent he was neither going to speak nor acknowledge her any further, she prayed she hadn't made a mistake.

He was going to make her spend the night alone anyway.

TEN

Keir rubbed his jaw. The rain went from a downpour to a drizzle as the night came and went. Minute by minute, the dreary wet landscape appeared through the sky's gray veil that had overshadowed it for the last sixteen hours.

Behind him, Echo snored softly, tangled back up in musty blankets on the cot in the corner. She had fought sleep, even after he had reassured her he would keep watch and would wake her if the need arose. She was safe with him.

Echo was painfully innocent, he could tell.

And she was stubborn as all hell.

For a woman who was capable of surviving on an alien world, Echo lacked the skills to hide her responses to him.

Which made her either afraid of him and was trying to hide it, or she was attracted to him and didn't realize it. Her cheeks had flushed when he'd caught her chin, and her eyes had dipped to his mouth.

The moment had staggered him.

He'd parted his lips for her, had wanted to press his mouth to hers, to take her lips and kiss them, and to see how she would react. He'd wanted to see if she would have pulled away or kissed him back. And if she had kissed him back, would she had let him go further?

Rubbing his lips with his fingertips, Keir cursed and dropped them. Finding out what would happen wasn't worth jeopardizing the mission. And, even if she was naïve, so was he. He had nothing but contained disdain for humanity as a whole, he didn't like them.

Echo was a beautiful woman, a *free* woman. That was all. Any male, a Cyborg or otherwise, would agree.

Keir frowned. His thoughts kept circling back to Echo.

He didn't like imagining anyone else finding her beautiful.

Hearing a shuffle behind him, he cocked his head. Echo moaned and turned in her bedding.

He straightened his neck. He would get his answers one way or another.

Echo groaned with emotion, and he heard her blankets being shoved aside. The wires in his chest buzzed with excitement. She was waking up. Keir closed his eyes.

"Is the storm over?" she mumbled.

"Almost," he answered, his frown deepening.

She padded over to him on socked feet to stand at his side. She rubbed her eyes and tied back her hair, completely unaware of the tension radiating from him, or of the erection he was barely able to keep hidden, despite his systems interfering.

"Give me a minute to wake up and get my head on straight, then we'll head to the compound." She yawned. "I'll need to check in with the others before we can get to it."

Get... to it?

"Did you sleep well?" he asked, unable to keep the strain from his voice. After how they ended things the evening before, they'd spent the next few hours in awkward silence.

"Better than I have a right to," she answered. "Did you sleep, or did you just stand there all night?"

"I stood here all night."

"Right, because that's normal for you. I need a shower." She sighed. "Maybe tonight."

He didn't respond, instead, he waited for her to tug on her boots as he watched her reflection in the window. Afterward, she folded the cot and blankets.

When she was done, he faced her. "Ready?"

Her clothes were wrinkled, there was a sheen of sleep in her eyes, and despite being tied back, her hair was crimped. Even bedraggled, she was beautiful.

Humans stared at *him*; he didn't stare at humans. Yet he wanted to stare at her. She was meant to be stared at. It was uncanny. Echo's features were nearly symmetrical. After she had fallen asleep, he'd leaned over her sleeping form and calculated them. Whoever her parents were, had given Echo their best genetic material.

"Yeah, I'm ready." She cracked her neck, acting oddly comfortable with him this morning. "Let's get this show on the road. I'm hungry."

His lips tweaked. "Even idioms have made it here." Echo looked at him confused, and he shook his head. "Never mind."

"We'll have you off this world before the heatwave, I promise," she said, heading for the door and opening it. She dashed out into the rain.

He followed after her.

Echo jumped on her bike and tugged on her helmet, nodding to him once before she took off. He stared after her until she was a dot on the horizon. She seemed to be running from him. Even now, even after they had spent a night together and he had kept her guarded, she was running.

Eyeing the dark clouds she was headed for, Keir clenched his jaw.

Breaking out his wings, he caught up to her a moment later.

Echo stayed on the road, making it easier for him to keep her in his sight today. After a few minutes and she didn't divert once, he relaxed.

The day brightened over the morning and revealed the aftermath of the storm. Everything was muddy, wet, and even drearier than before. His gaze roved over the soggy landscape without seeing it, honing back in on Echo. She sped away from him and predatory musings took over his thoughts.

His hawk loved a good hunt.

He dove for her, only to stop right before he snatched her into his arms and swooped back toward the sky. He did it again, nearly snagging a strand of her hair with his talon.

She didn't notice. She simply hunkered forward and focused only on the road ahead.

Wind whipped his hair, rain streaked his cheeks, and his talons emerged to slice through the air. He wasn't made for the confinement of spaceships, claustrophobic ports, or even cities. He was made for this, for the wilds. He wished he could share it with Echo, if just for a little while. She was too tightly wound. He wondered if she knew what the concept of *fun* was. If he caught her up and took her to the clouds, Keir was certain he could loosen her up.

He was made for the sky. The first time he had spread his wings and flown, it had been bliss. It had been the only part of his life that he had enjoyed. Day in and day out, he'd been paraded around after he had entered this universe. His wings, his hawk, had been the only thing to save him as he watched his brethren become real heroes from afar.

He had envied them.

When the war came to an end, he'd vowed that he would do whatever it took to never be beholden to anyone ever again. He would never be made into a fool.

Once his sanctuary was complete, and Keir had silent control over Titan's reestablishment, he would have no need for humans ever again. There was no place for them on his land.

He swooped down to fly behind and at Echo's side and waited for her to discover him.

The military base appeared in the distance, and his mission crashed back to the forefront of his thoughts. Echo drove straight for it, never once turning to search for him like she had the morning before. Keir resealed his talons, clawing them through the air one final time to end his fun.

The wind gradually picked back up, driving the remaining storm clouds away. The rain was no more than a drizzle in the breeze.

He lowered to the ground and hovered quietly as Echo stopped at the compound's gates and parked her bike within the shadows of the wall. She pulled off her helmet just as his suit rethreaded over his wings and he landed on the ground.

She got off her bike, turned and squinted at him.

"You really must be flying," she said, winded and fully awake now, reflecting his own invigoration. "I swear I saw you. In the corner of my eye." She examined his form, a smile forming on her lips. "Wouldn't that be something?" she mused wistfully. He straightened at her blatant perusal, hoping she liked what she saw.

He wanted her to like what she saw.

"I was flying," he said.

She shook out her hair and started tying it back up with a smile. "Right. Sure. Prove it to me. For real."

"No. Perhaps you should try harder when you search for me," he teased, reaching out and pushing a stray hair behind her ear. "Next time, look up, not back."

She went tense all over, and he dropped his hand, realizing what he'd done again, fisting his hand at his side. Her heartbeat blasted into overdrive, her lips parted, and she now stared at him warily. Keir cursed.

She cleared her throat. "I will. If there is a next time. Are you ready? I can take you to the old lab." She shifted away from him.

Bristling, he cocked his head. "I thought you wanted to check in with the others first?"

She moved farther away, clearly uncomfortable, and more curses soured his tongue. He hadn't meant to upset her.

"I'd rather get what you're looking for handled," she said. "They can wait a little. Clearly, the storm has already been through here. Unless you have more questions after last night, you won't need me once I remove the chains."

"Chains?"

"We've had to go old school with our security. A lot of the old setups have either been disabled, removed, or have broken over the last sixty years. Chains are cheap." Echo rushed through the open gates of the compound.

She was fleeing from him. Again.

"Lead the way," he gritted under his breath.

She quickened her step as he began to follow her.

He clenched his hands to keep his talons from emerging to snatch her against him, like he'd wanted too when he was flying behind her. Keir didn't like how she kept running from him now that he realized that was what she was doing. His hawk wanted his win. It wanted to sink its talons deep...

But, to his growing concern, the man inside him wanted far more than that.

ELEVEN

She headed toward the central buildings on the base. The drive had cleared her head, had calmed her, but hadn't fixed her growing problem.

Waking up to Keir had been a shock. He was the first thing she saw when she'd opened her eyes. Her joints had locked up and made her body ache viciously. It had been an ache she knew all too well. The clenching pressure between her legs that indicated arousal.

But it wasn't waking up to him that disturbed her, it was what she had done afterward...

She'd settled into the blankets when she had realized he wasn't aware. And for much longer than she'd ever admit, she had lain there, pretending to sleep. She had watched him and ached. She had pressed her curled hands under her chin to keep them from sneaking between her legs.

Why does he keep pushing back my hair? Echo's brow furrowed, all too aware that he was following closely behind her. The faster she walked, the closer he seemed to get. Stifled, she unbuttoned her jacket.

I've spent too much time alone. It was making her act like a fool.

Keir's footsteps crunched the gravel. Heat radiated off of him, and even though she fled from it—from him—she continued to feel his heat fight against the wind upon her exposed flesh. Echo veered away from the garages and buildings where most of the colonists worked and lived, hoping to avoid them until she lost Keir. No one needed to see her pretend to be calm when she was anything but. They needed her to be strong.

"This research lab is within the compound?" Keir asked.

"Yes, of course. I told you it was."

Was he hoping for a different answer or was he trying to make conversation with her? He could've talked to her yesterday evening if he'd wanted, but he'd done what so many Cyborgs did, and turned themselves off. For as much as she appreciated the space he tried to give her, it had reminded her how terribly lonely she was, and had nearly made her brave the storm, and his wrath rather than face it.

Echo peered at the clouds and prayed that they didn't part until Keir was well and gone from this world.

A gust of wind hit her, and she shivered, seeing a giant countdown looming over her head.

"It's just up ahead," she said.

Practically running to their destination, her keys felt like dead weight in her pocket. She stopped at the old security doors to the building and frowned. The door was unlocked. "It shouldn't be open..." She grabbed the handle and twisted.

Keir's hand snagged her wrist. She was forced to back away as he moved in front of her and opened the door himself. He paused on the threshold and bent his neck, peering inside.

"What are you—"

"Is the building supposed to be open?" he asked.

"No, but it's fine. Someone must have forgotten to lock it. That's all."

He raised his hand. "There's someone inside."

"What?"

Keir moved ahead and into the darkened foyer, tugging his gun strap forward.

"It's someone from the compound." She grabbed his arm. "Put your gun away. Jeez. There's no need for that. Seriously, no one here is dangerous. To either of us."

"And yet you beg for their protection," he murmured, shooting her stoney look.

She pursed her lips. That was true. Keir took his hand off his gun, and she relaxed.

Echo reached into her jacket pocket and took out the small flashlight she had on her keyring. Aiming it ahead, she called out. "Who's there? It's Echo."

She heard shuffling and went to the light switches and flicked them on. She turned off her flashlight.

"Echo?" a voice responded.

Madeline emerged from one of the offices, a hand

shielding her eyes. Bleary-eyed, she looked like she'd been crying.

Echo frowned upon seeing her, and headed in her direction. "What are you doing here?"

Madeline's gaze shifted from Echo to Keir, her eyes widening.

"I'm sorry," Madeline began, "I didn't realize—"

Keir stepped forward.

Madeline startled further as he approached her, overtaking Echo. "I thought the building would be empty. I just—"

"We didn't mean to scare you," he offered apologetically, cocking his head at her. "It's nice to see you again. Has the chocolate been to your liking?"

Madeline's mouth snapped closed. She eyed him from head to toe, fixating on his face. She smiled up at him. "Yes, thank you."

Echo chewed on her lip. The familiarity between them bothered her.

"Maddy," Echo chastised. "You shouldn't be out alone, not in your condition, and right before a burnout."

Madeline's gaze snapped to hers, the smile falling from her lips. "It's none of your business what I do."

Echo winced. "I didn't mean..."

Keir moved to Echo's side, taking Madeline's attention off of her. Madeline's smile returned.

She chuckled under her breath and shook her head, putting her hand on her lower back. "Sorry, pregnancy hormones. I didn't mean to snap. I know you worry, Echo."

"It's fine," Echo said. "No need to apologize."

Madeline ignored her. "Have you found what you were looking for?" she asked Keir.

"Not quite," he said politely. "But I'm hoping that'll change soon."

Embarrassed, Echo stepped aside.

"I hope so too, but I'm afraid this building holds only ghosts now." Madeline chuckled. "There's not much else here, if this is where you're searching for answers."

"If that's so, you're brave to face them, especially alone."

"I prefer them."

Keir cocked a brow. "You do?"

"Absolutely. They never question you. I like that about them. They don't care about your intentions, only that you're in their space. They just want to live, that's all. I get that."

"I haven't encountered many myself, so I wouldn't know, but those I have encountered had never been thrilled with my presence. Human ghosts are still human."

"Stay on Volun long enough and you'll encounter many. We have more ghosts than living residents now. Do humans not like you in their presence?"

"Some don't. Though, I've come to realize those humans may be my favorite."

"Oh?"

"They don't believe the lies that have been told to them by their superiors. They think for themselves and listen to their instincts."

"And what lie is that?"

"That I'm here to save and protect them with all the honor of a saint."

"And yet, here you are, asking me if I liked your chocolate."

They smiled at each other.

Echo wished the floor would swallow her whole.

"Well, you've come to the right place—oww!" Madeline's hand shot to her belly. "He's kicking. The little imp is impatient."

Keir's eyes dropped. "How far along are you?"

"Eight and a half standard months. Ten Volun months. Would you like to feel?"

Echo jerked, her fingers twitching when she realized Madeline wasn't including her. She only offered it to Keir.

He shifted on his feet, suddenly looking nervous as hell. "I—"

For as much as she envied him at that moment, she felt for him too.

"Yes," Keir said, stilling. "If you don't mind?"

Madeline's smile grew. "Not at all."

Keir raised his hand, his fingers outstretched. He took a step toward Madeline as he did, closing the gap between them. Gently, he placed his hand on her belly. She grabbed his hand and adjusted it to her left side.

Keir's eyes flashed, the light casting from them like deep purple storm clouds at midnight. "I can feel him."

Madeline didn't remove her hand off of Keir's. "He's going to run circles around me soon. If only his father was here to chase after him, right?"

"Yes, he will." Keir stared sharply at Madeline's belly. "We need more children like that. Circles can be fun."

Echo couldn't help but picture them together. Their happy union flashed before her eyes as quickly as Keir's had a moment ago. Was it because he'd envisioned it too? The beautiful babies they would have, the exciting life they would lead. Their conversation was so easy, so natural. Where it had always been a whirlwind of emotion, a battle being skirted, between her and Keir.

Echo had to stop it—stop this—before it was too late.

"Madeline," she said, announcing her presence. "Can we walk you home? The wind is picking back up, and the paths are still slick."

Keir pulled his hand off of Madeline's belly, and Madeline released him, turning to Echo. "I'm not afraid of the wind. It couldn't blow me away right now even if it tried." She patted her stomach.

"Can I?" Echo asked before she could help herself.

Madeline's eyes widened and then she nodded slowly, her smile dropping again. Echo gingerly placed her hand on Madeline's belly, ready for the woman to shove her away.

She didn't. Echo felt a fluttering beneath her palm, and a grin formed on her lips.

"Beautiful," she whispered, awed, feeling the baby's kick. "I didn't know they moved so much in the womb."

"Maybe if you spent more time in the compound, you'd know more," Madeline quipped.

Echo snatched her hand away.

Madeline didn't wait and ambled toward the exit. "I'll be fine heading home—"

Keir hooked his arm with Madeline's and began leading her back down the hallway.

"Watch your step," he said, as she peered up at him. "Lean on me if you need."

Madeline's eyes lit up. "I... Thank you."

He led her away.

Echo remained rooted where she was.

Who was she to stop Madeline and Keir from making a connection? It wasn't her place. Maybe it was a good thing...

When they were gone, Echo turned on her heel, and entered the office Madeline had exited from. Inside, there was nothing but an old desk and a wooden chair, pushed neatly under it. Besides the barred window behind it, the room was empty.

Echo pulled out the chair and sat down. Several minutes went by before she heard Keir return. She left the room and went out to meet him. The warmth in his expression was nowhere to be seen.

"Sorry for making you wait," he said.

"It's all right. It was nice of you to walk with her. I don't mind."

Keir's eyes sharpened upon her face, and Echo prayed he couldn't read her thoughts. "It's been a long couple of days, and I have not seen you eat, Echo. You said you were hungry. Humans can only endure so much."

"Perhaps," she said quickly. "I'm used to it, though."

"You shouldn't be. You should be taking better care of yourself, too."

She hated this line of questioning more than she hated watching Madeline flirt with him. "It's really not a problem. I'm fine, and I know I'll be able to eat soon. The sooner we get this over with, the sooner I'll be able to do just that. I haven't seen you eat either," she grumped. "Madeline likes you."

"I don't need to eat, as you already well know, having dealt with my kind before." Keir reached into his vest and pulled something out, handing it to her. "Take this. I should have given it to you last night. It's a field ration."

She stared at the object before taking it. Turning it over in her hand, it was a standard nutrient bar.

"Thank you."

His eyes narrowed on her.

"Come on." She licked her lips. "We're almost there."

They passed through the upper building and toward a large stairwell. She flicked on the lights inside and stuffed the bar into her pocket.

"You and Madeline have issues?" he probed as they descended the stairs.

"We don't."

"Seems like she's mad at you."

Echo's spine straightened, sensing his eyes on her back. "She has no reason to be. We barely ever talk."

"Maybe that's the problem."

"We're here," she said when the stairs ended and they

faced the chained-up doors at the bottom. Keir halted at her side as she found the right key.

Keir scowled. "This... is it?"

"Yes." She grabbed the chain and unlocked it. "It used to be behind several security doors, I've been told." Echo slapped her hand on the frame. "But they were uninstalled when the government shut this place down, probably to be reused on another site. There's not much left. Nothing at least to warrant anything more than these chains to seal it off." She unthreaded the chain from the handles.

"I expected far more security than this."

Hiding her face, Echo coiled the chain, placed it on the ground, and pushed the door in. She stepped through. The air was colder, older on the other side, tickling her nose. She strolled to the wall where the light switches were, turning them on. Inside, a sleeker, high-tech space lit up from the LEDs overhead. There were old biohazard signs and chemical routes placed out from the leftover pipes lining the walls. Everything was labeled.

Everything.

Jonah and her had chosen this place because it had been a laboratory long ago, but what kind? They didn't know.

Industrial rooms lay beyond down several sealed hallways, stripped clean of everything but for some machinery and benchware that had been left behind. Wherever Echo looked, dust coated everything, reassuring her the space had been undisturbed for the years between its last offworld visitor.

Keir's eyes glowed as he scanned the space, no doubt

recording it to his memories. An intensity had taken him over, making his hawkish features sharper than usual.

Echo pulled her lip into her mouth, watching him. Keir looked at everything intensity, not just this, who was she kidding?

"The rest of the space should be unlocked," she said.

The last two days had been stressful, but they could've been worse, much, much worse.

She was almost sorry that this was likely going to be their final few minutes together. He strode past her and into the space, bending his head this way and that. It was a curious mannerism, and one she hadn't seen from anyone else. No one she knew bent their neck so much. She almost wished she had asked Keir why he moved the way he did.

Echo released her lip from her teeth, growing wistful as Keir pushed open the door to a room and ducked in.

Digging her boot into the floor, she shifted and looked around, waiting to see if he had anything more to ask from her. But as the minutes built and the silence grew, she realized she'd been dismissed.

Keir went from one space to the next without further acknowledging her.

"If you think you can handle it from here, I'll leave you to your own devices," she called out to him, returning to wait at the door's threshold. "I only ask that when you're done, you put the chains back on the door and close the lock."

Down the hallway, Keir kneeled and swiped his fingers across the dust on the floor.

She prayed that he wouldn't see through her deceit. The bones of this space could've been impressive if it were still operational. It looked like it could've been a cybernetics lab at one point. It looked like the real one... kind of.

He stood and faced her, but his eyes were distant as he walked back to her. She handed him the chain and he took it.

He *was* dismissing her.

"Good luck, Keir. I know it's not what you were hoping for, but we all tried to warn you." Feeling like she should say more, offer him more, she added, "Don't take too long. You'll want to be gone before the clouds finish clearing from the sky."

He glanced back at the lab. "I plan on it."

Fingers twitching, she waited for him to say something more, for his intensity to return to her and to feel the pressure of it weigh her down. For him to bombard her with questions about how this place isn't what he'd been sent here to find. That she and the rest of the compound had no idea what a cybernetics lab even looked like.

She readied for that absurd argument, and to convince him...

"Have any questions?" she asked.

"No. I think you've answered everything." He returned to the hallway.

Watching him walk away, and then out of sight, she couldn't help feeling a little disappointed.

He was...*gone.*

It was over. He had no more use for her.

Deciding it was best to just let this end, Echo turned on her heel and bounded up the stairs before she could second-guess it. Pushing open the door outside, she inhaled as the wind wrapped her up.

She didn't have to keep lying.

Echo exhaled and rubbed away the tightness in her chest.

Now she could put the events of the last several days behind her, and hoped she never, ever saw him, or another of his kind, ever again.

TWELVE

Keir glanced around him at the doors, hallways, and laboratories—still recalling nothing about them.

Not even a scent or a feeling.

When he inhaled, he scented Echo. And just like that, she took back his thoughts. Her scent was like Earth's germanium flowers and wet grass—neither of which would be on or anywhere near Volun.

His skin prickled as her smell streaked through him. Keir halted, his skin never prickled. It had done so twice today. His skin had risen feeling Madeline's baby kick, and now again, inhaling Echo's natural aroma. She smelled too good, and he'd been enjoying it while they were together. Only now, it was beginning to fade since she had left. He inhaled harder, taking in as much as he could because he wasn't going after her to force her back by his side. His hands balled as he glanced at the exit.

She'd served her purpose.

It was time to let her go.

Yet, he couldn't shake the prickles on his flesh.

When Madeline had let him feel her belly, he'd been nervous—until the baby kicked. It wasn't every day that he touched a pregnant woman, nor interacted with a young human life. His nerves had shifted to envy when a dormant instinct slammed into his head.

It was an instinct he was certain should have been dormant forever.

His need to *nest*.

Reeling, his mind had crafted a vision of his own child being born—not created. A child made from his own seed. Echo's belly had flooded his mind. She was carrying his child.

There was a stirring inside his chest.

He shook his head to clear it of Echo and her smell, pushing her from his systems. But the tightness in his chest remained. The vision had unnerved him, and he was relieved when she'd left. Keir ran his hands over his face and straightened, glancing at the exit one more time before scowling and turning away.

He went deeper into the research space, seeding out his mind for any stray electrical currents he could usurp, mapping it out to send back with his report.

He'd visited a few cybernetics laboratories in his time. Ones that worked to create or to fix lifeforms like him. Those laboratories weren't militarized and were privately funded, offering body modification surgeries for humans who wanted to have more than what they were given organically.

Any other cybernetic laboratory that was still in existence were run by the government—like the one he'd been hoping to find. But those weren't equipped to make Cyborgs anymore—if they ever were—and were equipped to study nanocell technology instead. He was welcomed at these labs for testing and body part replacements, but they weren't what Nightheart was searching for. None of those laboratories could create a real Cyborg and sustain them all the way to adulthood.

Technology like that... cost a lot of money.

Since the war, no new militarized Cyborgs had come into existence.

He cost a lot of money. Unfortunately, he wasn't into self-mutilation.

Volun didn't seem like the place to keep billions of dollars of technology hidden away.

Chains bound on doors?

Even after half a century, Keir had expected something entirely different.

He palmed his mouth. Either way, it made no difference to him. Nightheart trusted him, and if the lab he was searching for was well and truly gone, he had to accept that.

Room after room, Keir scanned and memorized every detail. Old pipes and machinery lined the ceilings, traveling in and out of the rooms and deep into the walls. They were cold to the touch. Broken glass littered some of the corners, there were dust motes in the air, and in a few places, ripped-out wires hung from the walls and ceiling. The few machines left behind no longer had the proper equipment to be useful anymore.

Sleek metal walls, old security systems, everything about this place was dull and dusty from abandonment.

Keir pushed through another set of double doors and found a recreational space.

There was more old and broken equipment scattered throughout. But it wasn't the trash that caught his attention, it was the holographic shooting range, and the bullet holes in the walls on the opposite end.

Heading for the largest hole, he set down the chains and fit his fist into it, lining it up as if he'd punched it himself. Testing the wall with his other palm, he calculated the force needed to make such an indent.

Only a Cyborg could have punched a steel and cement wall.

Keir stepped to the side and punched the wall next to the first hole. The crunch echoed hollowly as debris went flying. He drew back his hand and compared the holes.

His lips twitched into a smile. The holes matched.

Echo had been telling him the truth all along.

Maybe there was some hope for humanity after all. He straightened and glanced behind him, no longer sensing her presence.

He frowned.

It hadn't occurred to him that Echo wouldn't remain to keep an eye on him. He looked down at the chains, recalling her telling him to lock up when he was done.

Why is she always running from me?

Keir shook the dust off his fist and headed for the exit, locking up the door as per her request. He didn't need any more evidence. The compound and the lab was nothing more than exactly what everyone had told him: a relic of the past. He'd been here for days and hadn't seen, heard, or sensed anything that would say otherwise.

Leaving the building, wind slammed into him, and he lifted an arm to shield his face. It was dark out now and unusually warm.

He'd spent years searching for this place for Nightheart. Now that he had found it, only to discover the place in ruins, humored him.

Good fucking riddance.

Keir couldn't ask for a better outcome. He would never have to wonder again if there were other Cyborgs being made to serve. He may have journeyed here for money, but he'd always planned to put a stop to his kind's creation. Humans didn't deserve their service.

Some humans.

The light flickered from a nearby lantern, drawing his gaze. He switched to night vision as a large branch flew past him and searched for Echo.

Breaking open his wings, Keir flew above the compound, pairing with his skiff at the same time. He flew towards it, his gaze searching for her. The wind thrashed his wings, wheezing through the platelets.

Besides a scattering of lights from the working lanterns,

the compound was quiet and dark. The colonists were all inside. He'd been in the lab for hours.

Keir landed beside his ship and ducked into it right as a piece of sheet metal cut through the air toward him. Scowling, he watched the metal tumble away to hit the side of a building.

Echo hadn't lied about the weather either.

Running his hands over his face, he needed to leave now if he didn't want to brave the heat with his skiff. His main ship would've handled it, but not the smaller vessel he came down in. He switched on his thrusters and readied for takeoff.

There was nothing left to keep him here. No servers, no leftover databases with information for him to mine. There were barely even any humans left.

He still didn't know who else had been here before him. Which one of his brethren had come searching for this place before him. If he wanted to find out, he'd have to stay here longer.

He leaned back and ran his hands over his head. He didn't like not possessing every piece of the puzzle. He also didn't like the position it would put him in. Keir had what he had come for, more than he could ask for. He didn't have to brave the military to get his answers.

Something banged against his skiff. Keir watched as a plastic bin rolled away, followed soon after by another tree branch.

Had Echo made it home? Was she safe? Her scent had long since left his systems and he...missed it.

Had she eaten? Had she listened to him?

He knew she didn't live inside the compound's walls. She would've checked in and then left.

He hadn't gotten the chance to repay her for her help. Considering that she had taken time out of her schedule for him, put him in her debt. Keir glanced behind him and at the remaining crates stacked in the space behind the cockpit that he'd brought with him to barter with.

Without dwelling on it further, he strapped in and drove his ship into the air, and headed in the direction of Echo's outpost.

THIRTEEN

THE TREES SHOOK as he landed outside her home, their giant leaves billowing viciously. The lights were on and he could see straight into and through the outpost. The main room was empty. Echo's hoverbike was parked under the deck.

She'd made it home. The tension between Keir's shoulders eased.

Regardless of the weather, it was his fault that the last couple of days hadn't gone her way. Making sure she was all right and paying for her time was the least he could do.

Keir moved to the back of his ship and grabbed the first crate off the stack. Leaving his ship with the crate, he flew to Echo's deck. A hot gale enveloped him as he did. All around him the trees shook and crackled as branches snapped.

To his right, the dark clouds were lightening, as if something big and bright was approaching from far behind them.

The sun.

He tore his eyes away from the eerie glow and shifted the crate to his side to knock on the door.

He waited.

After a minute, Keir knocked again, moving to the deck windows. The room was still empty. Echo's boots and jacket were next to the door, and there was an empty cup on the counter. He walked farther down the deck to the windows that gave him a view into the hallway.

A half-dozen doors lined it, but only one was open. The last door at the end. A light was on inside the room where he couldn't see.

He couldn't sense her presence.

He set down the crate and went back to the front door, the platelets in his back expanding. He knocked again, louder this time. Pulling his knife out of his vest, he tried the handle. With one heavy push, the door opened inward.

Keir scowled.

It was unlocked.

A woman, no matter how capable, should never have the door to her home unlocked. It was an open invitation to predators.

"Echo?" he called out.

There was no response.

If this outpost was designed like the others around the compound, she would have heard him. He would have *heard* her.

Quieting his steps, he stalked down the hallway to the room at the end. As he did, he noticed things he hadn't seen from outside. There were markings on the walls, overly sanded edges, and the scent of plastic, rust, and... the deep seep of bleach and soap that had long ago soaked into the very essence of this place.

He stopped at the threshold of the last door.

The room was bigger than he expected. There was one large bed with a thick wooden frame up against the back corner and to his left. The bed was unmade and covered in numerous blankets, quilts, and animal hides, clashing together in pattern and color. It had to be Echo's.

The rest of the space had the same feel, a hodgepodge of accessories and mementos.

There were clothes hanging off of a rod in the front right corner, random weapons up against the walls, and a giant animal hide rug across the floor. It was a beast he didn't recognize. On the right wall was an old wooden dresser with framed pictures atop of it.

Keir picked up a picture of Echo as a child. She was grinning and standing next to a man that resembled a younger Jonah, and was holding his hand. They stood beside a dead beast.

Keir cocked his head.

It was a commemorative hunting snapshot—the beast, their trophy. He set the picture down and faced the last corner of the room where there was a large metal door set in the center of the back wall. It looked like the ones he'd seen in the research labs earlier.

Hearing a very faint, hushed sound behind it, he moved closer. The door had to be thick and fully soundproof for him to discern so little from the other side.

Straining for more, he pressed his ear against it. The sound of running water could just barely be heard. His brow furrowed.

Cursing, he stepped back. *She's bathing.*

Pivoting away, Keir's jaw clenched. Echo hadn't answered him because she couldn't hear him.

No wonder why she hates my kind.

He moved to leave—and leave Volun entirely—when the door popped from its frame and opened, releasing pressurized air. Keir halted as steam poured out and filled the bedroom. Echo's body appeared, naked and dripping wet, half-turned toward him, drying her hair with a towel.

She was completely unaware of his presence.

Straightening, he was rooted to the spot.

Toned and pale, her body was exactly how he'd imagined it, taut with the muscles it needed to have to survive. Her breasts were small and pert, nipples peaked at the end. Stands of her wet hair escaped the towel to cinch around her face. There were several faint scars though no marks of old, deep wounds. No bruises or scratches. No real marks of age of any kind.

If she'd been hit by lightning like she had said, there would be evidence of it.

Swallowing thickly, Keir stared. He'd never met another woman like her, and yet he couldn't figure out why that was. Echo wasn't just beautiful, she was... perfect. There was a wildness about her he recognized, and something untamable—or unattainable—that he couldn't place.

If he hadn't felt like he'd spent the last several days

chasing after her, maybe he would have had her figured out by now.

She was assured in the life she led, that was obvious. It had taken him a lifetime to find the same certainty in his path, and even then, he doubted his choices often.

She moved the towel down her arms as the steam dissipated. Unable to look away, Keir followed her every move. The muscles in his chest strained and tightened, and a heavy pressure flooded his limbs. His wings ached to be set free. He thought about saying something, anything to get her to cover herself. He couldn't.

There were no words.

Any second now, she was going to discover him and there was nothing he could do to change that. She would never trust him or his kind again. Frowning, Keir's cock hardened and pushed against his pants.

He looked down at his bulge in horror. He didn't want her to fear him. Not her.

Echo's eyes drifted up and caught sight of him.

"Wait—" he said, lifting his hands as she cried out and dashed to the wall to her left where a panel was.

Her fists hit the panel in a flurry.

"This isn't what it looks li—"

The floor fell out from under him. Darkness enveloped him with a resounding *thud* as he dropped. "Echo!" he roared, recovering the moment his feet hit the ground. The hole above him closed.

Sheathing his knife, he braced to shift. His wings made it halfway out before they stalled.

But his systems lagged and short-circuited from the effort. They didn't respond further. Something was stopping his commands. "Echo!"

There was no response.

Keir fell to his knees and grabbed his head, internal sirens blaring through his systems. The breaks in his signals were worsening, he couldn't stop them. He tried to fight them off. Then one by one, the sirens in him died.

He was rebooting.

He wrenched his eyes closed, staving it off for as long as possible, gritting his teeth so hard the metal in his inner jaw bent. His half-shifted wings jerked and dropped upon him, burying him in their weight. He struggled to stay conscious as his ability to see vanished.

"Echo," he gasped as darkness stole his mind.

FOURTEEN

She didn't move from the corner of her room until there was silence, and even when there was, Echo remained frozen in fear. She was afraid that if she moved, the trapdoor would burst open and Keir would come flying out and finish what he had started.

Echo edged from her spot, clutching her towel to her chest. She snatched her clothes and rushed into the shower room to throw them on. Afterward, she went back to her bedroom and snagged one of her guns from the wall. She leaned against it and pointed the gun at the trapdoor.

So far so good.

Another few minutes passed. She slid down the wall.

Slowly, Echo lowered her weapon.

Keir wasn't coming out. He couldn't. He was trapped. It was done.

"Fuck," she hissed under her breath as the reality of her

situation hit her. "Fuck. Fuck, fuck, fuck." Echo got to her feet. "Not again. Fuck!"

He had no reason to come find her. She had shown and told him what was necessary, what he had asked for. Now, he was trapped like how Ares had been trapped. Only this time, she was alone. She was in charge.

Echo caught her breath and tried to calm down.

It's going to be okay. I'm safe. Everyone is safe.

He's trapped.

Echo moved towards the trapdoor and walked around it twice before kneeling at the slatted peephole in the middle of it. Shifting the slats so it opened, she leaned forward to peer inside. Strange, pointed shadows met her and she frowned, uncertain what she was looking at.

"Keir?"

When there was no response, she left and found a flashlight. Shining it through the slats, her frown deepened.

She could see Keir's face, part of his legs, and one of his hands, but the rest of him was covered in a mass of jagged metal. Sharp plates jutted out and bent over his still body. Echo shifted closer to the hole and followed the jags with her light.

The metal covering him was attached to his backside, lined up with either side of his spine. Her brow furrowed. What she was seeing didn't make sense. The drop was barely twelve feet. The gap wasn't big enough to cause significant damage to a human, let alone a Cyborg. The rug covering the mechanism was supposed to cushion the blow as it fell inward.

He was going to wake up any minute now, and when he did, he was going to be furious. He would want answers.

Echo drew back.

They're wings.

He'd been telling her the truth. Her face scrunched.

Keir was a shifter. One of the rarer, more worrisome classes of Cyborgs.

She'd never be able to go up against a shifter class Cyborg out in the open. Hands shaking, she set the safety on her gun and put it aside. A gun wasn't going to help her anyway, and she had no intention of shooting him now that she was safe. At least now Keir couldn't use his wings against her. He couldn't use *anything* against her where he was, electrically or physically.

She leaned forward.

"Keir?" she called his name again, concerned.

His wings moved and she jerked back.

He'd just invaded her home, her room, and saw her naked. He hadn't said anything to stop it.

He watched me. Echo's lips pursed. *He had a knife.* She shouldn't be concerned for his well-being.

Echo shot to her feet when she heard a groan and quickly shut the door to the quarantine chamber, shifting the tapestry on her wall back over it to hide it from view. She then left the room and snatched a bottle of water, some jerky, and gathered them in a small pail.

Without Keir's systems keeping him healthy, she was going to have to take care of him until she figured out what to do next.

That's what she'd had to do with Ares.

Something hit her deck, and her eyes shot to the windows. Pitch darkness met her, but the burnout was imminent. The increasing volatility of the wind hailed it.

The situation she now found herself in hit her like a warship.

Calling Jonah wasn't going to solve anything. He would want to put an end to Keir's life. Immediately. That would be his solution to the mess they were now in. He'd only spend the entire time trying to convince her it was for the best if he didn't outright try and end him. Or worse, Jonah would want to tell her dad.

She feared what he might do if confronted with Keir without her mom to keep him calm. He hadn't been awake since she had left.

She was alone in this. She wasn't going to risk Keir's life. Not unless things got out of hand.

Only... Keir wasn't here for himself, he was here on behalf of another. Killing Keir would only solve things for a little while. Someone would show up looking for him, possibly another Cyborg. She wasn't going to get lucky twice.

Echo squeezed her eyes closed. She didn't want to kill Keir, not without speaking to him first. She didn't want to kill anyone. She hadn't been allowed to talk to Ares, and when she finally got the chance to check in, he'd been unresponsive. It had been different.

No, she was alone in this. At least until the burnout was over. Thankfully, for now, everyone would be too busy to realize anything was amiss. She'd have time to come up with something to tell them when they asked where Keir was, and if he had departed.

His ship... I can't hide his ship. Shaking her head, she set that problem aside for later.

Echo returned to her room and kneeled beside the trapdoor. Putting the supplies into a tiny chute beside the door, she dropped them in, quickly closing the chute back up. Clutching her hands together, they still shook. She curled and twisted them in her lap.

After she left Keir yesterday evening, she'd been certain she would never see him again. She'd left the building and went to find Jonah, but ended up at the compound's hospital when Jonah wasn't at the garage. She ended up helping Sarah and Todd fix one of their storage freezers in preparation for the heat to use as a back up if their main one failed. It had been on the fritz for months.

The busy work had helped get her head on straight from her time spent with Keir. She hadn't felt good, leaving him the way she had. Echo sucked in a heavy breath. It had dredged up her loneliness. She had felt like there were things left unsaid between them and she didn't know why. They owed each other nothing.

The near kiss, the way he brushed back her hair, the... heat of his gaze. She whispered her fingers across her lips and then dropped them. She needed to stop fantasizing.

She'd read too much into the interactions and she was just beginning to put the whole episode behind her when she discovered him in her room with a knife in his hand.

She had to have read too much into them, right? Now, she wasn't sure.

Echo curled her hands again and pressed them into her lap. Because why else would Keir be here? Unless he figured out she'd been lying about the lab and had come to call her out on it?

Was that lie worth breaking into her home and bedroom? Was it worth doing so with a knife? He didn't need a knife to hurt her. Was that what he had planned on?

Her cheeks heated furiously. He'd also seen her naked.

He'd been staring.

She had glimpsed the massive tent between his legs.

Echo swallowed the ball in her throat with a shiver and pressed her face into her hands.

It wasn't long after that before she heard Keir stirring below.

FIFTEEN

SOMETHING *CLANGED*, and his eyes opened.

He groaned, finding his thoughts muddled and his body sluggish. Keir pulled his hands beneath him and pushed off the floor.

He collapsed.

He clenched his fists and settled, checking his systems for damage, testing each processor and limb. Basic information was delivered back to him, his failsafes having gone into effect. He groaned again, pushed his body onto its side, and bunched up his half-shifted wings with only the strength of his muscles.

"Keir?" Echo's voice called down to him, soft and hesitant.

Blinking, he searched the darkness for her, his eyes landing on the thin strips of light directly above him. A shadow moved across it.

Confused, he watched the shadow as he went over the events leading up to his captivity.

I was going to give Echo the rest of the supplies I brought.

Keir wrenched his eyes closed, and tried to figure out what had changed between now and when he'd last seen her.

There was a reason he was here, and he couldn't calibrate the possibilities without a steady charge and electrical currents. His thoughts were slow. *Human* slow.

He'd wanted to see Echo one final time before he left Volun. *My mission's complete. I brought the rest of the supplies to give her... I wanted to say goodbye...* Keir had to think this over several times before he was certain that it was the truth. He didn't have his records to actively pull from to verify it, and he needed to be certain his thoughts were his own. Lifting his hand, he massaged his forehead.

I saw her naked.

And wet.

Fuck.

Echo's nudity hit him, bringing everything crashing back like a tidal wave. She had caught him standing in the middle of her bedroom, watching her as she dried her body. Keir cursed. His eyes went back to the slats of light as his cock twitched.

Ignoring it, he sat up.

The shadow moved, and he heard shuffling.

Echo had probably thought he'd been there to hurt her. She already didn't trust his kind. He should've expected this, but he'd been too focused on her safety, and then her nakedness, to realize how his appearance in her bedroom would seem to her.

Keir lips twisted. He'd fucked up. *Bad.*

Staring at the light, he waited for her to call out to him again, almost too nervous to call out himself. His thoughts were still muddy and the need to beg for forgiveness was ripe on his tongue. When there was only silence, his eyes shifted to the dark room he was in.

Heavy shadows clung to the walls.

The room was square and had metal grates embedded in the floors and walls around him. It was half the size of Echo's room. The ceiling was high enough for him to stand, but the room wasn't long enough in either direction for his wings. Above him was a short tunnel and at the top, the door and the slats with light.

There were no other lights, furniture, or accessories within the space. There was only the rug that had fallen in here with him, and a pail with a bottle of water inside. He tested the closest wall with a hand; it was cold to the touch.

Pushing to his feet, he staggered from the weight of his wings. Keir stumbled about the perimeter.

Several of the walls had dents and scratches on them. Exploring them with his fingers, he knew they'd been made by another of his kind. Just like the hole he'd discovered in the recreational room.

He wasn't the first Cyborg to be trapped here.

Keir moved to the center of the space and turned full-circle. His hair brushed the ceiling.

"Echo," he called to her at last. He could feel her fear and anxiety through the thick metal between them. He could practically taste it. "Echo, I know you're there. Answer me."

The shadow moved and the slats above him widened a degree.

Slowly, Echo leaned over and he caught sight of her eyes, her mouth.

Their eyes met and her throat bobbed. Thankfully, she'd put on clothes. They stared at each other, neither one willing to speak first. Worry etched her features and he could tell she was afraid.

I'm not the first.

That thought righted his shoulders.

"There are probably a thousand thoughts running through your head, just like there are in mine, but why don't you open the hatch and let me out so we can talk?" he offered, hoping he sounded reassuring. "We can figure it out together."

It was, afterall, his fault for being here. Whatever *here* was.

She moved away, and he lost sight of her. But then she returned with a flashlight in her hand. Illuminating the space between them, she directed the beam at his feet.

"Are you hurt?" she whispered.

Keir squinted and glanced down at his body and his half-shifted wings. "No."

"Good," she said, sagging slightly and licking her lips.

"Your wings... I didn't know what they were at first. I thought—"

"They can cause me damage if I am unable to finish shifting them. To do that, you'll need to release me—"

"I can't."

He scanned what he could of her face. "Why?"

Her lips parted, then shut. Then parted again. "You were in my room and had a knife in your hand. Why would I let you out? You were just standing there, staring," she said, voice hitching. "I'm not an idiot. You've come to hurt or threaten me."

Keir winced. "It's not like that." He lifted his hands in an act of submission. "You didn't answer, and I assumed you might be in trouble. I couldn't hear the water."

"In my own home? Here, on Volun? Where I know everyone and I've lived my whole life? If I'm going to be in trouble with anyone, Keir, it's with you."

"You didn't answer—"

"Stop. How am I supposed to believe that? You're a Cyborg. Your kind doesn't make mistakes, not like that."

And there it was... It was in Echo's tone and the way she said the word *kind*. It bothered him. Whoever had hurt her did so enough to leave a lasting impact. He glanced around the dark hole he was in, and to the markings on the wall. Most of his systems didn't work here. Only his most basic connections made it through his body's processors.

It wasn't just some fight or words that had been thrown her way, not if she had a trap like this under her room, a trap that prevented electromagnetic interference. To even set up such a space would take an exceptional amount of work, money, resources... Or enough fucking fear and motivation to cover the rest.

It was more than just a simple Faraday cage. Keir touched another wall and ran his hand down the cold stone. The room wasn't carved directly into the mountain. He could sense something beyond the walls obscuring signals and keeping his signals from making connections.

There had to be more than just a trap hidden in Echo's home, there had to be a lot more for him to not be fully functioning.

Keir gritted his teeth.

"Echo." His voice was grave. "Listen to me and listen to me clearly. I don't know what happened to you in the past nor who hurt you, but I am not like them, and though I know you have no reason to believe me, I would never, ever hurt you."

He couldn't even if he wanted to. The idea made him ill, and it had nothing to do with codes. He'd known her for a short amount of time and he had grown to care about her wellbeing.

"Then why are you here? What were you doing in my room?" she whispered.

Her hand trembled where it rested.

"I wanted to repay you for your help," he said carefully. "Given the circumstances."

"You couldn't wait until morning? Was it that important?"

"I had planned to be gone by then."

Stifling silence filled the space between them again. Echo's fingers strained on the slats.

Keir continued, "If you need proof, go to your front door and look outside. There should be a crate from my ship full of supplies on your deck."

"How do I know you're not lying and the moment my back is turned, you're going to try and break free?"

"You and I both know I'm not going anywhere."

"You're not even going to try?"

"Aren't I? Right now? I may not be entirely human, but I can empathize. I would rather you release me and save me the effort."

"You seem certain I would do such a thing?"

"I know you will because you're smart—"

"Hah!" Echo burst out in nervous laughter. "Smart? You don't want me to be smart, Keir. Right now, you need me to be a goddamned idiot."

His brow furrowed as she rose to her feet. She left, then came back with several weapons in her hands.

"I'll go check for a crate because I want to believe you, but don't call me *smart*. It's antagonizing," she growled. "I know what I am and what I'm capable of—I don't need you telling me what I am or am not. Nothing about capturing a Cyborg is *smart*."

With that, she left him.

Keir listened to her footsteps until they receded down the hallway and out of earshot. When he knew she was gone, he cursed under his breath. It was going to take more than a crate of supplies to convince her to set him free.

For as good as he was at convincing people to do things they shouldn't want to do, he was having a God-awful time with it when it really mattered. Echo was the type to smell bullshit from a mile away.

Keir kicked the rug at his feet and found his knife. He sheathed it.

Echo needed to tell him what had happened here because the longer he was left with his theories, the darker his thoughts became. He glanced at the markings left upon the wall.

Who had made them and where were they now?

Keir's hand clenched as his eyes roved over the tight shadows in and around the hole. His body shuddered.

He wasn't meant for a cage.

SIXTEEN

Echo opened her front door. Shielding her eyes from the wind, she found Keir's crate. She grabbed the handle and dragged it inside. Once safely in her living room, she kneeled beside the box and unlatched it.

Inside the crate were neatly packaged tools and medication. Each sealed and wrapped in degradable foam casings. She dug through the contents and discovered batteries, flashlights, screws and nails, as well as cloth, gauze, matches, soldering wire, and even a tarp. She checked everything over twice; there was nothing out of the ordinary, nor anything incriminating.

Echo sat back on her heels, gazing at the mess she'd made. Everything in the crate would be useful, if not to her, then to someone else.

It doesn't mean he's telling the truth.

The crate didn't explain why he'd been standing in her room with a knife in his hand.

For a terrified moment, it had been Ares who'd been standing there instead of Keir, with his long, tied-back flaming red hair and military uniform. He'd returned to exact revenge.

But it's not Ares in the hole, it's Keir. Her stomach knotted. Ares was dead.

Echo rose and looked out her windows. The night had faded, and the clouds had turned a dark gray-red. The clouds were higher in the sky and thinner than the evening before. Wiping her palms on her pants, sweat beaded her brow. The landscape was lightening with dawn, giving the rocky outcropping and trees outside her home a pale, red glow.

It would only be a matter of hours before the clouds were gone entirely and Volun would be in direct view of the sun. She'd be missed at the compound today if she stayed and dealt with Keir. Someone would come looking for her.

Echo inhaled and returned to her room. She knelt beside the trapdoor.

Keir was waiting for her. His eyes met hers. "Did you find the crate?"

Something buzzed and Echo jerked upright. She twisted to her bedside table where her earpiece shook next to her wristcon.

She reached for them and put them on. Her hands trembled.

"Echo, the crate?" Keir prompted.

Jonah's name flashed on her wristcon.

Echo closed her eyes and answered the call. "Jonah, I know. I'll be there soon."

"Goddamned base is red as a battlefield after a slaughter this morning," Jonah said. "The Cyborg's ship is gone. Did you get rid of him?"

"Echo?" Keir prompted again.

Echo fled her room, shutting the door behind her.

"Echo," Keir called after her. "Wait!"

She went back to the front of her house. She couldn't risk Jonah hearing him or finding out. If Keir thought his circumstances were bad now...

"What's going on? Are you still there?" Jonah quipped in her ear.

"Yeah," she responded. "I'm just moving to a better place to talk."

"The Cyborg's ship is gone. What happened? Did you get rid of him? Are you heading in now? We could use the extra help getting the older folks moved down."

"I'll be heading out shortly."

"Good. We missed you yesterday. We could've used your help. Damn Cyborg and his damned timing."

She winced, guilt gnawing her chest. "I'll be there within the hour. But don't wait for me, I have a couple things to finish here first."

Jonah grumbled. "The wind last night damn near blew my workbench away. Took Building B's door right off its hinges. It's going to be a rough week, and that's without a Cyborg standing over our shoulders. He is gone, right? Echo? Please tell me you took care of it?"

"If his ship is gone, I assume he got the answers he came for," she lied blithely. "Either that, or the weather scared him away. I left him outside the old research space before heading home to take care of a few loose ends."

"You left him?"

"Yes."

Jonah paused. "You sure that was a good idea?"

Was it? At the time, it seemed like a great idea. The best idea.

"He didn't need me after I let him into the unit. We both know he didn't need me, or anyone at all, to begin with. He could've torn through our compound if he had wanted to." She shrugged. "We parted on good terms, and I asked him to replace the chains on the door when he was finished."

"He believed you? And here, I thought we were going to have a whole situation on our hands again. Finally some good news. Maybe he had been telling the truth, who would've thought?"

Echo winced. "He had no reason not to believe me..."

Or so she had thought.

"I'm going to see his ship being gone from the field as a good sign. But when I get a chance, I'm checking on that door to be sure."

Echo faced the hallway leading to her room. "Yeah..."

Jonah continued. "Gregory and I worried that you might take a liking to him. Linda's going on about how he'd make a great match with Madeline. But who wants to take on another man's baby?"

"Yeah..."

"Yeah?"

Echo shook herself. "Sorry, just lost in thought. I need to get ready. See you soon." She shut off the call before Jonah had time to say anything more, and headed back to her bedroom.

Quieting her steps, she pushed open her door and entered.

"Keir," she began, nearly apologizing for her rudeness before thinking better of it. She returned to the trapdoor and searched for him. "Keir?" He walked into her line of sight. There was dirt smudged across his pale features giving him a devilishly criminal appearance. His wings were partially straightened out behind him now. Echo's brow furrowed.

I caged a... a bird? Keir's eyes pinned into hers, and she tried not to be intimidated. She wished he'd attack, threaten her, or try and break free. It would be easier if he did. He wasn't going to make this easy.

He canted his head. "What's wrong?" he asked, all pretenses gone from his voice. His eyes narrowed.

"I'm needed at the compound."

"Did you find the crate?"

She nodded.

"Are you going to let me out?"

She parted her lips then flattened them. "You know I can't," she said even though the words hurt.

A look of frustration flashed across his face but then it

was gone. "What do I need to do to prove to you that I'm not here to hurt you?"

Echo's chest tightened. She shook her head. "I don't think you can."

"You can't keep me down here forever. Eventually, you will have to let me out." When she didn't respond, he continued, his tone sharpening with warning, "The man I work for, the reason I'm here at all, will come looking for me, Echo. Do you understand?"

She pulled away from the slats and wrenched her eyes closed. Echo pressed her palms to them and groaned. She'd forgotten about Keir's boss.

Of course he would wonder what had happened to Keir if Keir vanished on the job. She didn't have to ask Keir what would happen if his boss got involved. The warning in his tone told her enough. His boss was another Cyborg, afterall.

She was better off being the one in the hole, not Keir, with the way she felt right now.

"Release me and I will leave, and you will never have to see me again," he said.

Had she made a mistake? Should she just release him now and hope for the best?

Faces flickered through her head. All of them beings who depended upon her. Could she risk it? Risk them?

There were too many lives at stake.

It wasn't just about her.

Keir had seen the security door in her room. He could've seen the other one behind it as well. That alone was enough reason to silence him and to tread as carefully as possible.

"I will try and be back soon. It stays cool down there, even in the worst of the heat. You'll be comfortable," she told him. "I'll keep the slats open and the light on while I'm gone. We'll... talk... when I get back." She rose to her feet and headed for the door.

"Echo," he called after her. "Don't run from me!"

She paused and clenched her hands, holding her tears at bay.

"Be careful," he said, his voice lowering.

I always am.

She left.

SEVENTEEN

Jonah rang her comm a half-dozen times by the time she arrived at the compound and parked. The day had barely begun, and every joint in her body already creaked. Sweat beaded her brow, and the heat already made it hard to breathe.

She second-guessed every minute she was away from Keir and the growing problem of having him locked in a cage. Echo feared leaving him alone.

The industrial garages appeared ahead of her. They were all closed up except for Gregory's, where a dozen or so people were readying the space within. She waved at them.

Using her net, she unhitched the crate Keir gave her and placed it inside and to the back where other supplies were sitting. Echo left it and the contents in it for anyone who might need them in the days ahead.

Glancing around, dozens of beds were being set up in the back, sectioned off by family groups. Some colonists were already setting up their spaces, while others could be heard arguing. She spotted Linda carrying a load of linens in her arms with a scowl on her face.

With a quick nod to Jonah across the way, Echo stripped off her jacket and got to work.

Before long, the sky cleared, and the garage door was lowered.

She helped wherever she was needed most, leaving the easier tasks for the older folks. She carried down beds, fixed Margot's wheelchair, prepped ice boxes, and made sure no one strained themselves more than they should. The heat continued to build, and she trudged on.

Keeping people inside was the hardest part. It always was. By midday, several people had already collapsed from sun poisoning.

Even when everyone was situated, and the fans were blasting, the air purifiers on max, Echo went from one task to the next, unable to stop.

If she stopped, Keir and her predicament returned, and right now, she needed them gone. She needed to pretend it had all been a terrible nightmare. With the weather rapidly shifting into increasingly dangerous territory, being with the colony was more important. Because unlike Keir, people didn't have failsafe systems to keep them alive. They only had each other.

"Echo, I need you!" Gregory yelled.

She found him in the back corner where there were several smaller rooms attached behind the garage, including an old lounge area, several offices, and a bathroom that no longer operated. It had been stripped clean and been turned into a freezer.

"What do you need?" she asked, following Gregory into the lounge. There was a worn sofa in the corner covered in blankets that reminded Echo of her own bed.

Gregory faced her when they were alone. Tired, worn, and shaking a little in his hands, his weakened demeanor put her on edge. When she was young, Gregory had been a force to be reckoned with, a big man that was likened to a juggernaut. He used to lift her on his shoulders and carry her around. He used to wrestle and train with her father. Now, he was just as tired and old as the rest of them.

"The ashtrax you brought the other day," he panted, wiping his brow with his own wet cloth. "I haven't even begun to butcher it. My hands..."

He lifted them to show her. They shook worse than she'd ever seen them. She took them into her own and squeezed them.

"Why didn't you tell me?" she asked.

"A man doesn't confess when he's vulnerable," he rasped, patting his face with a wet towel. "I thought with the Cyborg gone, you might have some extra time?"

"You didn't have to hide this." Echo squeezed Gregory's hands harder. "If you've been hurting—"

"You would have taken over butchering duties too. You're only one person, Echo. You can't do it all."

"But I can do more."

Gregory sighed and he tugged one of his hands free from her grip. He led her to the door. "Look at everyone, look how weak we are, and we're getting weaker all the time. Jonah and I have been talking..."

She cocked her head. "About what?"

"Leaving Volun. After the burnout."

"Right," she sighed.

"We've been discussing it. Hollin needs full-time care, Nathy can't even get out of bed most days, and Linda doesn't want Madeline taking care of them anymore so late in the pregnancy. My arthritis is slowly killing me, and the meds... There's never enough."

"I can go out foraging tomorrow."

Gregory glanced over her shoulder and then back to her, shaking his head. "Jonah contacted the EPED to schedule an exodus. He's already reached out to the southern compound to tell them."

Echo stood, stunned at everything Gregory was saying. He was being serious.

"Look at them. Look at us. We can't sustain this life anymore," he said, staring at the colonists. "We don't want to leave. None of us do, but we know we can't stay. We'll die if we stay."

"They know?"

"Most do. I didn't agree at first, but this morning changed my mind. This... this is unsustainable." He waved his hand at the space before him.

Echo faced the colonists—her family—and couldn't help but agree. She saw Jonah walking her way. She didn't know how to take the news. Jonah had been adamantly against an exodus her whole life.

"You tell her?" Jonah asked Gregory when he stopped before them.

"Does everybody know but me?" she accused. She wasn't angry about their decision on the matter, only that it had taken place without her. It irritated her even more that it was becoming apparent that they wanted to keep her in the dark. That they had waited until now.

"I'm sorry, kiddo. We've been discussing it off and on for a while now. I was going to tell you the other day but then we had our little trespasser arrive and I didn't want to burden you further. I needed you sharp."

"Sharp?" Her lips parted. "So you decided to keep it from me? When I should have known from the very beginning?"

"It was all talk until—"

"Until it wasn't! That's how it always is!"

People in the garage quieted and looked at them. Echo balled her hands and ducked into the room and out of sight. Gregory and Jonah followed her, closing the door behind them. She tried to understand, tried to put herself in Jonah's and Gregory's shoes, but this was her home they were talking about, her family, her everything. Leaving had always been a shadow hanging over her head but it had always been something to worry about *later*.

She thought she had more time.

"Echo," Gregory said, putting his hand on her shoulder. "I don't know your burdens like Jonah here does, but we want you to come with us. We're not leaving Volun without you."

"I can't leave," she snapped, facing them. "I can't."

"You can," Jonah warned.

"You don't understand—"

"I do understand, Echo. It's why I've allowed you so much more freedom than everyone else. Why I trust you and no one else with some of the most important tasks. Everyone in that room behind us might have once been soldiers and civil servants in their youth, but those skills faded with age, with time. Unlike them, you're in your prime, a product of your mother and father. We need you, but you don't need us. You never have. I had hoped you would leave with Hanna years ago, but you didn't. You stayed for him, for them, deciding to hide with us, choosing to preserve something that's been gone for a long, long time."

"That's easy for you to say. You don't have someone you're trying to protect!"

Jonah frowned and glanced at Gregory with worry, and in doing so, sweat dripped from his bushy beard. "Gregory, could you give Echo and I some privacy?"

"Right," the other man grunted, sharing one last pitying look with her before leaving the room.

When he was gone, Jonah sat heavily on Gregory's sofa, huffing and wiping his brow again. He sighed. "Echo..."

"It's not that easy for me to leave. You know that," she argued. "Of all the people in this universe, *you* know better than anyone else. Putting this on me right now, at the beginning of a burnout, is unfair. You should have told me you were considering leaving Volun when you first talked about it with the others. I had a right to be there."

Jonah's face fell further, and a sadness filled his eyes. "Perhaps you're right, but others needed a chance to digest the idea without influence."

"What are you saying?"

"That if I had brought you into the conversation earlier, you would have reacted the same way you are right now, and that would kill the idea before anyone else had a proper chance to think on it. They love you, you understand? Gregory, even Linda, and all the others, they love you. They respect me, but they don't love me like they do you, Echo. I couldn't let you sway their opinions."

Her chest tightened. "You'd think I'd convince them to stay? I'd never do that."

"I couldn't chance it. I don't want *you* to stay, girl, that's my problem. I can force the others, I can't force you."

Echo's lips flattened. She loosened her trembling hands. "If you and everyone else wants to go, then I won't stop you. I never would," she said, her voice lowering. "I just... would've liked to have known sooner." Echo thought of all the people outside the room and how she'd known each and every one of them her whole life. Saying goodbye to all of them, all at once? Probably for the last time?

"I'm sorry," Jonah sighed again. "I wasn't trying to hurt you. I wanted you to see that we've decided as a collective, and I hoped that—"

"That I'd see this and join you? That they would convince me to leave too?"

Jonah nodded.

"I can't believe you would do that," she whispered. "After everything."

"It wasn't supposed to be like this."

"Like what?"

Jonah shook his head.

"I don't understand. What did you expect? That I'd accept this news because it's hellish right now? You waited until the burnout to put this on me? And for what? Guilt? A way to convince me to accept all this with ease because it's the right thing to do for everyone outside this room? How could you possibly think that and put me in this situation? What about those who aren't in that room? What about them?"

"They have made their choices—"

"Not all of them! They can't!"

"I wanted to tell you sooner—"

"Why didn't you?" she bit out.

"Stop it, Echo!" Jonah snapped, startling her. "For fuck's sake, you're not his fucking daughter."

Echo stilled. "What?"

"The man you're trying to protect, he's not your father. Auryn isn't your father."

"I-I don't understand..." Had she heard him correctly? Her hands began to shake again.

Jonah rested his elbows on his knees and rubbed his eyes. "I wanted to tell you when your mom decided to leave, but she made me swear not to. I didn't understand it at the time, because if she had just told you, you'd leave with her and none of this would be an issue. But when I think back on it, I think she was frightened. Hanna had to be terrified. She was always scared that whatever choice she'd make, it would be the wrong one. Not after the incident with Malin. She didn't want you to know."

Echo's ears clouded with fuzz. Her chest thundered. "Stop, please. This is my home, and I'm staying. Nothing you say will change this. I need to get back to work." She rushed to the door and grabbed the handle.

He was going to lie to her and make her think Auryn wasn't her dad? He was going to bring up Malin?

"Echo, wait!"

She fled before Jonah or anyone else could snare her further. Catching Gregory's guilty, flustered face on the other side was enough for her to flee into the brutal heat.

Enveloping her like water, the heat closed in around her, and she gasped, looking up at the sky. The clouds were wisps upon an open pinkish-gray landscape. The edge of Utha's sun could be seen just behind the giant planet, blasting her with light. The weight of it nearly brought her to her knees. It was so beautiful and so very deadly. Forcing her eyes away before she blinded herself, there was a haze rising up around her.

She wanted to scream. She wanted to hit something. Echo pressed her hands to her mouth and wrenched her eyes shut.

Volun was all she'd ever known. What would happen to it if she left? And who else could be her dad, if not for Auryn? Thoughts swirled her head, making her dizzy. Did she really want to know? She'd grown up with many father figures, but she always knew she was part Cyborg. She'd known since puberty, when suddenly, she'd turned into a woman over the period of a single week, and her parents had told her.

Jonah was just using whatever he could to convince her to leave. Echo looked down at her hands. She'd spent the majority of her life lying about what she was, even to those in the colony, so if Auryn wasn't her father, who was?

Malin?

The door opened behind her. Echo turned to find Madeline stepping out. She curled her arms over her chest.

"You shouldn't be out here, Maddy," she said, facing the sky again and hiding her face. "The burnout's begun."

Madeline joined her anyway and handed Echo a water. "I'll go back inside soon. I just needed a break. Everyone's getting their medication mixed up. And even with the fans, it's beginning to smell in there. Anyway, I always like to see the sky at the beginning before the steam gets too bad. Are you okay?"

The question took Echo aback. "Yes."

"I think that's a lie. You looked pretty upset a moment ago."

"It was." Echo sighed. "I wish it wasn't."

"I figured as much. So is it true?"

Echo bristled. "Is what true?" Did everyone know something she didn't?

"Are we really leaving? There are rumors going around, and the way you stormed out..."

Echo's shoulders sagged. "I don't know. It appears so. I was just told."

"Well, fuck."

She looked at Madeline in shock. "I don't think I've ever heard you curse before. You don't want to leave?" She eyed the woman. Madeline was wearing a dress that was too big for her, despite her belly, and like everyone else, sweat soaked her clothes.

She couldn't imagine what might be going through the other woman's mind. And 'well, fuck,' was as good a clue as any.

"Why would I?" she said. "I know nothing about the way other people live. I've never left Volun before."

"Me neither."

Madeline nodded and glanced down at her belly, rubbing it. "I never pictured raising my children anywhere else. Well, I never pictured anywhere else, ever, for anything. It scares me. Change scares me."

"You could stay… if you really wanted to."

Madeline laughed and Echo immediately felt silly for suggesting it at all. "And going at it completely alone? I don't think so. I wouldn't even know how to. I can't hunt or trap. I can barely even start a fire without a match."

"I'm staying," Echo whispered. "You wouldn't be alone." She stared hard at her boots. Echo had no idea why she said it, but she felt better knowing she wasn't the only one who didn't want to leave.

She was also scared. She didn't want to admit it, she

didn't have Madeline's courage. Admitting it wouldn't help anyone anyway.

Madeline's laughter died, and she turned to face Echo. It was the first time she and Madeline had talked in a long time without others around. Though to Echo's shock, Madeline was considering her words. She gazed at Echo distantly, as if imagining the possibilities.

"You don't have to decide today or tomorrow, or even next week," Echo offered, her voice softening. "I don't have to either. We need to make it through this week first. And who knows, maybe something will happen between now and then?"

Madeline smiled but it didn't reach her eyes. "True. Too bad Keir left. He would've been a big help today. I wish I had known he was leaving. I would've said goodbye."

Echo looked away. "Yeah."

"He was a lot nicer than I thought he would be, considering everything I've heard. I was a little awestruck when I first saw him. I never thought I'd meet someone as handsome as Ares. Too bad Cyborg's can't have babies."

Echo's unease returned and her eyes slanted back to Madeline. Echo's throat tightened and she nodded stiffly at her. Her thoughts shifted to Keir, to her dad. She had to get back home soon.

"He was." Echo turned toward the door. "There will be a lot more handsome men to see if you decide to leave," she said with a fake chuckle, wanting the mood to remain light between them but also extremely uncomfortable with Madeline's words. Maddy didn't know about her parent's personal history, there was only speculation. And no one had speculated on it for many years. Echo wished she had speculated on it more because right now was neither the time or place. "Come on, let's get you back inside before you burn. I can barely breathe out here already. I don't even want to know the kind of strain you're putting on your lungs right now. The last thing we need is for you to go into labor."

"Could you imagine?" Madeline guffawed.

No, Echo wasn't even going to try and imagine the nightmare that would be. Her mind blanked before she even went there.

Madeline followed her inside, and they parted ways. Echo avoided Gregory and Jonah for the remainder of the afternoon, busying herself by preparing food and dividing up the remaining food stores, and pretending absolutely nothing was amiss. The rest of the day crept by. The distractions weren't enough anymore.

When the sun was finally hidden behind Utha and the skies darkened, she could barely keep her eyes open. Half the residents were fitfully sleeping when she slipped out and headed for her bike.

During any other burnout, she'd have remained in the compound until it was over. No one was expecting her to leave. Even at night, it was risky leaving the safety of the walls.

She almost made it home before her bike overheated. It stuttered to a stop a half mile away.

Leaving it behind, exhaustion slammed into her as she

trudged the rest of the way home. When she finally made it inside, she was drenched in fresh sweat and she couldn't see straight. She snagged several bottles of water, drank one down, and carried the other to her room.

"Keir." Echo dropped to her knees, shoved the water into the shoot, and lied down next to the trapdoor. "I'm sorry."

She yawned and passed out.

EIGHTEEN

Finding his thoughts darkening, and the stillness beginning to fray his mind, Keir searched for a distraction while he waited for Echo's return. He crouched, busying his hands by lining out the platelets of his wings and fitting them together, folding them back up. The pointed edges cut his fingertips, and he made a mess of blood across the gleaming metal. Using the water Echo had left him, he cleaned as he went.

Hours passed as he delicately righted his extra metal limbs, and the work helped clear his head. When his wings were firmly tucked away and his shirt rethreaded, he leaned against the wall and closed his eyes.

The door to the outpost banged open.

Sitting upright, his eyes went straight for the slats. After a few minutes, Echo entered the room and settled beside the trapdoor. Panting filled his ears, her gasping breaths.

"Keir, I'm sorry."

He waited for her to explain. When she didn't, he stood and moved to the middle. She'd gone silent.

"What happened?"

Worry slammed into him when she moaned in response.

Reaching up, he was still an arm's length away from the slats. All he could see was the ceiling of her bedroom, a little bit of her hair.

She didn't take care of herself, not nearly as well as she should. As he waited and listened to her raspy breaths, Keir was certain she'd extended her abilities. Again. Whatever happened that had sent her to the compound, had kept her there all day. In that time, if he hadn't had his wings to focus on, he'd have gone crazy wondering what was going on.

He'd seen the storm, the tornados, had been pummeled by the wind. It was enough to kill a human who wasn't prepared. Accidents happened all the time and bad weather was only going to increase the odds of them occurring.

"Echo, answer me," he demanded. "If you're going to pass out, at least pass out on the bed," he growled. He scented her. Perspiration filled his nose. It was gritty but not unpleasant. Although it was thick, and thickening by the second.

She needs water.

She stirred. "I don't know what to do," she mumbled, her words ending on a hitch. "I've always known what to do."

Was she crying?

Keir frowned and glanced at the markings on the wall.

Something told him she was a victim in all of this, not an enemy. Over the day, he realized there was no way Echo could have built this trap alone. Not without help.

And she had tried to get him to leave Volun. She and the others. She hadn't planned to trap him. In fact, he was certain she regretted the whole situation entirely.

Trust.

She needs to trust me.

Keir sighed inwardly, his stomach churning. Then he cursed under his breath because his stomach never churned. How the hell would he get a human to trust him? Get *her* to trust him?

Fucking up could see him trapped here for a long, long time. A predatory bird in a dark cage. He'd lose his shit. He'd go numb. He wouldn't have a choice.

But most of all, fucking up could hurt Echo further, and the way his chest constricted and his hands clenched at the thought of that happening meant he cared for her. In a way he'd never cared for a human ever before.

"This is what you're going to do," he said. "You're going to get up and get into the shower. You're going to drink enough water until you think you might burst. And then you're going to bed."

A few moments passed before she responded. "Why do you care so much?"

Great question. Keir's shoulders bunched. "Because I'm not getting out of here if you die on me, and those at the compound need you." He'd use her sense of guilt against her if it meant she wouldn't die tonight from dehydration and heat exhaustion. He was fine playing the villain when it suited.

"Fine," she rasped, sounding worn down and annoyed.

He heard her rise and move across the room. A few minutes later, the shower turned on and he settled down to wait.

Minutes passed as he listened to the water. The door to the shower hadn't been closed all the way based on how much he could hear. There was movement although not much, and he pictured Echo curled up on the floor, huddling under the spray.

His hands clenched tighter.

He didn't want to imagine her naked, but he couldn't help it. Tawny skin, dark lashes glistening with water drops, and her toned body flooded his mind, and with it, his body's reaction to seeing her in such a way.

Keir's gaze fell to his groin, where his cock lay trapped underneath. Blood rushed to it, making his cock harden painfully, and he couldn't fight against his body's reaction. His shaft pushed against his pants, and kept pushing, expanding, battling the control he tried to muster.

Licking his teeth, he scowled and gripped his bulge and tried to push it back down, but the harder he tried, the harder it got.

Echo moaned.

He dropped his head back, hissing between his teeth. *Fuck me.*

She moaned again. This time, he cocked his head, honing in on the sounds she was making. It wasn't even pleasurable moans that had left her; they were moans of exhaustion. What kind of male was he getting excited over the possibility of something that was absurd? His life had no room for a companion.

He was Nightheart's agent. Though missions came sparingly, Keir had given his brethren his loyalty. And Echo said it herself, she wasn't leaving Volun. His missions sometimes spanned months and were often dangerous. She would never be willing to come with him, nor would he even want her to.

Nor would he ever want to leave her behind... if she was his mate.

The very idea of something more between them was absurd.

Because if he ever took a mate, it would be for life. His hawk wouldn't allow it any other way. And until very recently, his hawk had been a bitter loner and Keir's only companion.

I'm not trying to mate her. I'm trying to get her to trust me. Keir's scowl deepened when he realized he'd been rubbing and squeezing his length the entire time.

The water turned off, making him tense up. He shot to his feet and paced to keep from touching himself with fantasies about a woman who was on the verge of collapsing.

Echo left the shower, and the lights overhead dimmed shortly afterward. She stumbled and cursed, and then he heard linens shift as she crawled onto her bed.

Keir canted his head again. *She listened to me.*

She had done exactly what he'd told her to do.

Hating the silence that clung between them, he moved to the center and looked up, hoping he'd be able to see her. There was only the ceiling. Was she waiting for him to speak first? Was she waiting at all?

Had she already passed out?

He'd waited all day for her, worried about her, trying to figure out what was going on here and why he was in a cage. She would head back to the compound at first light, leaving him to stew another day, wondering if she'd return to him at all. He couldn't let that happen. Not on his watch.

He opened his mouth to speak.

"So you're a shifter Cyborg?" she murmured.

Keir's mouth closed and then opened again with barely suppressed relief. "Yes."

"An avian bird-like creature, I suppose? Like a razorbeak?"

Her voice was low and muffled, breaking through a shell of exhaustion.

"Not quite so alien," he said. "I've been spliced with the DNA of a red-tailed hawk, a predatory bird from Earth. They died out long ago. We're not as well known. Most people who have seen me fly aren't aware that my wings are more than just wings. That I'm more than just a Cyborg."

"What does it feel like?"

"What does *what* feel like, Echo?"

"Having that kind of nature inside of you? Being able to fly? It sounds... so nice to just be able to fly away. To fly anywhere you want too just because you feel like it, because you can."

He frowned. "What happened today at the compound?" She didn't sound like the woman he'd spent the last couple of days with. Defeat tinged her voice.

"You first."

"Me first, okay." Keir unclenched his fists. They shook, and his frown deepened, staring at them.

He licked his lips. "It's a blessing and a curse. Each of my facets is. For as much as they're all a part of me, my instincts still fight calibrated reason. Emotions are either overwhelming or barely felt at all. There are times I want to give into each side, and there are just as many times where I fight them. It's about maintaining balance because there are three different egos and each one wants to dominate. The codes I've been given, the nanocells that make my creation possible, they barely keep each ego under control. Every shifter has this problem."

"Is that why your kind is often so... angry?"

Keir glanced at the markings left on the wall. "We're not all angry. Some of us revel in the power we've been born—created with. But we either keep the delicate balance going, or we let one side win. Some of us might not always be able to help it."

He scowled at his cock.

"How is any of this a blessing?"

Keir sighed. "Freedom, power, fearlessness. We feel every emotion but can, if we so choose, temper them at will. Our bodies are nearly indestructible, we're hard to kill. And when control is lost, or thrown out the door, it's exhilarating. There's nothing like jumping off of a mountain and soaring away, of knowing you can do such a thing, and not die. There's nothing like breaking free from society's structures and having the universe in your hands. Nothing like Titan..." he trailed off, picturing the planet he had made his home.

The bedding ruffled. "Titan? The planet?"

"Yes."

"I've read about it. The humans' first colonized world. The closest planet humanity has ever found to Earth." She yawned. "The Trentians ravaged it."

"Yes, long before my creation. It's where the war officially began. It's why I'm here, Echo, why I'm really here."

The bedding shifted, and his eyes shot to the slats, hoping he'd catch sight of her.

"Titan or the mission?"

"The mission is a job, one I believe in because..." He shook his head. Telling Echo he'd spent the last sixty years bitter and hating humans wasn't easy. Lying to them and leading them to their deaths was something he may never come back from. Sharing his profound embarrassment and shame wasn't something he was ready for, if he'd ever be.

"Because?" she prompted, her voice lowering with sincerity.

Keir swallowed, feeling more vulnerable now than he'd ever felt being paraded and belittled as a glorified mascot. He was a war machine, not a puppet.

"Because the Cyborg I work for is willing to give me the

means to help me restore the planet. Because I can relate to him. He has more power and resources than any one of us. And because he's just as fucking bitter as me," he gritted.

Maybe they were close because Nightheart was the only other Cyborg Keir personally knew who could fly. Nightheart understood the visceral need for *freedom*.

Echo's footsteps padded toward him, and a shadow fell across the flats. She sat and leaned over. Her face appeared.

Keir inhaled sharply. She was as beautiful as ever, even distorted with shadows. Though her eyes were tired and haunted, her features taut with strain, she was beautiful.

Her eyes found him, holding his softly, tiredly. Her vulnerability was on display, where he kept his hidden.

"What does this other Cyborg want with the cybernetics laboratory?"

"He wouldn't share information like that with me, with anyone. None of us would. I'm doing a job for him, not with him."

"You are, Keir, right now. You are sharing with *me*. Only me."

His jaw clenched and he shifted his eyes away from her. "It's my turn to ask questions."

"Haven't you been already? You've been asking questions since you've arrived here. What more is there besides this?"

"Apparently they were the wrong ones," he growled, returning his eyes to her. Her gaze had gone distant, staring at the shadows at his feet. "What happened at the compound today?"

Her face fell. "Jonah and Gregory moved everyone into the garages to keep them together. It wasn't easy…"

"The truth, Echo. I want the truth."

She leaned back. "That is the truth."

"Why are there markings down here that would have only been made by another of my kind? Why is there a quarantine chamber at the back of your home? And for both our sakes, why is there a Faraday trap under your room? What aren't you telling me?"

She flinched but then her gaze hardened. "Why were you in my home in the middle of the night?"

"I told you why."

"I don't believe you."

"It's the truth all the same."

"And I'm telling you the truth too!"

He wanted to grab her, shake her, force her to give everything up. Except he couldn't. She'd incapacitated him. All he had to rely on to save him was his damnable humanity. Even his hawk had gone dormant, hiding so it didn't have to be aware of how trapped it was. He wasn't about to have an existential crisis at a time like this.

He peered down at his body, the way it strained and reacted to Echo and everything she did. Since their first encounter, it had been like this.

"I wanted to see you," he confessed, and with the words leaving him, some of the tightness in his chest eased. "I had to see you. At least one more time."

Her brow furrowed. "Why?"

"I would have regretted it if I didn't."

He needed her to say something, anything. The tightness returned to his chest, worse than before, constricting his heart like a tourniquet. There was nothing he could do to protect himself from the admission now that it was out, no systems he could rely on to show him through terabytes of data, research, and documentation that being vulnerable, and a Cyborg, was remotely logical.

"Say something," he urged. "Please."

Echo winced again, and his heart felt like it was falling from his body. He pressed his fist to his chest.

"Please," he begged.

Her lips parted, and he inhaled sharply.

NINETEEN

"Why did you want to see me?"

"Fuck," he hissed and rubbed his face.

"Why?" she demanded. Did he... like her? She could scarcely form the words in her mind for fear they'd make her face something she'd become sensitive about. She liked him. That was hard enough for her to admit already. She hadn't wanted to leave him back at the laboratory and it wasn't out of fear of discovery or fear of him. It had taken distance from him to realize she had almost...enjoyed their short time together.

"I don't know... I just... needed to."

Echo settled down on the floor, resting her face beside the slats. She blinked rapidly to clear the tears that wanted to form. She tried to convince herself that he was lying to her just to get her to release him, but this was nothing like that. His voice was sincere.

It shook her, made her chest heavy. She brought her hand to her mouth and hid her breaths.

"Everyone is leaving." Echo shuddered, too afraid to confront what he was telling her. He'd wanted to see her again? One last time? Had she succumbed to heat exhaustion or had she heard him correctly? It was safer, for both of them, to pretend both of those were true.

She hadn't liked his interaction with Madeline. It had taken her some time to realize that it had been jealousy that she'd felt watching them converse with such ease. Why couldn't it be that way with her?

"What do you mean leaving?"

"Jonah contacted the EPED for a colony exodus. They told me today."

"The EPED is coming here?" he shot out, the softness from before gone.

Her brow furrowed. "I... assume so? If Jonah has put in the request."

"Echo" —Keir's voice lowered— "I'm here on behalf of the EPED."

"What?" That made her pause. "I thought you said you were here on a mission for another Cyborg?"

"The Cyborg I'm working for owns the EPED."

"He..." Her palms instantly clammed up. "The Earthian Planetary Exploration Division?"

"Yes."

The EPED was run by a Cyborg?

"I thought...The EPED was run by the government."

"At one point, it was. Nightheart took it over shortly after the war ended and has run it privately since."

Nightheart. This other Cyborg's name was Nightheart. Her lips flattened.

"You're not happy about this."

"No. I can't leave with them... I can't..."

But what if Jonah said was true? That Auryn wasn't her father?

"Why? There's nothing but ghosts. The other woman said it herself. Leave. Go to Earth, Elyria. Join me and come to Titan. What is so important about Volun?"

"Join me and come to Titan."

She rubbed her eyes to clear the tears wanting to form. "I can't."

"Yes, you can."

"It's not that simple, Keir."

"Then explain it to me. Start from the beginning."

She curled up on the floor. If Keir worked for Nightheart, he worked for the EPED too, and the EPED was coming. Would the other Cyborg come here too?

"Echo?"

"Please," she begged. "Stop. I'm so tired."

"Who hurt you? What is so damn important that you won't leave?"

"I killed him!" she cried. "I killed him—do you understand? I killed him!"

Keir went silent, and Echo held herself prone, too afraid to move. She pressed her fist to her mouth, digging her teeth into her skin. When Keir remained silent, she couldn't take it anymore.

He wanted to know what had happened with the other Cyborg, and now he did. Now, he had to face her situation from her eyes. Damn him. She closed her eyes hard.

"Say something," she begged when the silence continued.

"How?"

His voice was... not what she'd expected. He didn't sound furious. Echo blinked her tears back and moved her hand off her mouth.

"Ares came here six years ago. But he wasn't the first to die..." And now that she said it, the pain of who Malin could be to Echo, terrified her.

Because she was not fully human, she was much stronger, could endure far more, and was near-impervious to sickness and even pain. Her body had always healed and healed fast. She'd broken more bones than she could count, been bitten by wild animals, gone days without sleep, without rest, water, food, whereas everyone aged around her, worn down by the same things. She kept going, nearly unfazed. Only her emotions twisted and spiked.

She'd stopped aging several years before Ares showed up. She'd been watching everyone else around her grow older and older, even her mother. It had never been more apparent than when she was near Madeline.

It was why Echo unconsciously avoided her whenever she could. She saw Madeline grow, become something more, and change, when she herself had stopped completely.

"Ares," he stated under his breath. "Who else?"

"Malin," she whispered. "Did... you know them?"

She heard Keir begin to pace.

"No."

She licked her lips. "You don't seem mad."

"He hurt you? Ares?"

"He hurt my mother. He tried to kill her."

"And are these markings his?"

"Yes."

"Malin, was he down here too?"

"I... My father killed him. At least that is what I was told. But I don't know what to believe anymore. He built the trap you're in, because of Malin. He built it when my mother was pregnant with me."

He stopped pacing. "How did you do it?"

She saw the flash of his eyes burst from the trap and she leaned back over it. Their eyes met.

Echo shuddered. "We left Ares down there, for months, without food or water. We blocked off the room, and only my mother was allowed to enter, her or Jonah. But I could hear him... Even when my mother and I moved back to the compound, even knowing I saved her life." At least she thought she had. "The guilt of what was happening was too much. I could hear him." She didn't tell him her body had reacted to Ares. Like he had tried, for a time, to connect with her straight through her cybernetic cells. "I snuck out one night and came back. Came to see if he was still down there, and when I saw him unmoving on the floor. I was relieved. But then he groaned."

She had wanted to talk to him, ask him the things she couldn't ask her parents. Ares had been out in the universe, he knew more than they did.

Her parents feared her fascination.

Echo shook her head, recalling the horrible minutes leading up to Ares's death and how he looked at her. "I couldn't let him live on endlessly like this either. It was cruel." He'd flooded her with rage. He'd goaded her without ever speaking a single word. She didn't know how he had, only that being so close to him after all those months, she'd been overcome with the need to end his entrapment, any way she could. "I left and returned with a knife and cut his throat—"

Keir scowled. "That was dangerous."

She'd done more than cut his throat. It had been like her hands had moved without her mind controlling them.

"It was a risk I took and one I don't regret. He didn't try to stop me. He barely even bled." She inhaled a shaky breath, reliving the fear of that moment, how she had lost herself, and how it could have gone terribly, horribly wrong.

"What did you do with his body?"

"I..."

"Echo?"

"Why aren't you furious? Why aren't you scared?"

"Because if Ares did what you say he did, he deserved his fate."

"I wish I believed that..." She winced. "Do you deserve yours?"

"You're not going to kill me, Echo. Of that I'm certain."

"How do you know?" she snapped. "We only met days ago. Ares had been around much longer than that."

"You're not cruel or an idiot. You know I'm not here to hurt you or anyone else. Ares let you kill him. If he had wanted to survive, he would have. And just because you destroyed his physical body, doesn't mean his mind is dead."

A sad burst of laughter released from her throat. "Is that enough, though?"

"Yes."

The way he said it made her pause. His voice held so much certainty that she was taken aback. Everything he'd told her so far had been the truth. It was easier seeing him as a villain. Yet he'd done nothing to warrant the title.

Echo tightened up into a fetal position again, tensing all her muscles, letting her choice strain her completely before uncurling and pulling her body up to stand.

She was going to take another risk. A bigger one than dropping down into a dark hole with a man who could be baiting her to do just as such. She was going to make this choice before it was taken from her.

Trembling, Echo walked to the trapdoor panel and, with tired fingers, released the trap. She leaned against the wall and waited for Keir to climb, to either hurt her... or leave.

Silence filled the room.

After a moment, her curiosity got the best of her, and

she slowly moved to the open hole. Standing where he'd been before, Keir looked up at her when she approached. His expression was hard, unreadable.

"You're right," she whispered, wiping her cheek. "I'm not cruel or an idiot. Leaving you in there would make me into someone I don't want to be. Something I never wanted to be." She got on her knees and reached her hand down, praying she wasn't making a colossal mistake.

She believed that he hadn't come here to hurt her, despite finding him in her room like she had. It didn't make sense. And if she was going to try and trust him, the only way she'd know for certain would be to set him free and level the playing field.

There was no other solution besides killing him and it hurt her to even think of that option.

With his eyes sparking, Keir reached up and grabbed her hand. Echo helped him from the trap, releasing him after he climbed out like she'd been burned. She sat on her bed and waited for his scorn. For his retribution. She deserved it and worse.

She was unable to look at him directly as he stood in the center of her room, his head cocked back and forth, studying her. His mannerisms and quirks suddenly all made sense. Knowing he was not only a cybernetic man, but an animal too, answered some of the questions clawing at the edge of her mind.

He took a step forward and stared down at her. His eyes flashed and then remained bright as his systems turned on. Echo waited on edge, tense for an attack. And she still couldn't meet his eyes to save her life. She didn't think she could handle seeing the hatred and disappointment that she was certain would be there. Not from someone she had grown fond of so quickly.

Except instead of leaving or lashing out, arresting and taking her to the nearest port for sentencing, Keir turned and walked into the quarantine chamber.

He began to strip.

She sat upright, confused. "What are you— Do you want me to—"

"Stay," he ordered. "I won't be long."

Opening and closing her mouth, Echo's cheeks reddened.

He unsnapped his straps, pulled off his boots, the few items attached to his body, then tugged off his vest. She looked away but couldn't help glancing back.

Directly behind him was the security door leading to the real cybernetics laboratory. The secret back passage into it that only she and Jonah knew of, where the rest of her lies were laid bare for him to simply discover. All he had to do was turn around and walk through that door.

Everything was there, waiting for him. He only had to open the door...

She glanced at Keir again, and he was almost naked. Unable to look away this time, Echo stared, hard. She'd seen men naked before, on numerous occasions, but not a male like Keir. A God among men. He pulled his undershirt over his head, revealing his tight, muscled body. He was exactly how she imagined he would look, too good to be real. Too good to be remotely human, and yet he was, very much so, and she was just beginning to acknowledge it.

His hands moved to unclip the latch of his pants. Heat rushed through her and her throat constricted.

"Your wings?" she rasped, still waiting for his retribution. The fact that he was casually stripping instead confused her greatly. "Where do they fit?" The question left her before she could stop it, but talking about his wings was better than staring at a cock he was certainly about to reveal.

Her lips parted as she trailed her eyes over the beautiful lines of his body, his arms, abs, and back. She anticipated the rest of him, her heart rising in tempo. A bulge had formed between his legs, sending her into a tailspin. Her eyes widened, knowing its meaning.

Keir crooked his head and turned away from her then. With his bulge now out of sight, she relaxed slightly. She licked her lips.

If this is how Keir would punish her, he knew her far better than anyone else.

His skin was pulled open along his spine, revealing thousands of thin metal platelets that expanded outward as the seam widened. There was no spine, no ribs, just metal, moving and shifting, emerging out from inside him, like a perfectly fluid machine. A living machine that moved organically, working as a body would with a billion pieces all in play.

The wings barely emerged before they disappeared back within him and the seam closed tight.

When it did, she realized he'd completely removed his

pants. Her gaze dropped to his backside just as he turned for the water valve.

She looked away, but looked back when she heard the water.

Facing the wall, his outline was fully on display, including his cock, which was hard, thick, and erected. There was a slight, upward curve to it. She pressed her thighs together. It was long and pale and proportionate to his body.

He squirted soap into his hand and proceeded to wash his hair, his body, all the while she watched mutely, her thoughts whirling.

The heat dancing through her pooled inside her chest, between her legs, and she lay down on her bed, making herself comfortable.

He was clearly letting her watch him, and so she was going to take him up on it.

She trusted him now. More than anyone.

How was that possible?

How?

When he turned off the shower and reached for the very same towel she'd used earlier, he finally looked her way. Their eyes locked as he dried his body, stepped out of the chamber, and walked to the bed, completely naked. Echo shifted back on her bed and made space for him.

It was as much as an apology as it was a chance to see how far she could place her trust in him.

When he hesitated, she knew she'd made the right

choice. Keir wasn't going to hurt her. He was never here to hurt her.

He crawled into her bed, eyes intent upon hers. He reached behind him and turned off the lights. Echo scooted towards him and pressed into his side as he settled. Resting her head on his chest, she hooked a leg over his to make sure he couldn't rise without her notice, and he slowly curled his arm around her and held her against him.

"Sleep," he murmured.

Darkness stole her away.

TWENTY

ECHO WOKE up lying on her back, gleaming eyes staring down at her from above. Heat pressed into her from every side, but it wasn't stifling or thick. It wasn't from the burnout.

Staring up at Keir, she held still as his gaze trailed up and down her face. He wasn't holding her down, he was holding his body above hers. All of her clothes were still on, warm and undisturbed upon her frame. She didn't dare move.

"Your features are symmetrical, too symmetrical," he stated, his eyes flicking everywhere at once.

She inhaled slowly, her gaze dropping to his bare shoulders and chest. He was still naked. Shadows distorted his lower body from view.

Echo stamped down the need to fight him off. At this rate, he was going to find out whatever he wanted to know, and there was nothing she could do to stop him, except convince him to keep the same secrets she did. She'd made the first move, he'd made the second, and now it was her turn. And even if he didn't keep any secrets...

It was out of her control now anyway. She was trapped underneath him.

He wasn't going to let her run away.

Cyborgs don't like losing control. Keir's words hit home. This was a losing battle.

She nodded stiffly. "I know."

He dipped his head, his gaze piercing. "It's rare, symmetry like yours. When I first saw you, my system briefly considered you a mecha, or an android."

She waited for his eyes to sharpen, for him to figure her out. To realize, in a way, he was right. But he pushed off her and onto his back, surprising her again. She faced him and leaned up onto her elbow.

He stared at the darkness above them. "I didn't mean to wake you. Go back to sleep."

"Sleep is the last thing on my mind," she whispered.

"You've been out for three and a half hours. Human bodies need more time to recover than that. I'll try not to wake you again." He moved to rise from the bed. "Unless it's with food."

Echo grabbed his arm. "Stay. Don't leave."

If he left, he could leave for good, and that brought fear right back to her heart. Despite all that had happened, she'd been comforted knowing exactly where Keir was when she'd had him trapped. Now that he was free, he would leave, sooner than later, and she wasn't ready for that.

She wanted to continue trusting in him. She wasn't ready to say goodbye.

Keir looked at her. "Why? I'm trying not to frighten you."

She pulled him toward her, and he molded to her wants, even when she pushed her body under his arm and rested her cheek on his chest. He remained tense, and even tenser still, when she placed her hand on his chest and hooked her leg back over his. "You don't frighten me." *Not anymore.*

She felt more control of the situation than she had when he was trapped beneath her room.

Keir's own tension infinitesimally lessened, and with some of his own hesitation, he curled his arm and pulled her against him. She nuzzled him. His skin was velvety soft and warm, like a human's.

"The morning will come soon enough," Echo breathed. The lies would start again.

Except minutes ticked by, and neither one of them dared to move. Time seemed to slow down to a crawl. Keir remained strained beneath her, and she was becoming more aware of their bodies and where they touched. She almost wished she could fall asleep again because she ached to trail her fingers over his chest and to feel him but was too uncertain what doing so would mean to both of them.

Echo breathed in his scent. She shouldn't be getting attached to him.

She wasn't leaving Volun. Following him to Titan was a nice fantasy, but it wasn't possible for her. With Jonah and the others leaving, there would be no one left to make sure her father would remain alive, secure. If everything he'd sacrificed his life for would remain living as well. Even if Auryn wasn't her biological father, it didn't change anything. He'd raised her as a daughter, loved her mother.

The stories she'd heard of Malin clicked into place. It was always her mom who'd brought him up, never her father. To Echo, Malin was just another Cyborg who'd caused chaos here, and that had all happened before she'd been born. Had her mom loved two Cyborgs?

She only wished it was easier to talk to her mother. Numerous questions teetered at the tip of her tongue. Questions she was certain her mother would sigh at. And bringing it up to her father... Echo wasn't certain how he'd react. She ached to glance at the shower and the door beyond.

Keir's fingers threaded into her hair. "Sleep," he whispered, playing with the strands.

Goosebumps rose across her arms and legs, and she tried not to strain against Keir and beg for more. "I can't."

He groaned. "I apologize—"

"My face, my body is completely symmetrical, except for the damage it has received over the years." The words flowed easier than she had expected.

Keir's fingers slowed their movements.

"I can go days without sleep, even a week, if my mind doesn't get so tired, and if I remain hydrated and fed. The burnout is always taxing though. I can endure a great deal of pain and recover from it quickly. I'm also stronger, stronger than anyone in the compound at this rate."

His fingers stopped their caresses. "What are you saying?"

"I've stopped aging."

Keir had gone completely still. Unless he directly took her blood, their nanocells were shared, or he studied her for a long enough time, he wouldn't be able to tell she was anything more than human. She was telling him otherwise.

Jonah knew. Others speculated. She was certain Gregory had an idea. Madeline and a few others as well. Cyborgs couldn't have children, she'd even been told Cyborgs couldn't procreate. Yet here she was. But she was told to not discuss it, and so she never had.

Auryn told her she was his daughter, to keep that knowledge to herself and leave it at that. It had always been enough for her.

So whoever her real biological father was just didn't matter. He'd been a Cyborg, and a Cyborg helped raise her.

"You're the progeny of one of my brethren," he said, figuring it out.

"Yes."

"You're rarer than I am." His voice lowered with awe before hardening. "Who sired you?"

Her face scrunched, her heart jumped and she whispered, "I don't know. I thought" —she shook her head— "I thought it was Auryn, but now..." How could she answer his question without saying too much? It was a subject she'd barely had time to consider if fully comprehend.

Keir's expression molded with confusion. "Auryn? I've never heard of him. You don't know?"

"Auryn raised me but Jonah says he's not my biological father." She lifted her head, her heart quickening. "There are others? Like me?"

His gaze streaked across her features again, serious and... disturbed? He was tenser than before.

"Yes. Our progeny are all currently living and residing in Ghost City to be protected and kept away from humans who would see them as nothing more than an object to be studied. Is your... Is Auryn or your mother not aware of this?"

Echo frowned. "No. What's Ghost City?"

His pinning eyes moved away from her. "The only Cyborg-run state. A massive warship we claimed and made our own after the war, kept hidden from all who are not connected virtually or tied with a Cyborg by either blood, marriage, or matehood. Perhaps they thought you would be safe here."

Echo sat up to study him, hoping he'd look at her again. His arm had dropped from her body.

"Is something wrong?" she asked.

"I don't know. Yet." His voice had numbed.

Feeling her stomach churn, and embarrassment heating her cheeks, she turned and moved away, and the moment she did, she felt his gaze again.

Knowing that she wasn't the only one did make her feel relieved, but it wasn't what she had hoped for.

She'd wanted to kiss him. To know what it was like to be that close with another. To be that close with him.

She'd wanted more than that.

She just didn't want to do it knowing he'd probably find out her biology in the process.

"Echo, what's wrong?"

"I'm just more tired than I thought I was."

He sighed and sat up, cursing. Hearing his feet hit the floor, she glanced over her shoulder.

"I can't be in this bed with you anymore." He rose and walked to his clothes that were still piled in the open quarantine chamber. She turned back toward him as he continued to speak. "It's best if we keep our distance from each other. For both our sakes. This"—he waved his hand stiffly—"is dangerous."

He tugged up his pants but not before she glimpsed his very stiff erection.

"Is it because of what I am?" she asked.

He cocked his head.

When he didn't immediately answer, anger struck her. "Tell me, Keir. We're being honest here, aren't we? Help me understand."

He pivoted, walked back to her, grabbed her by the neck, and pinned her to the bed as he leaned over her. She gripped his hand, even though he held it gently but firmly in place. His eyes were wild, searing her flesh; she strained against him.

"Help you understand what?" he growled. "That if I kiss you, mate you, it would be for life? I like to know what I'm getting myself into before I make life-altering choices. And from the moment I've met you, nothing has been clear! I'm plagued with thoughts to nest!" Fury flashed across his face, even when his gaze strayed to her lips. "Auryn—or whoever your father is—will kill me, Echo, you belong to him, and now knowing what you are... Only one set of nanocells can dominate. He might kill me anyway just for sharing your bed with you. Until I get some answers, real answers, there is nothing between us. There can be nothing between us!"

"So now you're scared," she shot out. Heart racing, she quivered under his hand, unable to help her excitement.

Her wristcon buzzed on the table beside her bed. She was startled, but Keir kept her attention. It continued to buzz, ignored.

Keir leaned into her until his face was above her own. Some of his hair fell into his face. "Scared? You have no idea what true fear is."

"And you do?"

He scowled.

"You're scared," she goaded, pressing against him.

"You're not scared enough. Cyborgs don't take from one another. We don't steal from one another. We have a code. We have territory. *We're brethren.* We do this so we don't war amongst ourselves."

"I never asked you to mate with me, Keir. What does some code have to do with it? I'm not something to be owned."

His eyes flashed at her words. Heat pooled between her legs, and she writhed under him, uncaring of his words. Every fiber of her being vibrated.

His lips twisted. "Codes have everything to do with us. You are one of us!"

"Am I? I want more with you. Can't you see that? I *want* more. I want to know more, too, just like you."

His hand gripped her throat, his fingers pushing into her skin, but his furious eyes fell back to her lips. "Lies. You're trying to kill me," he snarled. "First the trap, now this. What else will I find out when my back is turned? Are you trying to claim me, usurp my cells, without me knowing? As far as I'm aware, this is just another trap!"

"Usurp your cells? I don't know what that means..."

"There's a reason Cyborgs don't mate with each other!"

"I wouldn't know," she whispered, confused. "I've never even been kissed."

"Fucking hell," he snapped, eyes narrowing on her mouth.

She shivered. "I've never been touched."

With a growl, he slammed his mouth on hers.

Echo gasped, her lips forced open roughly. His tongue drove between them. Keir's hard press to her mouth took her by surprise, if only because he'd actually done it.

Loosening his hand around her neck, he dropped it to press into the bed beside her head. He kept his mouth firm upon hers, his tongue inside, pinning her. She couldn't turn away, couldn't push him off of her if she tried, and she didn't want to try. His lips were brutal and she was swallowed whole. Echo wrapped her legs around his hips and trapped him in return. She pushed into him and fought his mouth with her own.

His mouth gentled, and some of the tension buzzing off of him dispersed as she cupped his cheeks, tempering her own movements to show him what she sought. What she craved.

Complete and utter connection with another being. Even if they only had a few hours to pretend, she'd wanted to experience that with him.

Keir threaded his hands into her hair, lifting up to peer down at her. The light from his eyes nearly blinded her. She blinked rapidly as hers adjusted, holding his face so he wouldn't move away. Echo pressed up and dabbed kisses on his lips, tasting and exploring them, replacing the remnants of his viciousness with something sweet. Keir groaned and lowered his body. He deepened the kiss.

He needs reassurance as much as I do.

With that thought pulsing through her hazy mind, she dug her nails into his scalp and grabbed at his hair.

She didn't know how to ask for more.

"Don't fear me either," she begged between kisses. "I don't want anything else. I'm not asking for more."

He grabbed her hands and thrust them above her head. "But I want more," he growled, making her heart race.

Tangling his tongue with hers, he moved fully onto the bed and over her body. She pushed against him, over-whelmed with the need to keep their bodies locked. She feared if she didn't, he'd fly away, his words would be lost in the wind off his wings.

"Echo, Echo, Echo." His hold on her tightened. He then let go of her hands and moved them down her body, clutching her, feeling her, his fingers straining everywhere, leaving their marks.

Keir rose up again and looked down at her. She inhaled and reached for him, running her hands down his chest. His muscles twitched wherever she touched. He held himself over her, staring hard, while she explored his body.

She shimmied, waiting for him to kiss her again, and when he didn't move, she began second-guessing again.

"I want to..." He ran the back of his hand over his mouth. "I need to..."

"I don't want you to stop," she said.

His eyes flashed. "Then I won't." He dove back down, a predatory gleam capturing his features.

With his lips devouring her jaw, neck, and shoulders, she gasped and released an exhilarated laugh. "I'll protect you."

He growled and cupped her chin, pushing his thumb into her mouth, driving his hips hard between her legs. "Baiting my ego will only keep my mouth off you." He sucked and nibbled the crook of her neck. "Only one of us will win."

She responded by doing the same with his thumb, sucking it into her mouth.

He shunted his hips roughly against her, driving her up the bed, clutching her jaw, and working his thumb around. She sucked harder as he stroked her with every drive of his pelvis. Pleasure streaked to the crux of her legs and her insides knotted deliciously. Straining limbs and hands groped and caressed, sending her into a frenzy. He jerked up, popped his thumb from her mouth, and took hold of her shirt, ripping it down the middle. Her pants went next. She rose with him, unclasping the buckle on his pants and yanking them down his hips. In moments they were both naked.

Keir spread her legs wide, lowering over her, forcing her to lie back down into the bedding. His hawkish features sharpened as his eyes flurried over her body, settling briefly on her face, her breasts, and between her legs.

He was everywhere at once. A whirlwind. Until he wasn't, until his face was between her open legs.

"Mate," he rasped, staring.

Heat surged through her realizing what he was saying but not wanting to comprehend it. Fear quickened her pulse as his fingers gripped her skin. "Mate?"

"Yes, Echo, *mate*." The heat from his mouth rushed over her sex.

She tried to look at him but his face was between her splayed legs, tilted down. "What are you doing?"

"Learning everything about you. If we go through with this, I'm taking everything. You are more beautiful than I could have ever imagined."

He pressed his lips to her center, and she buckled. "What are you doing?" she gasped again, louder this time, because he hadn't answered the question she meant. What did he mean by mate, other than... sex?

He held her still. "Kissing you, nesting you."

"I didn't mean—"

"I know." Keir pressed his tongue firmly upon her and licked from her backside to her clit.

Echo strained, her mouth hanging open, as he did it again, and again in rapid succession, lashing his tongue over every secret and sensitive spot. She cried out when his fingers parted her folds and he drove his tongue inside of her next. Demanding yet malleable, his tongue plunged in and out of her, sending her into a flurry. It was all happening so fast. He probed and licked all the right places, places she wasn't even aware could be used for pleasure, while pushing the tip of his tongue to her most sensitive spot within. She dug her heels into his back and shook.

Her wristcon buzzed again. His fingers dug into her skin. "Keir!"

He lapped her harder, plunging his tongue in and out of her quivering sheath. She clenched around him with each shallow, wet thrust, dropping her hands to her bedding to pull and grasp at it.

"More," she urged, her shock and embarrassment diminishing, stolen away by his dancing tongue. She was close, so close. The fingers of one of his hands strummed her clit while the other lowered to caress her intimate backside. She bucked her hips.

Blood rushed through her veins, and it felt like every nanocell in her body was sprinting to her core. "More!" she screamed as the pressure intensified, the pleasure dizzying.

He pinched her clit hard, and she unraveled with a thankful sob. Pushing at him, body thrashing, years of tension, of fantasies expunged from her as an orgasm ripped from her body.

Keir's tongue and fingers vanished mid-writhe. Near craven that he continued, Echo whimpered, reaching for him, only realizing at the last second, that he was lining his cock to her opening.

Yes. Wait! Yes. Her lips trembled.

Yes.

Flashing, stormy eyes caught hers as his thick tip pushed into her. *Yes!* His white light blasted away the shadows of her room as he held her hips prone. Their eyes glued, she bucked her hips again for more, and he thrust.

Brief, beautiful pain sliced her core as her final barrier tore open.

"Stolen," he hummed, making her whole body writhe again just from the sound.

He pushed deeper, widening the tear until he lodged his length firmly inside of her, locking them together. Without pumping, without pulling out, he held her hips and kept them like that, feeling her sheath flutter and pulse from the last clenches of her climax. The pressure skyrocketed as her body accommodated to his, forced to adjust completely. He was big, long. Like his body. Dark spots dappled her vision, partially blinded from the light emanating from his eyes. A startling gasp fell from her lips as his wings shot out from his back. They stopped short of hitting the walls and destroying her room.

She hadn't expected sex to be like this, she hadn't expected him to penetrate her at all.

His hands tensed on her, holding her in place while she tried to move upon him, to relieve the terrible pressure growing again inside of her. Now that her clenching had eased, she needed more.

Keir stared at her as he thrust again and again, his expression rapt with determination.

Soon, she was right back at the brink. Echo fought for it even though he was denying her, pulling out and stretching her continuously. Her jaw clamped.

"Please," she begged, moving her hips in small shunts, trying to match his fervency.

And then heat filled her, and an exceeding amount of wetness. Keir's eyes wrenched shut, and he arched his back, driving her hips up with a pained groan, driving her up with him. His cock twitched and expanded, forcing her body to take it.

A smile tugged at her lips as he came, slowing his thrusting down at first, and then speeding up until her whole body vibrated from the quick, almost unseeable movements. Even as her orgasm faded, her excitement continued to grow. Watching him lose his mind, knowing he wanted her just as much as she wanted him, almost elicited another climax from the sight alone.

She'd never felt so wanted before.

He fell upon her and pressed his face into her neck, arching to keep his cock firmly inside her despite his size. She locked her legs around him as he calmed down and pumped shallowly, still groaning as if he were in pain. His seed continued to spill.

He licked her neck, her ear, rising up to run his mouth all over her face, then down to her shoulders and chest. He continued pumping throughout it all.

This dangerous Cyborg wanted her. *Her.* She'd take what she could get before it all came to an end.

She relaxed into the bedding as he moved over and around her. He pulled out to lift her legs into the air and bare her sex between them. With his eyes spotlighting her core, he pushed his fingers back inside her.

Echo's breath hitched. "What are you—?"

"Claiming you."

Glancing down at what he was doing, she saw him pushing spilt seed back inside of her.

Her chest constricted as the implications of what he'd said earlier and what they had just done dawned on her. Echo tensed and pulled out of his grasp. "Keir, stop. I can't get pregnant."

Was this what had happened to her with Ares? Had Ares found a way to infiltrate her over the months of his captivity? Echo's body tensed. It was hard to think on it with Keir stealing her mind.

He recaptured her and held her legs up, his eyes lighting upon her face. "No." He pushed more of his seed inside of her. "And I'm not trying to get you pregnant, not yet."

She startled and stopped, processing his words, as he went back to holding her legs up and licked her lips nervously.

"Let it happen," he murmured, focused solely on her and what he was doing. "Let it happen."

Echo's lips parted as an image of Madeline flashed across her thoughts and her pregnant belly. The wristcon buzzed again and she jerked, her gaze slicing to it on her bedside table.

And then she felt the pressure, the heat—an electrical shock deep in her womb. It was unlike anything she'd experienced before.

She gasped, jolting again, fuller than ever before, like she was about to burst. Sparks exploded throughout her core, coiling and constricting deep within her. Keir lowered his body over hers as his nanocells invaded.

"It's up to you now," he whispered against her ear.

Echo barely heard him. Her mouth fell open in a quiet scream as each and every fiber of her being erupted in pleasure.

TWENTY-ONE

KEIR HELD Echo as he programmed the nanocells inside his seed to take her over, also proving Echo's truth about her heritage. If she'd been fully human, there would be nothing to fight, nothing for his nanocells to do but make sure his seed impregnated her, but he wasn't programming them to do that; he needed to stake his claim first.

Echo was his now.

She'd been his the moment they'd met. His hawk had known it; it was the rest of him that had convoluted his instincts. He hadn't wanted to do a damn thing but watch her, study her, be with her since he'd followed her outside the compound that first night.

He had no idea she was more like him than he would have ever guessed. Echo was a rare bird and she belonged to him now, if she accepted it. Keir was determined to make her accept him.

His nanocells would live inside her, bolstering her own,

solidifying their connection until either his death, their part-ing, or she destroyed them.

She moaned, pressed her body against his, then twitched, moaning again. He kissed and petted her, memo-rizing every detail, only to caress and worship her some more, giving her as much pleasure as he was able while her body adjusted to his invasion. Moving down to return his mouth between her legs, he slid his tongue back inside her.

Their essences coated his tongue, making him hunger for more.

"Keir, I'm scared," she whimpered. "This isn't what I... *meant*."

He opened his eyes and looked at her, lapping her dewy, sweet-tasting pussy.

"Don't be scared," he hummed and licked. "Don't be scared of me."

He didn't want Echo protecting him from anyone. That was Keir's job now. Once he knew how to contact her father, Keir would confront the Cyborg himself. He was eager to prove himself, he always had been.

Taking on Echo's protection, and keeping her nature hidden from all those who would use her—study her—was something he knew he needed to discuss with the Cyborg that had sired her.

How far did his claim on her go?

Keir lifted up, trailing his gaze over her flushed skin. "The choice is yours." He slipped his fingers inside her tight sheath, excited by the ease of being allowed back inside of her. He wouldn't mate her again, not until she was physically and emotionally ready for it.

The wires in his chest shook erratically. Was he ready for round two? Keir frowned, brought his fingers to his lips, licked Echo's essence off of them, and returned them to her sheath to stoke another orgasm out of her.

He'd never slept with a human before, let alone a human born from one of his brethren. He'd never had the desire to do so, even though he had an entire network of knowledge on the subject in his head. How to please a human woman, how to touch them, how to pleasure them... Until now, he had never cared. Now this knowledge had flooded his head, and he was beyond hard to begin his training in it.

Keir finally understood why so many of his brethren had taken on mates. The lives of Cyborgs held little pleasure—whereas a mate gave nothing but.

He added a finger and caressed the sensitive ridged spot inside of her.

"I'm not leaving," she cried, clenching her thighs around his hand as he played. "I can't. This is all... too much!"

"I'll take care of your father," he mused, petting her faster.

It had to be her father that was forcing her to stay on Volun. However he was doing it, Keir would find out. If she was afraid and in hiding because of her biology, he would keep her safe. He'd take her to Ghost City and to Dr. Cagley, who was as close to an expert as anyone could be on the children born from Cyborgs. She was the only Cyborg woman who'd carried a baby to term, and that had been many years before any other progeny had been born.

Echo's body shook as she opened her mouth, giving into the orgasm he'd coaxed out of her. She pushed at his hands and then grabbed them, keeping them in place, moaning and wiggling all the while.

Warmth flooded his chest, knowing she wanted him there. He was determined to make their first time together pleasurable.

He'd never been wanted like this. Needed like this. Nothing about Echo and him felt manufactured. Even with the lies and secrets, everything had been... natural.

Keir was beginning to understand. It had just taken him being trapped with his systems off to realize how so many of his issues had to do with humanmade events and their damning codes—their inability to face the things he'd been created for, thinking a billion-dollar machine would not only solve their problems but could also be used as a spectacle to sell lies. His entire existence had revolved around it.

Echo was a surprise, something that shouldn't have been, and the first person who had made him feel remotely bad for his own disposition. He'd been bitter. He still was. He may always be.

But he wasn't bitter when he was with Echo.

She eased back into the bedding, sprawled out in languid exhaustion. Satisfaction filled him, seeing her in such a state. Her skin was flushed red, her lips well-loved, her sex pink and glistening from his saliva. His cock was harder than it had ever been, and he wanted nothing more than to cover her with his body and thrust inside her.

He had more than half a century of celibacy to make up for.

Keir withdrew his hand, lifted off of her, and grabbed a bath towel from a wall hook, wetting it under the water in the quarantine chamber. Unfortunately, their time was limited.

Echo opened her eyes when he returned with the towel.

"I think it's stopped." Her voice was a *woosh* of air. "W-what did you do to me?"

"Programmed my nanocells to flood you, to bond with yours."

It took her a moment to react. Her brow furrowed deeply. "Why?"

He reached out and curled his finger around a loose strand of hair that had fallen into her face. "Control, Echo. I can't call you my mate without it."

Her kiss-reddened lips parted and pursed. She sat upright, drew a blanket over her chest, and looked at him like she was readying to yell and beat him down with loaded questions. Keir exhaled softly, readying for it.

He couldn't help himself. He'd decided she was his mate and couldn't leave her in the control of another of his kind—blood-related control, that is. It had warred with instincts he was only beginning to understand and process. Licking his lips, he pondered how he was going to tell her this without being trapped in another cage.

A loud noise sounded, startling them both.

Tensing, Keir pivoted for the door and blocked it as Echo jumped to her feet. The banging grew louder, and a voice called out with urgency. Echo threw on her clothes, signifying the end of their time. Clenching his hands, irritation spiked for the interruption.

"Shit, shit, shit," she cursed. "It's Jonah." She snatched her wristcon and looked at it, worry deepening her features. "He's here. He called. He called four times!" She winced and met his eyes. "Oh god, what if something happened?"

He gritted his teeth. "It's barely the crack of dawn." Keir left the bedroom to answer the door and send Jonah packing. Emergency or not, he and Echo weren't done.

"Wait!" Echo yelled after him. "He doesn't know you're here!" She jumped on one foot, tugging her boot on with the other. "Keir stop!"

Keir didn't care about Jonah's mistrust of him. Frustrated, he yanked open the front door. Heat blasted him, enveloping him in a stranglehold. It was much thicker and more stifling than he'd expected under the rocks Echo's home was built within.

Jonah's eyes widened upon seeing him, but the surprise didn't last long. "You," Jonah accused. He was haggard and sunken, and his skin sagged from sweat, which glistened the wrinkles upon it. He carried an umbrella-like device that was strapped to his back, blasting him with air and misting water from above that immediately steamed and dissipated. Jonah's hand clutched the doorframe as he leaned his weight against it.

The man was soaked, crusted, with bloodshot eyes. Did anyone on this moon sleep? Keir scowled.

He'd never seen a colony ruled by so much toxic stubbornness.

"Where's Echo? Why are you naked?" Jonah croaked. "What have you done to her?" His voice rose with a hitch.

Keir grasped Jonah's shirt and hauled him inside. He retrieved a chair and forced Jonah into it. "Don't move," Keir ordered, leaving him for a moment to throw on his clothes and return with a canister of water from Echo's icebox.

Echo left her room and rushed to Jonah's side as Jonah snatched the water from him.

She crouched beside him, her face a mask of worry. "What happened? What's wrong? I just saw your comms. Is everyone okay?"

Keir balled his fists. The constant state of worry Echo was in was growing old. He was close to throwing her over his shoulder and taking her off this world and ensuring she never returned.

She'll have nothing to worry about on Titan.

Jonah shakily tore the cap off the water, eyeing Keir with disbelief and anger. "You weren't answering your comm," he panted, turning his anger on Echo. He proceeded to chug back the water.

Echo cringed. "I was busy."

Keir put his hand on her shoulder and squeezed.

Jonah's eyes shot straight to the exchange. He lowered

the canister and wiped the back of his hand across his mouth, disapproval in his exhausted gaze.

If only Jonah was Echo's father.

He'd be easy to deal with. Fuck, Keir would take Jonah to Titan too, if it meant putting a stop to the struggle Echo faced. She didn't have to endure this life just because she feared discovery.

"Madeline's gone into labor," Jonah said. "Too busy to answer four separate calls?" His gaze bore into Echo. "I thought something had happened to you—I thought the worst!"

Echo stood, her face hardening even as it paled. "Madeline's in labor? She's not due for weeks."

"She's due now apparently, and we need you at the compound," Jonah said. "You should have never left last night! Do you know how long I searched for you, thinking you'd passed out somewhere from heat exhaustion?"

Echo sprinted away and grabbed a pack lying on the ground by the icebox. She started stuffing it with supplies. "I'm sorry," she said, "I assumed you had fallen asleep with the others. I should've answered your comms."

"Yes you should've! What the hell were you doing that you couldn't?" he blustered. "You need to start explaining, right now, why you lied to me!"

Jonah tried to rise, but Keir intervened and pushed him back into his chair. "Catch your breath old man, or we'll be dealing with two emergencies."

"Don't you dare tell me what to do! I know my limits better than any borg'."

Keir didn't remove his hand from him even as Jonah struggled.

Echo scurried about, packing. "I'm really sorry, Jonah. Madeline can't be in labor. Oh, fuck, oh fuck." Her eyes had gone wild, and all traces of the last several hours had vanished from her face. "The baby can't be born during a burnout. It's too dangerous."

"How long has she been in labor?" Keir snapped at Jonah.

"A couple of hours, you son of a bitch! Let go of me or I'll have the EPED here arresting you by the end of the week! Did you leave the compound last night because of him, Echo? Why was he naked?"

Echo's head popped up, she faced him and Jonah. "My bike. It died."

"I'll take you," Keir answered.

"Your ship is nearby?"

"This wouldn't be a problem if you'd never left the compound!" Jonah yelled. "Let go of me!"

Keir squeezed his hand on Jonah's shoulder. "Shut up. I'll fly you there. It'll be faster. We can be there in minutes."

"F-fly, like—like you and me up in the air?" she stuttered.

"Yes."

She nodded slowly, swallowing. "All right. Okay. Let's go. They might need me. I should be there."

Keir released Jonah, who'd stopped fighting and was sulking now instead, and strode over to Echo, catching her before she could flee out the door. He cupped her cheeks and leaned in. "We are not done, you and I. Not in any sense of the word. Let's go help your friend."

Stunned, her eyes widened. He released her and walked out onto the deck.

"Echo, wait just a damn moment—" Jonah began.

Through the window, Keir saw Jonah rise and come after them.

"I'm serious, Echo," Keir muttered, catching her eyes. "We're not done." His systems recalibrated to keep his internal tech cool to battle against the staggering temperature.

Jonah stopped at the door and clung to it, winded.

She nodded, and it was enough for Keir. His sentiment had been as much as a warning as it was a threat and a promise. He did not like leaving things unfinished. And her request for a single night was not going to be nearly enough for him. He could've left Volun the day before if he hadn't felt there was more between them that needed attention.

Nothing goes unfinished.

"What's happening?" Jonah wheezed. "What are you guys doing?"

Echo jerked and faced the human.

Keir answered. "We're leaving, and you're staying here to rest, old man. You won't be good to anyone dead."

And with that, he pulled Echo tightly into his arms and launched into the air.

TWENTY-TWO

She barely registered the flight, only wishing it would be over with soon because she knew when they landed she'd be within the compound and closer to Madeline. Until she saw Madeline with her own eyes, nothing else mattered. She couldn't let the rest matter. Not right now.

Madeline and she weren't close because of Echo, because of her own problems, but it had never stopped Echo from wishing for more between them, even knowing Madeline wanted more too.

Echo feared if she let her emotions and mind wander again, even registering being flown through the sky in Keir's arms, that the guilt festering inside her would explode.

The baby was early. He was coming during a burnout, when the medical station suffered the most, overcrowded by everyone with heat stroke and exhaustion. Amongst all the other things that flared during times of high stress. It didn't matter if everyone here had lived through prior burnouts prior. Shit always happened, and people suffered.

It was time for them to leave. Echo wholeheartedly agreed on the exodus now that she had time to stew on it. Even if it was done by force.

A baby should not be born on this moon, during a time like this, when there were far safer places out in the universe for them.

When they landed, she slowly unhooked her legs and arms from Keir's body; she'd wrapped her body around him to hang on for dear life during their flight. That closeness had only brought everything that had happened between them flooding back into her thoughts.

In a single night, everything had changed between them.

She ached, twitched, buzzed on a microscopic level. Something was happening inside of her body. Thankfully it was lessening, and right now she had no other option except believe Keir; that it was her choice in the end, despite his fervency in the matter. She willed the sensation away. It was too hard to focus on it and everything else that was going on.

Keir had been fierce, almost possessive with her after they had kissed. It was like a wall had shattered around him after she had opened up to him. She'd reeled and basked in it.

Only now that their time had abruptly ended, she wasn't sure if what they had shared had simply been passion, or something more.

What did he mean by nest?

Keir steadied her and she opened her eyes. Echo pulled out of his grasp, seeing Gregory's closed-off garage. "Thank you."

"You're welcome."

Echo was unable to meet Keir's eyes. She went into the garage to search for Madeline, needing the stirring in her chest to stop.

Gloomy, low-lit darkness met her on the other side. Everyone was either sitting or lying around from heat exhaustion, sipping water, or just beginning to stir. The air was ripe with the smell of sweat despite over a dozen industrial fans going on full-blast and air coolers at max. The medical equipment that had been brought down, including the gurneys, were being used by some of the other colonists.

She caught Gregory's eye from where he brewed a pot of coffee in the back.

He walked to her. His eyes strayed over her shoulder and to Keir, who'd followed her inside. "Thank god you're okay. He eyed Keir warily. "I thought you left." Gregory looked back at her. "Jonah was losing his mind, worried something had happened when you didn't answer his comms. We couldn't find you. Madeline—"

"I know. I'm sorry. I should've told you I was leaving last night. Madeline?" she prompted. "Where is she? The old medical hall? Home?"

"Home in the dormitories. She refused to go to the medical hall, saying something about contractions being too far apart and being uncomfortable there. Linda and Sarah couldn't convince her, and who's going to wrestle a woman going through labor? Where were you?"

"Home too," she answered, glancing at Keir. "Thank you, Greg."

"Glad you're safe."

Echo turned on her heel and left the garage.

Keir snatched her against him again and flew her to the door where they had met the first night.

"Thank you," she murmured. Her stomach was doing flips from all the flying, and from being so near him. She wasn't used to it. At all. She was so used to keeping everyone at a distance, she'd forgotten what it was like to be held by someone. Echo straightened and went to open the door. He stopped her.

"Are you sure she even wants you there?" he asked. "And you need to stop thanking me."

Echo paused. She wasn't a midwife, and had no clue how to help deliver a baby. She and Madeline's relationship had never been the easiest one.

Only, they'd grown up together, despite their differences, and they shared a life that no one else could really relate to anymore, if they ever had. Echo missed Madeline already, knowing Madeline would leave with everyone else. Echo didn't know why, only that she did.

If Madeline and the baby didn't live through this, Echo would never forgive herself for not doing all that she could to make sure that had happened. She needed them to be safe.

"Yes," she answered. And even if Echo had Madeline

wrong, Echo was determined to do what she could to help regardless.

Keir pushed the door open for her, and together they climbed the stairs.

When they arrived at Linda's apartment, the door to her place was cracked open. Echo heard voices inside.

She called out. "It's Echo. Can I come in?"

After a short pause, someone yelled. "Come in! We're in the kitchen."

Echo turned to Keir.

"I'll wait here." He pushed a stay strand of her hair behind her ear. "If I'm needed, just call my name. I have never delivered a baby, but I have the field knowledge in my systems."

She blushed, pushing the rest of her hair over her shoulders. "Thank you, for everything. I mean it."

He gave her a look of scorn and she wanted to hug him.

"Go, and no more thank yous. I do this because I want to, understand?"

Her cheeks flushed harder, and she fled inside.

There were a half-dozen women in the kitchen and living room, including Sarah and Linda, fussing about. Sarah, Gregory's ex-wife, had been a nurse at the base long ago and was attending to Madeline, who was bowed over on the couch. Linda was on the other side wiping her daughter's brow. Echo knew all of them, some better than others, especially the only man in the room. Todd, Sarah's current husband, was a nurse as well, and had stitched Echo up several times in the past.

Several hugged her, telling Echo they were happy she was there, as she made her way across the room to Madeline. Maddy was now dressed in a thin shift, soaked with sweat. The single fan in the room was aimed directly at her but lined against the walls were several air coolers keeping the space remotely temperate.

"How is she?" Echo asked.

"Terrible," Madeline gritted out.

"She's doing good. Seven centimeters dilated and progressing quickly. It won't be long now."

Madeline's face wrenched, and she went quiet with strain.

Suddenly feeling helpless, Echo glanced about, nerves vibrating. "Is there anything I can do?"

"I'll let you know. Right now, it's just about waiting and keeping her as comfortable as possible," Sarah said.

Linda cooed and comforted her daughter, whispering encouragement. Todd handed Linda a fresh wet rag.

Echo stepped back and searched for a spot where she could be of use. Madeline groaned and bowed over again. There was an IV attached to her arm and a myriad of medical equipment on the table beside her.

Linda chanted. "Breathe, breathe."

Finding nothing she could do to help, Echo stood where she was, glancing at the door. "I can grab—"

Madeline reached for her. "Echo."

Echo went to Madeline's side where Sarah made room for her. She took Madeline's outstretched hand and squeezed it. "I'm here."

"Stay, please."

"I will," Echo said. "I'm not going anywhere. I'm sorry I wasn't here sooner."

Madeline's eyes slitted open. "I'm scared. The weather..."

"Don't be. We're all here for you and your son. We won't let anything happen. *I* won't let anything happen. The heat won't last."

"Promise?"

"I promise."

The fear in Madeline's eyes stole away all of Echo's.

Echo cupped Madeline's hand with both of hers, feeling more grounded than she had in years. "You have this," she whispered. "We both do."

Madeline clutched her back.

The next several hours crawled by. Echo and Linda took turns comforting Madeline as Sarah watched over and monitored Madeline's progress. Todd managed the medical equipment and drugs. The added heat made everyone slow and tired, the high stress of the situation elevated it, and as morning crept toward midday and the time between Madeline's contractions shortened.

There was ample water and supplies. Keir had gone to work outside the apartment so no one had to go far and brave being outdoors any more than necessary. He even began fixing the broken fans and coolers that had long ago been set aside, delivering them to the apartment. Talk of the Cyborg amongst the group had become a much-needed diversion. When they realized he'd brought Echo to the apartment, and had actually flown her there with *wings*, they turned on her with questions.

Questions Echo had no idea how to answer—at least some of them.

Keir was endearing himself to them and her need to thank him only built now that he'd warned her against it.

Mate?

Did he think sleeping with her, filling her with his seed, meant they were married? Echo shook her head and tried to remember the time her mom and dad had been together.

They had never been married, not like others in the colony who wore bands and rings. But they had been a team. Her dad had put her mom on a pedestal... He had always remained near here when possible. She couldn't recall ever seeing them kiss though she remembered her dad's embraces when he held both her and her mom at the same time. He always hugged them like he never wanted to let them go.

Echo chewed on her lip.

She'd also discovered that the majority of the colony was unhappy with Jonah's decision for an exodus, making her aware of how very stubborn they were.

And how much like them she was after all.

So she kept her head down and focused on keeping Madeline calm, all the while missing her own mother, and wishing she could ask for advice on what she should do about Keir. When Sarah ordered everyone but her and Linda out of the apartment, Echo was equally relieved and nervous about what rumors about her and Keir were going to be spread around the colony.

Thinking of him warmed her cheeks, sent her heart racing, and tightened her throat to the point it was hard to breathe.

Her stomach filled with butterflies each time he entered her thoughts, knowing he was right behind the door a room away, recalling what they had done just hours earlier. Her responses excited and unnerved her, recalling the way he brought her to climax with his fingers, his mouth, his cock, and what his promise to finish what they'd started ultimately meant...

And how much she risked having let him free and trusting him.

Have I made a mistake?

She forced her mind elsewhere.

So when Sarah checked Madeline's cervix and announced it was time for Madeline to push, Echo's increasing restlessness was teetering at the edge.

Madeline had been moved to her bed hours prior, started to bear down at the urgings of Sarah, who'd gone from checking her dilation to actively delivering a baby in the span of a minute. Madeline's cries escalated, her body straining with every fiber, intensified. Linda encouraged and soothed, holding her daughter. Sarah barked out orders, sending Echo and Todd scurrying about for whatever supplies were needed at the time, all while demanding Madeline to push as if her life depended on it.

And for Echo, she took those words to heart, barely able

to look at Madeline without tears flooding her eyes and prayers on her lips.

"I can't, I can't," Madeline cried. Despite the room being cold now from the extra coolers Keir fixed, the woman was drenched.

"Push!" Sarah said.

Madeline screamed.

The smell of copper filled Echo's nostrils.

Cold washed through her. She didn't know anything about labor, deliveries, or babies. Was blood normal? She was shaking and inwardly begging for everything to be okay when a hand closed around hers and squeezed. Glancing to her right, she saw Keir standing beside her.

"Push!" Sarah commanded again.

Keir brought Echo's hand to his lips and placed a kiss on the back of it, catching her stunned expression. He then released her and went to Madeline's side and took hers. Startled, Linda and Todd hesitated, but then continued what they were doing when Keir began softly encouraging Madeline to push.

Echo cupped the hand he just released and rushed to his side, looking at Madeline. "You can do it," she urged. "You're the strongest damn woman I know!"

"He's crowning—push! He's almost here," Sarah said.

Madeline screamed.

When she sagged into the bedding, and Sarah stood with a baby in her arms, everyone collectively shifted into action. Sarah quickly cleaned and checked the baby over, Madeline turned into her mother's arms, Todd cut the umbilical cord, Keir stepped away, and Echo moved to Sarah to help her, grabbing fresh towels and water.

With the soft wails of an infant being brought to his mom for the first time, Madeline burst into tears as Linda shifted Maddy's blouse aside to help position him on her chest. Holding her son to her, Madeline laughed and cried, making everyone else do so too.

Helping Sarah and Todd clean Madeline and the bedding, Echo beamed through tears of her own.

"We need to keep mom and baby cool," Sarah announced as they finished up. "Madeline needs to rest and stay hydrated. She and the baby will need to be attended and monitored. I'd like to take them to the medical hall as soon as possible."

"Can we give them a little more time?" Linda asked, rising from Madeline's side.

"No, let's go now," Madeline rasped. "I want to make sure Simon is okay."

Simon? Echo loved the name.

"We'll need to clear it and ready it for you first," Sarah said. "I'll go do that now and come back to get you when it's ready."

Echo stepped forward. "Let me know what I can do to help." She looked at Madeline and baby Simon fussing on Madeline's chest.

Echo's chest warmed furiously.

And suddenly it became too hard to look at Keir. Heat reddened Echo's cheeks as she tried to hide her envy.

Family, a baby, love... Her throat tightened, though her smile softened.

Madeline caught her eye. "Echo, please stay with me?"

Echo stepped to her side. "Of course. I love his name."

Madeline petted Simon's fuzzy head. "It's after his dad."

Echo never knew who the father was, nor had she ever thought to ask. She figured it was one of the men who'd come to Volun for deliveries, a crewhand, a merchant.

"I'll go with Sarah," Keir interjected. "Take all the time you need."

He followed Sarah and Todd out of the room. Watching him go, Echo's heart squeezed. She missed him immediately. It was just Madeline, Linda, and Echo now. She turned back to them.

"I like him," Linda announced. "More than this Simon of yours. He should be here. I think Keir would make a better husband."

Echo swallowed, stopping the urge to stake her claim on him.

"He's only got eyes for Echo, Mom, and Simon doesn't know I'm pregnant," Madeline said. "If he did, I'm sure he would be here."

Linda narrowed her eyes. "When I get my hands on him—"

Madeline huffed. "Not right now. I'm tired and hot, and can barely hear with all of these fans."

Echo stood. "I'll go get some water."

"Wait. Mom, could you leave us for a minute so Echo and I can talk?"

Linda hesitated but sat up. "Sure. Let me go get the water." She eyed Echo curiously before walking away.

When she was gone, Madeline turned to Echo after checking on her son, who had fallen asleep.

"He's beautiful," Echo whispered.

She wanted to know what Madeline wanted to speak to her about. Though she itched and desperately wanted to hold Simon just as much, Echo would settle on asking for the honor later.

"He is," Madeline agreed. "He's perfect."

Echo licked her chapped lips.

Madeline sighed, her features falling. "I have a favor to ask you."

"What's wrong?"

Madeline winced and shifted higher on her pillows. "I hate asking—"

"Please don't. It's okay."

"Everyone always needs something from you, from the two of us... It's hard to ask for help."

"I want to help. You more than anyone." It was the truth. Tears rushed Madeline's eyes at her words, and Echo moved closer. "Don't cry. Please. If you cry, you're going to make me cry. I think I've cried more over the last day than I have in years."

"Ugh. I hate this!"

"I know. Me too. The men outside would just call us women with their affectionate disdain."

Madeline sighed and wiped her eyes. Echo wiped her own.

"Fuck them," Madeline suddenly laughed.

"I agree."

"Fine. Okay. Here I go..."

Echo's smile returned. If Madeline could ask for help, then maybe she could too. Maybe there was some hope for both of them.

"I'd like to stay here, on Volun, with you. Me and Simon, at least for a little while," Madeline rushed out. "There. I said it. I asked." She wrenched her eyes closed. "It's a lot. I know."

Echo stilled.

She hadn't... expected that.

"I..." she started, "Why?"

"Simon."

"Simon?"

"His father," Madeline said. "He's a crew member on EonMed's ship. They're scheduled to return next season, and if the exodus happens sooner..." Madeline shook her head. "We'll miss him. I don't know how to reach him."

"You want to wait for his father?"

"Yes."

So, the baby's father had been a crew hand.

"It would be dangerous," Echo said slowly, uncomfortably. Echo could take care of Madeline, but an infant too? Alone? "Have you told your mom?"

Madeline sighed. "No. She won't understand. She'll tell me I'm not thinking straight."

"If she plans to leave, and you try to stay... You have to tell her, Maddy. Linda isn't going to leave without you." *Or her grandson.* "She's going to want to know why and waiting for a man," Echo swallowed, "She needs to know."

"I'm not worried about my mom. I'll take care of it when that happens. I just... I don't think I can do it alone. Be here alone. I could if it was just me but baby Simon too?"

"The shipment might be canceled if the colony leaves. It might never come," Echo reminded her.

"It'll come. Simon promised he'd return."

Echo chewed on her tongue. "And if it doesn't?"

She'd just told Madeline to ask her for anything, but this? Echo didn't think Maddy had thought it through. Yes, it would be easier if it were just them, but that didn;t account for everything that could go wrong, nor being stranded if something did.

Madeline's face scrunched. "I've already thought about all of this, Echo. All of it. It's the only thing I *can* think about anymore. If I leave, I may never see Simon again and tell him about his son. And if I do, how will we find each other? I don't know where the colony is going, if it's staying together or breaking up. I've heard how hard it is for women to travel through space, the cost, the questions, the added security to keep us from the Trentians. And he's a crew-hand, he doesn't have the money to search for me, nor I him."

"Have you tried contacting him?"

"Not since the last delivery ship arrived. I was able to send a message out."

"That was half a year ago..."

Madeline grabbed Echo's hand. "I know it's a lot to ask. A lot of responsibility. Please consider it."

Her stomach twisted. "I don't know."

"Please? If I'm with you, I'm sure the others will let me stay. I'm certain."

Echo wasn't. Jonah didn't even want Echo to remain behind. Both she and Madeline, and a baby? There was a lot more to consider than that. There was her dad, Keir, the lab... She shifted uneasily.

"Keir has a ship," Echo offered. "I bet he has the ability to send a message to Simon."

Madeline paused, her lips parting. "Do you think he would let me?"

A week ago, Echo would've said no, but now... "Yes."

"That would... that would be good. I thought he only came here on that skiff, not a ship."

She cocked her head at her friend. "I believe he has another one." He would have too to have traveled here. "We'll get a message to Simon, and then we'll consider what to do next. Does that sound good?"

None of it did to Echo. She could already see the pandemonium of what would happen if Madeline tried to stay. It was a problem that nobody needed. How was she going to tell Madeline that?

"Yeah."

Echo stood. "You need some water and rest. I'll send your mom in. We'll talk more about it later. You should tell her," she added before stepping out of the room and hearing Madeline sigh deeply in response.

She found Linda waiting in the kitchen, ice water in hand. She went into the room as soon as Echo departed.

Turning back, she saw Linda take the infant from Madeline after she handed her daughter the water.

Linda would never let Madeline stay, especially not with her grandson.

Needing air, Echo left the apartment and headed for the medical hall to find Keir.

TWENTY-THREE

ALL ECHO WANTED WAS an icy shower and to return to a time when things had been simpler.

Then she remembered, there had never been simpler times, only simpler moments.

Seeing Keir speaking to Todd in the shadows outside the building that housed the medical hall, she beelined for them. Her heart thumped, taking Keir in. She felt indebted to him and she had no idea why, and she was annoyed now that he kept calling her out on saying thank you. Last night had been nothing like she'd planned, and she wanted more of it, of him. Keir looked up and straightened as she approached.

"What's going on?" she asked, lifting her shirt to wipe her face.

"Your medical equipment is out of date," Keir said, his voice raspy as his gaze wandered all over her, making her blush. "And much of it is in need of serious repair. Half the chemicals you need to run a functioning medical pod are missing, and there is nothing here for proper neonatal care. I'm going to retrieve my ship from space. Todd and I were discussing specifics."

"You have a medical station on your ship?" she asked.

"I do."

Echo licked her lips and his eyes shot to them. "Madeline wants to send a message out too, using your comm system, if that's okay?"

Keir cocked his head and peered at the sky, looking from one place to another. "That's fine. I should head out now, while it's getting dark, if I want to be back by morning."

"I'll go check on Madeline and Simon," Todd said, excusing himself and shaking his head.

Echo watched him walk away before turning back to Keir. "Is something wrong? What were you two talking about?"

His eyes slid from the sky to hers. "We were bartering the price of my medical equipment and resources."

"Oh... Right." Echo hadn't even thought about the cost of Keir's help. At least not in terms of money. She stiffened. He'd been helping her a lot lately. "It's costly, isn't it, your lab's resources? How much?" She curled her tongue, wishing she hadn't asked. If the medical hall didn't have the funds for it, the compound would. She would.

The last thing she wanted to do right now was talk to Keir about money. The compound barely had enough to sustain itself with the resources it produced. But money was rarely exchanged between the compound's citizens. It was easier to barter.

Someone like Keir, who not only had his own ship and the funds to fly it, was probably not into bartering. Hard cash and credits would be worth more to him.

He hummed. "The same thing I told Todd. Nothing."

"Nothing? Are you sure?"

"I'm not going to make anyone pay to use my ship's medical equipment. I can be an asshole, but I'm not the devil. Does everyone here think Cyborgs are terrible?"

"Obviously not. That's mostly just me and Jonah. We mainly deal with other humans, so there's that. I don't think Todd knows you can turn into a bird..."

"A hawk. And I don't 'turn,' I shift," he grumbled.

She couldn't help smiling. "I'm teasing you." It was the first time they'd had a moment alone since this morning. His face was grim, and she realized today had been a long one for him as well.

He arched his brow. "You are?"

Then he cupped her face, leaned down, and kissed her.

Stunned, Echo held still as Keir's mouth moved over hers, soft and eager. He pulled her close, despite the heat, and coaxed her lips open.

She stared at his closed eyes, her mouth flooding with sweat, salt, and his tongue. His fingers threaded into her messy hair and tugged. When her shock subsided and she began to kiss him back, he pulled away. She gasped and sought more, but his mouth was gone.

"Do you want me to fly you home, or do you want to stay here?" he asked.

Reeling from the kiss, Echo blinked. "I'm staying here tonight."

"I figured as much. I just wanted to be sure before I left and retrieved my ship. Are you okay?"

She straightened her shoulders. "Are you?"

His brow furrowed, he searched her face. "That remains to be seen."

"What do you mean?"

"After Madeline and her baby are situated, and the rest of this"—he waved his hand outward—"calms down, we're going to have a nice, long talk, you and I. Whatever happens after that, we'll see."

"Yes," she agreed, her throat tightening. "We'll see."

He continued to search her face, and she held her ground. She was done being intimidated by his kind. She had nothing left to prove except that she could be brutally honest as well.

Even if it hurt.

Even if it meant retribution upon her. Even if he'd just kissed her out of the blue and left her wanting more.

Keir reached up and pushed a strand of her hair behind her ear, making her heart bleed. "You never answered."

She curled her arms over her chest, wishing he didn't make her feel so vulnerable. "Answered what?"

"*How are you?*"

Her shoulders drooped. She was feeling too many things right now. "Tired," Echo decided.

His eyes narrowed like he didn't fully believe her. "Go back to Linda's and get some sleep. I'll meet you there in the morning."

"What about moving Madeline to the medical hall tonight?"

"We're not taking her in there. She's safer at home where it's cool and clean. We'll move her and the baby to my ship upon my return. I can do a full scan on both of them and take her to the nearest spaceport if there's an anomaly."

"All right."

He cocked his head again. "All right?"

"It sounds like a good idea," she agreed.

Keir leaned forward, putting his face before hers, pinning her with his stormy gaze. She jumped but quickly recomposed herself.

"Progress," he said, straightening away, no longer appearing so grim.

She frowned. Now it was her turn to be confused. "Progress?"

"You're beginning to trust me, Echo."

Echo glowered. "Go get your ship, Keir. We're literally burning daylight."

He gave her a smirk and it immediately lifted her mood.

She couldn't help smiling back. "Go. Before I change my mind."

With his smirk firm on his face, he launched into the air. Echo raised her fingers to her lips and touched them, wishing he'd swoop down and surprise her with another kiss. She watched him fly away, marveling at the power of his metal wings and the way they glinted with the last light of the day.

TWENTY-FOUR

THE HEAT DRAGGED on Keir's wings and limited his air supply sharply at higher altitudes. Thankfully, he didn't have to stay in the air long.

Already connecting with his planetary ship, he dropped down beside it and ducked inside. Besides a few fallen leaves atop of it, his ship had been undisturbed for the duration of his captivity. His updating diagnostics reassured him that it had weathered the heat without any issues.

Keir switched on the thrusters, beyond ready to be off the moon and in the air. Because something was off, and he couldn't place it. Until he could, he didn't want to be away from Echo's side for long.

She hadn't accepted his claim. In fact, at some point during the day, her body destroyed his nanocells, leaving him mystified. He'd felt them die, he'd felt their tenebrous connection fade, and it had made him tense all day.

And yet, it seemed like she hadn't even realized. He'd

tried programming his nanocells to give her comfort, but it had been for nothing. He likened it to stress though he wasn't certain. He hated uncertainty.

His mood had dropped further because it wasn't only his fierce instinct to nest her that bothered him, it was that the air about the compound had shifted as well, leaving him on edge. His head hurt. It still did.

So did his heart.

Was it the fans, the heat, some unknown toxin in the air?

Echo?

Keir cupped his brow and pressed his fingers into his skin, debating if he should turn his pain receptors off. His heart felt swollen and vulnerable. His head—confused and illogical. The bitterness that was always present within both had been replaced. A deep prickling of concern had taken its place.

Cursing, he slammed his fist against his head.

Seeing Echo act so vulnerable with him and with Madeline's labor worried him. Her mind was racing with thoughts he wished he could decipher; he wasn't certain if Echo was racing toward or away from him.

He'd made the choice to put a claim on her, despite codes and territory. He did so without caring about the consequences. Except it was apparent she cared deeply about consequence.

Even more than me...

Keir inhaled and cooled down. Returning his attention to his ship's takeoff, something pinged his IP.

He stiffened.

Glancing around him, he tried to connect with the signal, only to find it gone. Dropping out of his body, Keir seeded outward, searching for where the connection had come from. Scattered electrical waves filled his vision, similar to what he traveled through days ago for Echo.

Volun didn't have relays. There shouldn't have been a connection made to him personally. Volun was unconnected from the network. And no one on the moon, nor in this sector of the galaxy, knew his personal IP. He would have been aware of such a relay within minutes of his first scouting of Volun. Cyborgs were always connected to the network, if there was a connection to be had.

The signal led directly to Echo's home.

Keir pulled back into his head and left his ship. Peering at the outpost through the trees in the distance, there was a light on.

He'd forgotten about Jonah.

The quarantine chamber, the door at the back...

The trap.

The signal got stronger as he flew towards the outpost. Jumping and then dropping atop of the deck, keeping his wings on standby, Keir's eyes roved over every detail around him. The pressure in his body intensified.

There was another Cyborg.

Through the deck window, nothing looked overly suspicious. Jonah's backpack was resting on one of the couches, but otherwise the room was undisturbed. The front door was unlocked.

He made his way to Echo's room. Jonah's sweat and the old aroma of his cigs were in the air. Sweaty fingerprints marred the icebox. There was no hint of blood, or death. All was quiet.

Déjà vu hit him as he stopped at Echo's room with his knife loose in his hand. Only this time, the door was wide open and so was the door to the shower. The door beyond was also open. The trapdoor was shut tight and uncovered. The bed was messy and unmade, making him hesitate. Echo's arousal still filled the room, and he pictured her lying on the covers naked, spread out before him.

An urge seized his mind to shield her with his wings and cover the illusion with his body, to mark her flesh, her very cells, with his being. She wouldn't be *his* until he did. He needed complete dominance of her, if only for a moment, to ensure she was his mate and his mate alone. He wanted to pierce the codes in her organic nanocells and infiltrate them with his own, threading his claim into the very fibers of her being.

Keir's eyes closed and the illusion vanished, but not his need. His cock was hard and there was no way to get relief. Without another glance at the bed, he left the room and walked through the quarantine shower to the other side.

He cooled down when Echo's bed left his sight.

Someone's waiting for me.

His eyes pierced the gloom ahead.

The smell of the tunnel beyond was nearly ozone, fresh and unfiltered, except for traces of Jonah and his unwashed stench. Dust motes scattered through the air. Sleek mountain rock, light tracks, and old chemical tags decorated every side, identifying piping that disappeared in and out of the walls, akin to what he would expect to see in an industrial laboratory that followed codes. The passage was larger than he expected and vanished around a bend ahead of him. It remained cool and untouched by the heat outside.

He followed it deeper and deeper. The walls morphed from rock to cement and steel; robot tracks eventually lined the ceiling and walls. He became increasingly aware this place was not connected to the compound, and with each step, new signals emerged to join with him. It wasn't attached to any place on the moon.

Coming upon two large security doors, and a hand and eye scanner, he paused to hack through it when the doors naturally opened for him.

On the other side was a large laboratory, spanning as far as he could see. Wires, machines, and capsules of every size were patterned out in rows. Wires hung like vines from the ceiling as if they'd been ripped apart. Broken viewing windows, smashed walls and doors gave the otherwise high-tech space a look of ruin and violence. Streaks of black ash marred the walls, and though it appeared as if someone had tried to clean it up, shards of broken glass littered the floor.

Lightheaded, he paused.

It was the laboratory he journeyed billions of miles to find. He knew it, instinctively, bringing his hand to his mouth to rub his jaw. He'd been here before.

And someone had destroyed it.

Faded voices emerged to prick his ears, and Keir headed

for them. They came from a room in the center that, at some point, had additional security measures all around it. Those measures had been destroyed, much like the rest of the lab's interior infrastructure. He took it all in; there was chaotic as well as tactical destruction to the space, as if it had been maimed twice.

Only for someone to try and clean it up afterward.

He didn't quiet his footsteps as the other Cyborg's signal was strong, poking at his systems. It led him toward the voices.

"He's here," a deep voice hummed. One he didn't recognize.

"About time," Jonah answered with a huff.

Keir turned the corner and faced the two men.

Jonah, no longer red, puffy, and sweaty from the heat, was sitting in a swivel chair massaging one of his knees. Keir's gaze landed on the Cyborg.

"Auryn," he said, loosening the hold on his knife.

"Keir," Auryn responded. "Welcome back."

The other Cyborg was naked except for a pair of cloth pants hanging low on his hips. Not nearly as tall as Keir, Auryn was bald and had an average build, but with a warmer, less ghastly skin tone. Old eyes stared back at Keir from a face molded by stress and tension over countless hours of struggle that not even the Cyborg's nanocells had been able to wipe clean.

He appeared as if he were in a state of deterioration.

Auryn hadn't been outside for years. There was a used-up and depleted quality to the Cyborg. He was attached to the giant reactor behind him with numerous tubes and wires. But from what Keir could see of it, the reactor had suffered the same damage as the rest of the lab. Though it still hummed with energy.

That energy washed over Keir in crackling electrical waves when, in reality, it should've blasted him.

Taking in every detail, he frowned. "You're keeping the compound alive. You're Volun's power source. You're stabilizing the reactor."

Auryn shifted, and the wires and piping attached to him moved. "Not quite."

Jonah eyed Keir wearily, looking as if he'd aged a hundred years since last night. "He's not providing energy to the compound. We have power stations and solar usurps for those. The burnouts provide enough solar energy to keep the compound running in between."

Keir cocked his head and sheathed his knife, knowing Auryn's eyes wandered over him curiously. "So you're keeping the reactor from breaking. The radiation—"

"Is being absorbed by microrobot sponges threaded throughout the walls and within the mountain around us," Auryn answered. "They're inside me as well."

Keir looked around the room. "It would make sense why I'm not reacting to it." He peered back at Auryn. He'd never heard of another of his kind being spliced with radiation clean-up technology; that tech was typically used for androids and other non-organic-based mechas. "Why wasn't I able to sense you or the reactor until now?"

"I'm shielding them."

Keir narrowed his eyes. "How?"

"The amount of energy being funneled straight into my frame is also being contained within, parsed out, and placed where I want it to go. I do not let it wander."

"You're not a shifter."

"No. I am not."

"And yet you welcomed me home. Shifter class and non-shifter class Cyborgs were made in separate laboratories."

That was fairly standard knowledge, based on what creation memories certain Cyborgs had, at least those who had shared them. The other laboratories were stationed closer to Earth and not as well hidden.

Auryn, remaining relatively limp and unmoving, lifted one finger in Keir's direction. "The humans here moved on from animal splicing. They found your kind limited in capability, weak in mind, often broken by instinct they couldn't code out. They had their fun, played with the possibilities and took what progress they made from you, and jumped off the next ledge." Auryn paused and looked at the wall to his right, his voice going distant. "It has always saddened Hanna. She wanted to work on shifters."

Hanna?

"Humans," Keir responded, but not without disdain.

Jonah grumbled. "Humans *and* Cyborgs."

"And Cyborgs," Auryn agreed.

Keir's face hardened. "You?"

"Malin," Jonah quipped. "When Lysander erupted into a

black hole and took out the Trentians' main fleet in the process, bringing the war to an abrupt end, the need for Cyborgs who could fight also came to an end. The military could not control you beyond the codes they placed inside you, and, knowing the gods they'd made, let you be free, and with it countless billions of dollars and knowledge stored within your frames. It was… their sacrifice… so you wouldn't turn on them one day. Making more battle tech, spliced with animal aggression, seemed idiotic to continue to fund. Needs changed."

Keir's head cocked to the other side. "Understandable. There have been no new shifters in generations, at least that I am aware of. But that doesn't explain this." He waved his knife at Auryn and the reactor. "The state of the cybernetics laboratory and the reason you're controlling a nuclear reactor." Keir's gaze slid to Jonah.

"For Echo," Jonah rasped.

Auryn moved, and both Keir and Jonah looked back at him. "Echo…" he mumbled wistfully. "And Hanna."

Keir gritted his teeth.

Auryn's head snapped up, eyes suddenly clear and filled with rage. "I'm awake now because of you. Unable to do what I must." His eyes shone with pure energy. Keir's stance shifted, readying for a fight. "Jonah tells me you've come here searching for this laboratory. Well, now you have found it, and its destruction. If you leave now and never come back, I will not kill you."

"This isn't about Echo," Keir growled. It was about Echo, but a whole lot more. If Echo was living above an unstable nuclear reactor, he was going to have to change that.

"My daughter will not be used by you for whatever reasons brought you here. She cannot restore your memories."

"Used?" Keir spat. "I'm not the one using her. I'm not here for lost memories. Take a good look in a mirror once a generation. It may do you some good."

"I keep her safe, protected, away from a universe who would only want to study and defile her. I've given her the means to be free from all of it. You will not have her!" The reactor hummed behind him. "Jonah had told me what you have done to my daughter!"

Keir bristled. "Echo's choices are her own, not yours. When was the last time you've seen or talked to her? She speaks of you like you're gone."

"Do not talk to me about our relationship. It is none of your business."

"But is she your daughter?"

"Enough!" Jonah scowled and stood. "Before you two bring the mountain down on us. We are on the same side, awful as that might be."

"Side?" Keir scowled. "I see no sides here. Only a deluded machine strapped to a nuclear reactor."

"Echo is leaving Volun with the exodus," Jonah stated as if he'd settled two Cyborgs aggressively going at each other many times before.

Auryn growled. "Hanna will never let her go."

Keir's lips flattened.

Jonah scowled. "Hanna is gone and I woke you to deal with Keir. You two can suffer together. But Echo cannot stay on the moon alone. I will not allow it. She's as much mine as she is yours."

Auryn faced Jonah and his eyes flashed white. "Hanna is not gone!"

Jonah stood and pushed out his stomach. "Have you gone mad?"

Hanna. Echo's mother, Keir realized. The one who left for Earth. He recalled the name from his first conversation with Jonah.

"She will be hurt, abused," Auryn's voice ratcheted, "if she is discovered! She will be seen like the others!" His eyes flashed again, brighter this time, making Jonah flinch away.

Keir raised his hand. "Stop," he commanded. He didn't have time for this now. He and his ship were needed back at the compound. "No one's taking Echo anywhere right now."

"Where is she? I want to see her," Auryn snapped. "I want to see Hanna."

Keir tried to keep up, only knowing something was off with the other Cyborg. Auryn didn't seem to be working as he should be. He wasn't being logical. "She's at the compound with Madeline and Madeline's baby. She's not here."

A flash of relief crossed Jonah's features.

Auryn grabbed a tube attached to his right shoulder and yanked it out. Jonah jerked and backed away as Auryn grabbed another. "I will go to her then." Yanking the second one out, the reactor shook.

"Stop," Keir ordered.

"Auryn, calm down." Jonah shuffled to Keir's side. "You need to go slower."

Auryn yanked another out and a *wooshing* sound filled the room.

A fresh wave of ozone filled Keir's nostrils. *Radiation.* He pulled Jonah's massive form to him and pushed the man outside the room. "Go!"

"Get your hands off of me." Jonah struggled. "I'm going. You two can kill each other, good riddance."

Keir released him, and Jonah spit at his feet.

Auryn continued pulling out wires.

Keir pointed Jonah to the exit. "Get to the surface and close the door behind you. Now."

"Stubborn motherfuckers always trying to tell me what to do."

Keir faced Auryn when Jonah walked away. "You could've killed him."

Auryn tore out another wire, ignoring him.

Keir's hand tightened on his knife. "No one is trying to take Echo away from you," he lied. *How long has this Cyborg been down here?*

Had Auryn ever left Volun?

He ripped another tube out.

Keir eyed the reactor behind Auryn as the *wooshing* built. "Auryn, calm down. What will happen to the reactor without you controlling it?"

"Nothing," Auryn hissed, stepping away from it now that he was free. "That's the problem."

Before Keir could react, Auryn slammed into him. Keir hit the wall with a crash, knocking his head back. He shot to his feet when Auryn plowed into him again, landing atop his chest.

"Don't." With his back pinned, his wings struggled to emerge. Keir kicked his legs out, throwing his fist into Auryn's face.

The other Cyborg recovered and met his gaze. His eyes were completely white. "Welcome home shifter," Auryn said, widening his blazing eyes and shooting pure nuclear energy straight into Keir. "No one comes between me and my girls."

Keir tried to cover his eyes with his arm, but it was too late. More energy than he'd ever encountered surged through him, sizzling him from the inside out. He plunged his knife into Auryn's chest.

White light eclipsed everything, and Keir's systems died.

TWENTY-FIVE

Echo woke to a baby's soft cry.

Sitting upright, she rubbed her eyes and looked around, finding that she was still in Linda's apartment on the couch. Soft light pierced through the thick curtains covering the windows, telling her morning had arrived.

Peering down the hallway to her right, Linda was passed out in her bed, several fans aimed directly at her sleeping form. Echo pushed her blanket off, folded it, and walked to Madeline's room.

Madeline was breastfeeding Simon on the bed. All traces of the labor were gone from the room—except for the extra fans and air coolers. Her hair was brushed, she wore a loose cotton dress, but exhaustion still shimmered in her eyes. Beside her and on the ground were several worn suitcases filled with clothes. Madeline smiled tiredly at her, and Echo took that as a welcome to enter. She closed the door and sat on the bed to Madeline's left.

"Did you get some sleep?" Echo asked.

"Some. I'm too anxious to rest for long."

Echo smiled down at Simon. "I bet."

"I did manage to take a long shower with Mom's help and packed some. I figured I might as well get us ready to leave."

"Jeez. I guess I slept enough for the both of us," Echo glowered. "I would've helped."

She had passed out shortly after returning to the apartment the night before. She'd made the three of them a late dinner and updated Madeline and Linda on the plans. Not entirely thrilled, neither Linda or Madeline were excited to leave but agreed that it was for the best to go to port and to a real hospital—as long as they were promised a trip back to Volun afterward.

"How is he?" Echo asked.

Madeline chuckled, and it was a beautiful sound. "Don't worry. You needed the rest. We tried to be quiet. As for Simon, he's hungry. Sarah said it might take a couple days for my milk to come in. It can't come soon enough." Madeline yawned. "Maybe I will rest some. Do you know how much longer Keir will be?"

"Good question." Echo rose from the bed and went to the window. Shifting the curtain, she looked out. "I don't see any ship tracks in the sky. I'll head to the airfield and see what I can find out. Good news, though," she said, facing Madeline. "There are some clouds in the sky today."

"I saw them when I checked earlier."

"Earlier?"

"This morning."

Echo paused. "How long was I asleep?"

"Half the day."

Echo's eyes widened. "Oh my god." She must've been far, far more tired than she realized. Maybe Keir's insistence for her to get more rest had been more than just concern on his end.

Madeline laughed. "It's the couch. There's something magical about it. If Mom or I can't sleep, we try the couch. It always works."

"Yeah." Echo brushed her fingers through her hair and tied it back. "I can see that. Will you be okay if I leave for a few? Or do you want me to stay until Linda wakes?"

"Go. We'll be fine." Madeline gently laid Simon in a bassinet at her side. "I bet there are people looking for you. If I need something, I'll call out for Mom."

"All right. I'll return soon. Get that rest."

Madeline yawned and curled up onto her side, facing the bassinet. "Will try."

Echo downed a glass of water and left the apartment, making her way outside. If it was close to midday and Keir hadn't returned yet, he would soon. The heat wasn't so piercing today, having changed into an aura across the cement. Glimpsing the sky and Utha's giant mass that can still be seen behind the clouds, she searched for ship tracks.

She swallowed back her anticipation. She was excited to see Keir arrive on his ship, commanding, intimidating, and with all the power and technological trappings to take her breath away. Except this time, it wouldn't be paranoia, fear, and worry clouding her upon his arrival, it would be with a ridiculous grin. She was grinning already. Hell, she was excited just to see him again and to tell him everything else that had been left unsaid. Echo wanted to be past it.

She was going to take him to the real laboratory and down to her dad.

She just had to wait for his return. She had to keep pushing through. Looking down at her dirty clothes and clammy skin, Echo debated going back and taking a quick shower, but decided against it as she neared Gregory's garage. She would have to find time for it later.

The panel was lifted high enough for her to walk under. Colonists lounged inside, conversing, playing cards, and eating and drinking. The smell wasn't so ripe today, and there were less people. Todd was among them, encouraging the more stubborn folks to rest. She asked him if he had any news in regards to Keir and he shook his head.

She found Gregory in one of the back rooms chopping up freeze-dried vegetables for a stew pot that was simmering. "Hey, have you heard anything this morning I should be aware of?"

Gregory looked up at her. "Nothing on my end. Todd announced the baby had been born, and everyone was fine. We're having a small celebration tonight."

Echo smiled. "That will be nice. I'm sure everyone is looking forward to it after the week we've had."

Things were beginning to calm down and it couldn't have happened at a better time.

"That's what I'm thinking. How about you? Have you seen Jonah? Been trying to reach him."

"Not since yesterday morning," she said. She hadn't thought about Jonah once, and she'd left him at her outpost. "Is he not around?"

"Hmm. He wasn't here yesterday either. I thought he was hovering about Linda's."

"No. He wasn't there." A niggle of worry bloomed. She checked her wristcon for messages, finding it clear. "I'll call him."

First Keir was late, now Jonah's missing?

"I tried. He's not answering."

"Maybe he's asleep?"

"Could be."

"I'll go check his apartment." She headed for the door but stopped. "If Todd hasn't told you, Keir is returning with his ship today and taking Linda, Maddy, and the baby to a nearby port."

Gregory grunted. "I'll lower the shutters so the others don't see him coming down. I've never seen so many fights break out since Jonah told everyone we're leaving. I don't think seeing a ship will do anyone any good with the way things are right now. The heat has everyone on edge. It's certainly making me regret my life choices."

She nodded. "I'll see you this evening."

"It'll be nice to have someone normal to talk to. I'll look forward to it."

Echo left Gregory and headed back to the barracks, her eyes on the sky. Jonah lived in a building adjacent to Linda and Madeline that had fewer and smaller rooms, once meant for singles or soldiers in training. Jonah had never left it, even when he had numerous options after the base shut down. His room from before was still his room now.

She bounded up the stairs to Jonah's floor and to his door. She knocked. "It's Echo."

She was met with silence. Knocking again, there was still no answer. Echo dug her keys from her pocket and let herself in.

She walked into the living room. It was messy with papers and empty water containers on every flat surface. There was a bowl brimming with cig butts on the table in the center.

He wasn't here.

Echo walked to his desk, which had tablets and more papers upon it and a cracked computer screen. Shifting through them, there were contracts and bills, correspondences with commercial suppliers. Coming across the EPED brand, she hesitated and lifted the tablet. On it was an extremely lengthy communication log, detailing Volun and the colony, and the application for an exodus grant. Jonah had been communicating with someone named Mia.

The reason given for the exodus: the degradation of the compound's military structure, including but not limited to the colony's inability to establish itself with new generations, inhospitable weather, and the continued degradation of once-established research laboratories and volatile technologies.

Echo lowered the tablet and groaned.

She already knew Keir worked for the EPED, and that Jonah had contacted them.

But Keir being here now—whether for another Cyborg or not—finally made sense. It wasn't a coincidence. Now that she knew the EPED was headed by Keir's boss, Jonah had practically handed the information over to them, even knowing the military had tried to wipe Volun's history— military history included—clean.

And for damn good reason.

If what they had been up to had gotten out to the public, and the Trentians had gotten wind of it, the war might not have ever ended.

Echo cursed and put the tablet down. She walked to the window and checked the sky again and then used Jonah's bathroom to take a quick shower. When she was done and there was still no sign of Keir nor Jonah, she headed back to Madeline.

Linda answered the door, awake and dressed when she arrived.

"Is it time?" Linda asked, letting Echo into the apartment. Madeline was limping around the kitchen at the back, icing some tea.

Echo rubbed her brow. "No. Keir's not back yet. Have you seen Jonah today? I'm looking for him."

"Thank god, no."

"Mom, stop," Maddy said.

"That man knows better than to come to my place, thinking just because he's some self-proclaimed overseer that he can tell us what to do and where to live—"

Madeline and Echo sighed collectively as Linda continued to blather and complain about Jonah. Madeline yelled over her mom, "He hasn't been by. Do you want some iced tea?"

"Thanks. No. I need to speak with him. I'll be back when Keir arrives." She dashed out before she was snared. Despite wishing to stay, Jonah's sudden disappearance worried her. And Linda's tirade in the matter wasn't going to help at all.

It was past midday. It would be evening soon, well past the time Keir told her he'd be back. If Keir had been a mere man, the extra time wouldn't have bothered her so much, but he wasn't, Keir was a Cyborg. His words and opinions were naturally based on calibrations constantly running in the back of his mind.

Her wristcon beeped, and Echo's gaze shot to the band.

Jonah's name appeared and she couldn't have answered it fast enough. She halted outside Gregory's garage.

"Where have you been?" she snapped. "I've been looking for you and no one's seen you. Madeline had the baby and she's fine, by the way. Are you still at the outpost? We need to talk."

"Echo," Jonah's voice wheezed. "You need to come to the outpost..."

"Jonah? What's wrong, what's happened? Why do you sound like that?"

"Auryn," Jonah coughed.

She stiffened. "What about him?"

"I fucked up, Echo."

"What did you do?"

"I told him," Jonah's voice erupted in another coughing spell. "I woke him. I told him about Keir. He was getting too close... You need to leave Volun with me and your family. Your real family. The ones who really care about you."

The blood drained from Echo's face as Jonah broke out into more coughing. "You woke him? You *told* him?"

"He's coming to find you," Jonah rasped. "You need to head home."

"He can't leave the reactor. It's unstable. Not during a burnout. I'm coming. If he's still there, tell him I'm coming. I'll be right there. Don't move."

"Echo, wait!"

She raced through the garage, searching for Gregory and his bike. People were already setting up for the party. She needed a bike. "What?"

"Keir's with him."

Her heart plunged into her stomach.

"Let's hope they kill each other." Jonah coughed. "And save us the effort."

She didn't have any time left to lose.

TWENTY-SIX

He stared at the piping across the ceiling, reading and re-reading the hazy biohazard indentures upon them, blinking out the char from his eyes. For a time, there was only white.

Slowly, his eyesight sharpened as his nanocells sought to repair the burnt outer layer of his body. He was mostly naked, mostly unskinned, and what was left of his scorched clothes and flesh hung in tatters around him.

Keir tried to sit upright. Pain crashed through him, forcing him back to the floor. Wrenching his eyes closed, he willed his cells to flush him with numbing agents, to dull out his pain receptors. When his eyes reopened, he found his legs and feet hooked to the reactor. The wires that had kept Auryn attached were now plugged into him.

He dropped onto his back and stared at the ceiling. The energy coursing through him from the reactor was probably the only reason he was still alive and functional.

Hearing a grunt, his eyes snapped to the source. His

metal fingers shifted into talons, sharpening to points. He heard another grunt coming from outside the room. Keir waited to see if the noise would move, or if he could discern anything else from it. When nothing happened, he began detaching himself from the reactor.

Keir's hand paused on a tube, his talons scraping the rigid metal. For hours he'd laid staring at the ceiling, feeling and seeing nothing but pure energy. White and staggering, there had been nothing else. That energy was inside him now, working his body into overdrive. While his mind was lost, the only thing that had kept him grounded was his need to get back to Echo.

He'd felt her. Somewhere inside of him. She had been with him the entire time.

Somehow she'd managed to brand her claim of him into his very being without his knowledge, and it had kept him sane.

Or, perhaps, she'd been there all along, having slowly usurped his own being and he hadn't had the courage to admit it.

He wasn't going to let his consciousness disintegrate and return to energy when there was more that needed to be done. There were people who needed him, truly needed him, that he didn't want to let them down. He wasn't created to let people down. He was created to give them hope, at least the ones he cared about. He'd realized that somewhere in the white void.

He was Echo's.

"I wouldn't do that if I were you," Auryn's voice said

from outside. It was rough and strained, sounding much how Keir currently felt. It had been Auryn's grunt he'd heard earlier. The other Cyborg was nearby and was either listening to him or watching him or both.

Keir ripped the tube out of his leg. "The reactor will hold." His voice came out just as broken. "The compound is far enough away. It will be fine."

"It's not the base I am worried about," Auryn said.

Keir gritted his teeth and finished pulling out the wires. The reactor rumbled and the energy flowing through him diminished with each disconnected tube. Getting his legs under him after the third try, Keir stumbled out of the room, talons outstretched for battle. He needed to get to Echo.

But first, he had her father to deal with.

Fortunately, there was a trail of black synthetic blood and ash for him to follow.

Stumbling deeper into the facility, Keir came across entire laboratory units that had machines and materials working within them. The interior went from cement walls, mountain rock, and heavy security measures—broken apart —transformed into an industrial, mechanized cybernetics zone. The air was cleaner, the lights maintained, and a series of training rooms and chambers emerged.

Glimpses of his earliest memories came back to him. Little details his eyes had kept that would have gone unnoticed in a memory wipe. The scuffs on the ground, how many lights there were along the walls...

His hawk saw everything, took every detail in, even the most mundane. It remembered slivers of memories that even Keir had a hard time piecing together when the whole picture was muddied. It took a lot of processing power.

Keir found Auryn hunched over on the floor in a cybernetics machine shop. He was leaning against the wall, his body just as mangled and stripped of organic matter as Keirs.

On the floor, several yards away, was Keir's knife. He picked it up as Auryn watched him; synthetic blood glistened on the blade.

There was a profound weariness in the other Cyborg's eyes. For a time, they studied each other.

Keir sat on the floor opposite Auryn, leaned against the wall, and set his knife aside. "I don't want to fight you." He cocked his head at him. "I didn't come here for that."

"It doesn't matter what you came here for, you're here now."

"Like with Ares before me? Malin before him?"

Auryn's now-dull eyes sparked at the mention of Malin. "Yes."

"Why?" Keir looked around. "Why were they here?" His eyes went back to Auryn. "Why are you here? What's the point in keeping this place running if there's no one here?"

"You...haven't figured it out?"

"If this is about Echo being your daughter, I assure you, since you've been down here, many other Cyborgs have had children—with humans and with each other. We've known such a thing was possible, fuck, since the war ended. It is extremely rare, yes, but it has happened. With how small our numbers are, keeping our progeny safe and protected has been... fairly easy so far for us to handle." Keir wasn't versed in the subject, it just had never been of interest to him until recently. "The majority of them live in Ghost City."

"So Jonah was right," Auryn accused. "You've had relations with her."

Keir slowly shifted his wings out from his body to flank his sides. "Is she yours? Or is she Ares's, Malin's?"

Auryn sat upright, pure nuclear energy surging to his eyes. "She is mine."

Undeterred, Keir continued, "Jonah told her otherwise."

"She is *mine*," Auryn repeated. "Jonah had no right!"

"Is he wrong?"

"Like every human man who can't have naturally what we have, he tries to steal it."

Keir bristled at Auryn's words; they hit too close to home. "You can't steal a human, they can't be owned." Controlled, yes, but not owned.

"And yet, he tries. Echo is *my* daughter. She does what *I* want her to do. I have raised her since she was a baby."

"So she is your daughter, but another's offspring."

"It does not matter who sired her," Auryn spat.

"Because you killed Malin, her real father," Keir guessed, "and she, in turn, killed Ares. Hanna ran. She left her daughter and fled billions of miles away to get away from you, from this... Whatever this is. I'm beginning to understand why."

"Do not talk of things you know nothing about! Malin committed treason, and Ares attacked Hanna, both deserved their deaths, their torment."

"Or was it you protecting yourself? Using Echo as a means to keep whatever it is you're down here for a secret?"

Keir couldn't be sure how much of an effect Auryn had on Echo, or if he had any control of her at all—if he ever had. He only knew that when two Cyborgs mated, or two pairs of nanocells were placed together, the dominant ones took over the weaker set.

Echo didn't have the control Auryn or Keir had on her microcodes. If Auryn's claim went further than just love, he may have tried to control Echo as a means to protect her, if not use her. He may have even done it without realizing it.

It wasn't mind control, not really. It was much more subtle than that—the combining of two beings. Only one Cyborg had complete control of his very makeup. Jack. And he used his cells as a virus.

Auryn sneered, pressing his hand to his chest where Keir had stabbed him. "You still think this is about Echo. If only it was so easy. If only... If it was, I wouldn't be down here, keeping a nuclear battery operational. Hanna!" he suddenly roared, as if he was calling out for her. His chest sparked.

Above them, the lights flickered.

Keir's head straightened and his gaze narrowed. "Then what is it about?"

Auryn called for Hanna again before returning his focus back on Keir. "She didn't tell you?"

"What are you talking about?"

"They're alive. They're *all* still alive. And if it wasn't for Malin, they would be living beings too. They would've been finished. They wouldn't be in perpetual limbo. The only thing that Cyborg did right was underestimate me." Auryn laughed but it sounded like it was full of self-deprecation. "They always underestimate me. Ah, what we do for our family..."

All sound turned to white noise in Keir's ears. He pushed off the floor and got back to his feet. He left Auryn behind. Searching wildly, Keir went deeper into the facility, opening doors, his wires vibrating. Auryn's sad laughter eventually vanished, leaving Keir in silence.

Alive? Who's alive?

The dread strangle-holding his systems didn't want his question to be answered.

Coming to a unit of closed, untampered security doors, déjà vu slammed into him again. He tested the eye reader, and when the doors decompressed and opened for him, he stormed past them.

On the other side, in vats, on work benches, and open-ended freezers, were partially created Cyborgs everywhere. Pyrizian metal in spades. A room worth billions.

And children.

Manufactured bodies, grown from test tubes, with parts scattered as much as they were placed together, threaded and spliced with the hard, living metal. Vats filled with cryoliquid lined the right wall, all filled with partially crafted beings, all in the process of being *born,* reshaped into the monstrosities they would spend the rest of their life trying to maintain control over.

Keir walked to a vat towards the back where the legs of a boy—grown to that of the age of an adolescent—were floating with wires coming out from its open thighs. Slowly, the legs bent and straightened, the toes curled.

In the vat beside it was the rest of what had to be the boy, now having grown into a man, but without his legs and legs.

Keir turned, finding the arms hooked to a series of computers on a workbench nearby.

"It's not just Echo I'm protecting. It's them."

He pivoted at Auryn's voice. The Cyborg leaned against the doorframe.

"They left them unmade. The humans left them," Keir said, looking back at the limbless, floating body of the partially made boy—half-man. "Why? Why would they do that?" The eyes of the man opened and looked at Keir. He was a pale, hairless, unnatural-looking ghoul.

Keir cringed. Half a century was a long time to be floating in liquid.

"I did not give them a choice. They tried to reclaim their prizes, those humans, but I didn't allow them to. I was the last Cyborg created here, that had not yet had his memories wiped. You see, Keir, they had moved on from splicing our kind with animal DNA towards the end. Your class was too hard to manage. So, they tried other ways to make us stronger, to give our kind an upper hand, and towards the end..."

Clenching his hands, Keir broke eye contact with the floating Cyborg and looked back at Auryn. "Fucking tell me already."

"They began using Trentian DNA, straight from a Xanteaus Knight. We had one here on Volun, a captive of war, brought here for interrogation and study. We could breed with them, that was open knowledge, but to create from them?" Auryn shook his head. "To make our own Knights, those not needing Pyrizian metal? A being as powerful as both Cyborg and Trentian, created with the codes of one of us, to infiltrate the Trentian homeworld and destroy our enemy from within? We already had a Knight on hand... The hard part was done. That's how."

Keir stilled, internal sirens screaming in his ears. "You're telling me that these—these are made from Trentian bodies?" The codes within him, the ones that urged him to distrust and to even destroy all Trentians probed his every thought.

"Yes."

Around him and in pieces were not just children, but children seeping with the DNA of what Keir had been created to destroy, what every Cyborg made during the war was created to destroy.

His heart surged and expanded as electricity streaked through him. Red washed over his vision. He tried to wrap his head around it but found his systems short-circuiting. His frame sparked. He balled and unfisted his hands again and again.

All the while, he knew Auryn was creeping up on him,

getting closer. The lights flickered again and two of the vats powered down only to turn back on at the front of the room.

"I can't let them die. I won't. I also won't let humans continue to play god. Not with us, not like this. Not after causing Hanna so much pain. Pain she didn't deserve to go through! When I realized what was going on here, I told Malin, the only other Cyborg still in attendance. He trained us all, even you at one point, I'm certain." Auryn shuffled closer. "He didn't believe me, not at first. It wasn't until the Knight vanished and Malin lost access to the cybernetics laboratory, that he began to suspect something. Except when he learned the truth, he decided to simply... destroy everything."

"Do you not harbor the same codes as us?" Keir asked, unable to look away from the vats and the terrible beings within.

A Trentian Knight wasn't just a normal Trentian. They were fierce, zealot warriors, and incredibly powerful alien beings. They fought in the name of their God, Xanteaus. A powerful entity housed within the center of the alien homeworld, or so it was speculated. Knights could take on a Cyborg one on one in battle, unlike a normal Trentian, and could do far more than that.

They had been brutal in their devastation before the first Cyborgs were created to fight them back. Knights led the alien's armies, their government. They had the power, with a single touch, to bind organic life directly to them and manipulate it for their means. The effect was irreversible.

All in the name of Xanteaus...

"The codes that urge us to kill them?" Auryn glanced at a vat with the body of a young child in it. "Yes, but they're not aliens. They're us. I was made with them, they are my siblings. As we are brethren, you and I."

Keir's eyes snapped to Auryn. "Are you one of them?"

Auryn was just a metal Cyborg, stripped of his flesh. Keir couldn't discern a difference between them except for his wings, talons, and a beak that was currently set at his human jaw bone.

"No. I was the last human body of the batch before the program changed."

"Are you... a shifter?"

"No..."

"You killed Malin to stop him?"

"When he realized I had spoken the truth, his solution was to simply... wipe the slate clean. He did not care what Hanna wanted."

"And what did Hanna want?"

Auryn halted when Keir said her name, turning to look around the lab. "Where is she?"

Keir watched him sharply. Auryn either didn't know Hanna was gone, or he refused to accept it. Either way, Auryn was not operating properly.

"Jonah left to retrieve her, remember?" Keir decided to lie and see how broken Auryn was. Keir needed to know what Hanna had to do with everything besides being Malin's lover. He glanced at the bodies in the vats and his eyes went red once more before he forced his codes to untangle the non-threat they presented. "What did Hanna want?" he asked again.

Auryn twitched, stalled, and then righted his frame. "She wanted to save them, and give them a chance. She had been working on them from the beginning. She's still trying to save them."

Keir's jaw clenched as he glanced at the bodies yet again. He understood Malin's reasoning for wanting to destroy them, more than he could understand Auryn and Hanna's reason for saving them.

The peace between the Trentians and humans was... fragile at best, and peace had only come about after devastating loss to the Trentians. It wouldn't take much to rekindle the war.

Keir shuttered his eyes. *Echo's protecting these Cyborgs too.*

From other Cyborgs, from humans, from... everyone.

It all finally made sense.

"How did you get the military to leave?" Keir asked, unshuttering his eyes to meet Auryn's.

Auryn shuffled towards Keir again. "After I destroyed Malin, I became a hero. But it didn't last long. Those in charge were fully aware of what was being done down here, and sought to cover it up. No one, not even another Cyborg, was to be aware of these new models. Hanna warned me. I was going to be wiped. They turned on me, and I barricaded down here and destroyed the main access points.

"The military tried to smoke me out. The more they tried to remove me, the more money it ended up costing them. I had every resource I needed to last for an eternity in this mountain and they knew that. Eventually, the base was shut down, not because of me, but because of what Lysander had accomplished. Partially-made Cyborgs were the last thing on anyone's mind, especially of the Trentian variety. Not now that there was a giant black hole tearing through commercial airspace. A black hole, created by one of *our kind*. It didn't matter *what* DNA they had. That kind of power..." Auryn shook his head. "Scared them. I could smell their fear even from down here."

"And Hanna?" Keir prompted.

Auryn's eyes blazed again at the mention of her name. "She had become aware that she was pregnant with Malin's child—a Cyborg's child, a traitor's," he sneered. "She was terrified of what that meant so she turned to me for help, not knowing who else she could trust. She managed to send me a message and escaped the compound. She gave birth to Echo down here, away from curious eyes, and for those first years it was just the three of us." The light dimmed in Auryn's eyes as if he were reliving the memories.

As if he were fond of them.

"Go on," Keir ordered, snapping Auryn back to the present.

"It took several more years for the military to completely give up on accessing the lab, and once they were gone, those who had chosen to remain were left without ships, without help. Jonah and his ilk took over the compound and filed for civilian colony status. And for years, all was well until the reactor started to fail..." Auryn was several yards from him now, still inching closer.

Keir loosened his hands. "And Ares?"

Auryn had gone completely still. "Hanna thought she could trust him because he was a Cyborg, because he had only journeyed here on his own free will. He recalled Volun in some minor way and sought to restore what he had lost. Hanna offered to do what she could in the matter to give him what he wanted, if only to ask for his help... He deserved his fate. He would still be down in the hole today if Echo hadn't pitied him."

Keir's talons clawed the workbench. Not, only did Auryn speak far too nonchalantly about another Cyborg's death, he had no idea how much it had hurt Echo. "Does Echo know any of this?"

"Know what?" a voice asked.

Their heads snapped to look at the door. Echo stood on the threshold.

TWENTY-SEVEN

She ran down in the laboratory; traversing old tunnels she used to play in when she was a child. She'd been banished from the place sometime after that.

Now, it was open and disturbed, the path leading deep into the mountain, unprotected. It was her job to guard it and the beings within. She'd failed.

"Keir's still down there with Auryn," Jonah had warned her minutes earlier.

Echo scrunched her face and quickened her step. She'd found Jonah, struggling on the couch, coughing. He'd been half-asleep with exhaustion and could barely look at her, his eyes ruddy and distant, and completely dehydrated. He'd looked half-dead.

She didn't want to leave him. He needed medical aid immediately. Gregory was on his way with Todd to pick him up and bring him back to the compound. But she couldn't remain by his side knowing Keir was with her father below, knowing what Keir might discover...

A glimpse at the reactor and the state of the room had told her enough. The burnt marks on the walls and the loud humming in the walls had solidified her fear. The air smelled... *wrong*.

Her eyes watered and her breathing grew labored. Not seeing Keir's and her dad's bodies sent her deeper into the tunnels, her fear spiraling. She headed to the place she dreaded most.

The cybernetics shops where her mom used to work, where the pieces of bodies used to be displayed all around her, where there were wires, chips, and codes.

Hearing broken voices, she slowed down to figure out where they were coming from, and made her way towards them.

"Does Echo know?"

Stepping into the doorway of the main laboratory, she found Keir and her dad talking in the back, or at least what was left of them. "Know what?"

Her lips parted with an inhale. Two humanoid machines, charred and smoking, turned their heads toward her at once. Both had deep eye sockets with glassy eyes and pieces of skin and other organic matter hanging off of them. Neither had hair nor clothes, but she recognized them both, even from across the room.

Horror-stricken, she forgot to breathe as she took in their appearances. Where Auryn's inner frame resembled that of a human man, Keir's... didn't. His wings, though plated and tight, were perfectly blended in and attached to his frame to make up his entire back, the backs of his butt and thighs, and even the bottom of his neck. The thin, sharp tips of those wings curved over his sides, ridging his inner frame under metal tubes and wires, like his wings were wet, and plastered perfectly into, inside, and against him. His wings framed him.

Even without features, and looking like he'd just walked through an explosion, Keir was a work of art. It reminded her of her mom's work.

But she knew her mom would've been much too young to have helped create Keir and bring him to life. Hanna had never worked on any of the shifters, they were before her time.

"Echo," they both said in unison.

Swallowing back her fear, her face went hard. Around her, the lab was failing, the reactor was dying. She didn't dare glance at the beings in the vats.

Her dad took a step toward her at the same time Keir did. But then Auryn rushed forward and snatched her against him. When she managed to glimpse Keir, he was right behind Auryn, appearing one microsecond from throwing Auryn across the room and butchering him. One severe look from her, and he backed off.

Trying not to shake, Echo pushed out of Auryn's arms.

His face plates shifted into a frown. "You never come down to visit me anymore," he said, his voice half-raw, half-mechanical.

"Hi Dad. I've been busy." She looked down at where his hand went to his chest. "You're bleeding."

"I'm leaking. How long has it been?"

Her throat constricted, eyeing the black liquid trickling out of him. "About six years."

"Six... years. That long?"

"We had a fight, remember? You told me not to wake you, that the reactor was too unstable."

"I don't recall. Where's Hanna? Why isn't she with you?"

Tensing, Echo straightened, seeking composure. "Remember? She left."

"Left? Where? Is she at the compound?"

"No," Echo shook her head, confused. It was hard to look at her dad for long with his face as it was; it was unsettling. It was like staring at her own failure. "She's not at the compound. She left for Earth..."

Echo glanced at Keir, who had lowered his talons, but remained behind her dad. He watched Auryn intensely, listening to every word, scanning Auryn a hundred times over.

All I need to do is get the two of them far away from each other.

"Earth?" her dad asked.

"Yes, to stay with her sister."

Auryn's frame stilled. Keir's talons lifted.

"When?" Auryn asked.

Echo grabbed her dad's hands, her brow furrowing. "Six years ago."

"But her work is still unfinished. What about the others? She wouldn't have left." Auryn looked at one of the benches. "There's so much left to do."

"She did, Dad, she left. She told you. She wanted you to join her, to give all of this up. And when you wouldn't listen to reason..."

"Hanna would have never left. That's not like her at all."

He didn't remember, she realized. Swallowing the ball now clogging her throat, she kept his hands trapped in her own.

"She was tired," Echo whispered. "She'd grown old. Remember when you used to tease her about her graying hair? The cane she needed after she broke her leg? Her hands couldn't do what they used to do. She tried to convince you that she'd done all she could, but you wouldn't listen."

"I..."

"What happened with Ares broke her," Echo breathed, blinking back tears. "*I* broke her."

I broke all of us.

Echo had been waiting for retribution for years after what she had done—even if it was out of pity—never wanting to acknowledge that her punishment had come for her long ago. And it had never left.

She'd chosen to stay because her dad had chosen to stay. Because she couldn't leave him.

Auryn tried to pull his hands from hers, but she

wouldn't let him. "I don't understand... This place was her whole life. We were her whole life."

"And she spent her whole life with us," Echo said gently. "She's old now. She didn't want to die here, surrounded by ghosts."

"What ghosts?"

Echo sighed softly. "Look around you, we're surrounded by them." Maybe Madeline was onto something. "Just look."

Auryn jerked away, and she let him go. His eyes flickered as he studied her, and she swallowed again, nodding. She pointed to her mom's old work desk where several pictures were resting atop of it. His gaze went to the desk before he strode over to it and took one of the pictures in his hands.

"Why can't I remember?" Auryn asked, voice low. "She is... old."

Keir grabbed her arm and dragged her back to the exit. "You need to leave. Now."

"I was going to say the same to you," she said, tugging her arm out from his grasp. "You shouldn't have come down here without me!"

"I was lured here by your... *father*. And would you have even taken me down here?" Keir snapped at her. "But none of that fucking matters right now because the reactor is leaking. I can smell the radiation, even from here. It means the nanostructures within are failing to break it down. You need to get out of here. Now."

Echo's eyes narrowed. "I'll be fine, you're the one I'm worried about. Let me handle my dad—"

"He's not your dad!"

Her eyes sliced to Auryn, who was still staring at the picture in his hand. "Lower your voice," she hissed, annoyed she even had to reprimand a being who should know better. "It doesn't matter. And I was going to tell you everything."

"When?"

"When there was some fucking time!" she practically screeched, her own voice carrying across the room.

"You should have told me that night—"

Echo lifted her hand, done with being told what to do by men, whether they were flesh and bone or not. "You're forgetting what's at stake here, for me, and for others, Keir. I've only begun to trust you. That does not extend to the man you're working for."

"Hanna has such an eye for patterns," Auryn mused. "She has a goddess's touch."

Echo winced again, and Keir tensed.

"This has nothing to do with Nightheart," Keir snapped again at her. "This is way beyond him now."

A hollow thumping noise sounded above, and half the lab's power died only to turn back on a moment later. The hollow thumping remained. Echo looked up.

Keir grabbed her and pulled her into the hall. "We'll finish this later."

She snatched her arm back again, turning on him. "Yes. We will. And this has everything to do with your intentions and Nightheart's, whether you like it or not."

Keir cocked his head.

She furiously pointed at the lab. "That Cyborg is my dad, and if he's taken into custody, he'll be dismantled for treason. My mom will also be arrested if the government gets involved again and they track her down. And the others, the unfinished ones, they'll die without Auryn, and that's not..." she bit her tongue and shook her head.

"What?"

"That's it."

"No, you were going to say something more, that's not... what?"

Her lips thinned.

Keir took a step toward her. "Tell me what you were going to say."

"I was going to say nothing," she quipped. "I finished what I was saying."

"No," Keir growled. "You weren't. You were going to say, 'that's not the real problem,' weren't you?"

The color drained from her face. "Please, don't."

He grabbed her and jerked her to him. "I know they're Trentians!"

His wings shot out and crashed into the walls on either side, then bent towards her like they were going to trap her, but they stopped short.

"That's the real problem isn't it?" he yelled. "You can't tell me because you don't know what I'd do if I found out! You don't know what I'd do, and yet, here I am, proving to you without even trying to that I'm not going to destroy them!"

His frame visibility shook.

Echo lifted her hands slowly. Her head and heart ached. "Keir, calm down."

"Calm." His wings snapped back inside him, and he released her. "Down? The longer you're fucking breathing in radiation, Echo, the less calm I'm going to be."

She took a step back when his hand thrust out and curled around the back of her neck.

He leaned in until she saw nothing but his metal features.

"I have never killed a Trentian in all of my existence, nor have I ever wanted to. I have never done any of the great deeds the universe has been told. I've never commanded. Even my title is a lie," he hissed.

She hated that she shook. That *he* shook. That he had found out at all, and that she hadn't been able to tell him herself.

Worse still, she hurt physically knowing, whether he liked it or not now, he was involved. She couldn't protect him from the truth. There was no turning back.

"Everything you might have heard about me was lies. Unlike Auryn, I was nor have ever been a hero, even to a single being. I'm a fucking fraud, Echo. What do I need to do for you to finally let me be what I was created for? For you to believe in me?" His voice lowered with grief. "Bare my soul to you?"

Echo brought her hands to her eyes, rubbing the tears budding in them away furiously.

"Tell me," he begged. "Tell me what I need to do." He

pressed his brow to hers. "Anything. I'm asking you to give me a chance, Echo."

"A chance?" she whispered.

"Please."

She sucked in a pained breath, closed her eyes, and parted her lips, telling him exactly what to do.

TWENTY-EIGHT

WITH HIS HANDS fisted around luggage handles, he carried the last of the bags onto his ship.

A crowd had come out to the edge of the field to see Madeline, Linda, and the newborn off, saying goodbyes, well-wishes, and words of encouragement through tears and even anger.

Except no one had come for him. In fact, the side-eyed stares from the group said more than enough. Their suspicion and uncertainty were more evident than even the end of a brutal heatwave.

Echo wasn't among them. He hadn't seen her since she'd ordered him to leave.

If this is what she needs, then so be it.

Keir glared at the colonists who caught his gaze, flashing his eyes at them. Most of them refused to look away, even at the threat he presented—stubborn to the bone.

He couldn't blame them for their wariness. His flesh had not yet regrown, and his metal interior was on display for all to see. It was...grotesque. He looked like an animal butchered, with only bones and sinew left. Although he was suited and clean, his face was not the one they had come to know this past week. He had also not reintroduced himself once he had returned with his ship from space, and only spoke to those he was giving transport to.

It was enough that they had eventually recognized him.

He peered up at the cloudy, gray sky. These people will never forget him. Not after all that had happened.

He'd got what he'd come here for. Now, it was time to leave and finish the mission.

Seeing another group head towards him from behind the crowd, he left the shadows of his ship. Todd and Sarah, with Greg and one other, rolled a gurney with Jonah lying atop of it. Awake and angry, Jonah glared at everyone who looked upon him, coughing all the while.

Keir met them beside his ship's ramp.

Echo was nowhere in sight.

Neither was Auryn.

"The ugliest Cyborg I've ever seen," Jonah said before falling into a string of coughs. "I won't...fly with...you!" Jonah tried to rise but Sarah slammed her hand down on his shoulder.

"Calm down," she said.

Keir looked from Jonah to her, noticing the bag she was carrying. "His?"—he indicated Jonah—"or medical equipment and drugs?"

"Mine. Todd and I discussed it. Jonah will need someone to care for him day and night until we get to the port hospital seeing as he refuses to be sedated. And it's better for me to go rather than Todd since he's better equipped to handle those remaining on Volun if something should go wrong."

"I don't need help, woman," Jonah fussed. "Don't come on my account."

Sarah sighed. "Unless you want to watch him yourself?" she asked Keir. "I figured one more passenger wasn't going to be a problem."

"No," Keir said. "You're welcome aboard. I'll have the AI set up another room for you, one by the medical bay."

"Thank you."

Keir nodded.

He turned to Madeline, Linda, and the baby as they approached. Linda carried the baby while Madeline limped with a make-shift cane. Tears were in their eyes, but Madeline was smiling, and that smile loosened some of the strain in Keir's limbs. He managed to unclench his fists by the time they stopped at the ramp.

Madeline's smile dropped when she looked up at him. "Your face... What happened?" She was the first who had dared to ask.

"There was an accident. Don't worry about it."

"Is that why Jonah's hurt?"

"Yes."

"Thank you for taking us to port." She wiped her eyes with her free hand. "I don't know how we'll ever repay you."

Madeline peered around, her face clouding with worry, glancing at Jonah and then looking away. "Where's Echo? Is she okay?"

"She's fine," Keir rasped, fingers twitching.

"Don't listen to anything he says!" Jonah barked and then fell into another bout of uncontrollable coughing.

"Quiet you," Linda snapped at him. "You just don't like someone else being in charge. If you don't want to die, I'd shut your trap, old man. I'd be happy to take this trip with my daughter and grandson without you."

Jonah turned his attention onto Linda as they devolved into bickering. Madeline took back Simon and gave Keir a pitiful glance before moving away to talk to Todd and Sarah.

A man Keir knew as Gregory stepped to his side and handed him a small package. "These are for you."

Canting his head, Keir studied the gift.

"Our thanks for all your help," Gregory continued.

Had he helped, though? He didn't think he had done more than anyone else. And he had done it for Echo, not for them.

"I've discussed this with Todd, I'm not accepting payment," Keir said.

"It's not payment. Don't just stare at it, open it," Gregory huffed.

After a moment's hesitation, he opened the package. It was a box neatly packed with an array of things. A wood carving of one of Volun's birds, a dozen rolled cigs that scented of something unfamiliar, and an old key. Keir lifted the key. "What is this for?"

"It's a symbol to welcome you back when you return. A key to the compound, for however long it's our home. It doesn't actually work. Consider it yours. Oh, and this as well—" Gregory pivoted and pulled something bulky from under Jonah's gurney.

Keir's portrait.

"No," Keir bit out. "I do not want that. Burn it."

Several of them laughed, and Keir realized everyone had been watching the exchange.

Gregory tucked the portrait under his arm with a shrug. "It was Jonah's idea."

Of course it was.

Keir pocketed the key, tucked his box under his arm, and turned for his ship.

The next little while went by in a haze. They got Jonah situated in a medical pod—where Sarah and Todd dosed him with muscle relaxants that put him right to sleep—and Madeline, Linda, and the baby were set up in the captain's room, where Keir had what little stuff of his within, removed to the bridge. Sarah checked everyone's vitals as Keir waited for them to be cleared for take-off, all the while, turning and twisting the key in his hand.

It looked like the one Echo used to unlock the fake cybernetics laboratory.

He hadn't seen her since he'd returned with his main ship, having left her with Auryn under the outpost. That had been yesterday evening. And if it weren't his promise to bring Madeline and Simon to port for medical treatment, he'd be with Echo now.

Wherever she was, he hoped she had long since left the cybernetics laboratory with Auryn and was now dealing with him elsewhere. Whether or not Echo's body was powerful enough to counteract the fumes she had breathed in, he wasn't sure.

Keir squeezed the key.

Every fiber of his being screamed at him to go to her, to force her away and remove Auryn, the lab, everything from the equation, but she made him promise, again, to do what she said.

This is what she wanted—for him to leave, to finish what he started, and to give her the chance to do the same. She needed time.

She was forcing him to do the one thing he didn't want to—for him to give up control...

And to give it to her.

Keir powered down his systems, blanking his thoughts, and just felt. His hands clenched.

Fortunately, she had given him the time to repair the reactor before he left, at least to the point it was no longer leaking, using some of the pyrzian metal from his wings, and his own nanocells to splice it into the non-organic metal.

Not once in all his life had he wanted to scream, roar, bluster and break something apart more than right now. Not even when he'd been trapped, caged in the dark, had he wanted it more. And he was about to travel billions of miles away from her, where if she were in trouble, he'd be unable to help.

She was his mate. The only one his hawk wanted, the only one *he* wanted. She was also more like him then he'd ever cared to admit, only better. She wasn't a fraud.

Echo had been right—he was an outsider. It wasn't his place to get involved in her world, even if her world directly affected his mission. He had no right to intervene. Volun was her home, its history was her history, and its residents were her family. Him being here was just an interference.

Except, he needed her close so he could claim her, and so she could rely on him. He couldn't do that billions of miles away...

But that was the agreement.

Complete the mission.

"We're ready," Sarah called out from behind him.

He turned to find the older woman, black hair short and curled to her head, on the threshold to his bridge. His ship was larger than most in the EPED's fleet, but still not big enough where he wouldn't be running into humans everyday for the next while.

"Strap in," he said, moving to his seat. "Anywhere is fine."

"I think I'll go and sit with Linda and Madeline and keep an eye on the baby."

"Very well."

She left, and Keir seeded into his ship, checking over the security feeds to make sure everyone abroad was following proper protocol. Giving them an update over the intercom, he locked up his ship and powered on the thrusters.

With a final glance at the compound before him, Keir pocketed the key and soared his ship into the stars before he made another choice he'd live to regret.

TWENTY-NINE

She cleaned her father's frame, helped him repatch the metal hole in his chest, and got him into fresh clothes. Auryn had calmed immensely once it was just the two of them again, and she wondered if it had something to do with the nuclear power dispersing from his body, or if it was just being with her that did it.

Before long, it was quiet, almost peaceful, and she relaxed.

Keir was gone. He'd left—he had listened to her. And now, no matter what happened, she knew he would be too far away to do anything about it.

When the rest of the lights dimmed around them, she took Auryn above and into the outpost, where they ate and Echo kept their conversation light. All the while, she had to remind him again and again that six years had passed, that her mom had left for Earth. Eventually, Echo gave up.

Auryn needed more than she could give him and

guarding him wasn't going to be enough any longer. He wanted her mom, and only her mom.

It made her realize how very little she knew about their relationship at all. How little she had paid attention. Had her mom been pretending all these years to love him?

And no matter how many solutions Echo tried to come up with in her head to fix the situation, none of them played out the way she wanted them too. None of them ended happily. Where Auryn was free, where the Cyborgs were saved, where she was also free to make her own choices without guilt, knowing everyone was safe and would remain that way.

She'd been here before. She'd confided in Jonah the last time. Only, she was alone now, and she was running out of time. The EPED was on their way and whether she liked it or not, things were about to change, and change drastically.

Begging Jonah to cancel the exodus was out of the question. She would never do that to the colony and force them to suffer for her parents' or her mistakes. They needed to leave.

It wouldn't have solved her problem anyway, it would've only prolonged it.

Echo peered down into her mug and the little bit of coffee left at the bottom.

"We should go to the compound," Auryn said.

"We can't."

"Why not?"

"Because they think you're gone, dad. They think you

left years ago with Ares. If you turned up now, looking like you do..."

She didn't even want to know what Keir was going to say to explain his lack of skin; what would she say in regards to Auryn? His appearance and return? The questions she'd be asked were enough to start a headache brewing behind her eyes now.

"They think I've left?" Auryn asked.

She licked her lips. "Yes. We've gone over this. You may have to manually search your memories." She didn't know how far her father had deteriorated, nor how he fully operated, she only had what he'd told her over the years. It was worse than she'd thought and she wished her mom was still around, if only she could run a full diagnostics on him—and potentially repair some of the damage.

But the more she thought about it, her mom was better off not knowing. When Hanna left, she and Echo had said their goodbyes like it may be the last time they'd ever see each other in person. Her mom wasn't coming back. She'd made it clear that she was done, and if Echo chose to stay, it was on her to survive going forward. Echo would not be getting help.

Auryn frowned. "Why would they think that?"

"Because that's what we told them when you did."

"I didn't leave."

Echo swung back the rest of her coffee and put down her cup, shoving it away. "We can't go to the compound today anyway because we have work to do."

Auryn hesitated then paused. "The energy from the reactor needs tending. The bodies will die without it."

She nodded and inhaled. "Yes, we need to take care of that. But I'd like to talk to you about something first."

"Hmm?"

Though Auryn looked little more than a machine himself right now, the being sitting across from her was her dad in every way that mattered. It helped, she supposed, for the questions she had to ask—questions she *needed* to ask. She studied him for a time as he, in turn, studied her. Gone was his tousled brown hair, his easy eyes, and quick smile. Even without features, his eyes were cracked, his countenance broken.

She'd wanted to wake him so many times over the last half-decade but had never had the courage to. There had always been an excuse, another task to finish, that kept her away.

The reactor had done a number on him.

Echo swallowed and came right out with it. "Was Malin my real father?"

"Malin was a traitor."

"Mom never thought so... And Jonah—"

He bared his mouth at her. "Your mother's relationship with Malin was a mistake. He was a traitor."

She licked her lips. "So she did have a relationship with him."

"You are my daughter, Echo. Not Jonah's, not Malin's, *mine*. I delivered you, held you in my arms, cared and protected you as I have cared for and protected all of

Hanna's creations. And I will do so until I am gone. That traitor is not your father. Where is Keir?"

Echo didn't react. She was afraid if she did, he'd see her sadness. "I told him to leave."

She'd told Auryn this already, several times.

"He can replace me below while I'm out. Bring him back here," Auryn demanded.

Echo swallowed down what Auryn was telling her. Had she done Ares a favor by killing him? Had he let her, knowing what was in store? Or had he been too weak to even protect himself?

She'd never know.

"Keir's gone, dad, he left Volun entirely," she whispered. "He's not coming back, at least not any time soon... He's safe."

"You let him leave? The planet?" Auryn rose from his seat. "Knowing what he knows?"

She stood up with him. "Yes. I wasn't going to have him end up like Ares," she hissed. "Or Malin."

Her father's eyes flashed, and she flinched away before she was blinded.

"He will bring the war straight back to our doorstep, the military," he growled. "What have you done?"

"What I should have done years ago. What I didn't have the guts to do before!"

"You're going to kill us all."

"I'm trying to put an end to this! It needs to end. What are you so afraid of? The war was over half a century ago!"

"Your mom and I are trying to put an end to this the right way," he roared.

"And she left because she couldn't handle it anymore! She's only one person, taking on a lifetime of work, meant for a team of dozens. She's old, Dad, old! Humans die too. They age, unlike you. We grow old and tired and we slow down. We don't have *forever* to depend upon! Don't you realize that?"

"She would never leave her children!"

"Yes she would," Echo screamed. "And she has. Because that's how it works. That's how it has always worked. Since the dawn of time!"

He slammed his hands on the table, breaking it into two. Echo took a step back as wood shards shattered at her feet.

"Bring her to me," he demanded.

Taking a deep breath, Echo looked up from the floor, coming to a decision. "She's down below, working. I don't want to disturb her." She lied easily. Almost too easily.

She hated herself for it.

Auryn relaxed. "Good."

Echo eyed him, wiping her clammy hands on her pants, hating herself more and more with every second. Auryn's short term memory was fried, though he still seemed to retain some things. If only he could retain the important parts. "The colony is leaving."

"So Jonah told me," he said, turning from the ruined table to look out the window. "Good riddance."

She licked her lips, and tried another tactic. "I'll be alone here if I stay..."

"That will be for the best. It will be easier to keep you safe."

Her chest constricted.

"Keir mentioned a place called Ghost City, where others... like me... live peacefully. They could help us, maybe? They could help you."

He looked back at her. "Are you willing to risk it?"

Was she? Her lips flattened.

He walked over to her. "Hanna will finish the Cyborgs soon and it won't matter. They'll be able to protect themselves and hide their nature from others, and when that happens, we can go there together, what do you say?"

Echo blinked back the tears that kept threatening to form in her eyes. It wasn't what she'd meant. She couldn't care less about her unique heritage, she could protect herself. She'd been hoping he would consider another solution. Any solution, so she wouldn't have to do what was evidently coming next.

"I would like that," she whispered.

His face softened. "Don't cry, little one. It's settled then. Let's go tell Hanna. I think she'll like the idea of being around those she might have helped rearing."

Echo nodded sadly.

Together they walked back through the outpost and down into the back entrance to a laboratory that had been shut away from the universe for generations—back down to a place she wished she had no connection to. Auryn brightened the dark path with his eyes as the rumbling of old piping and infrastructure hummed around them, groaning at the brink of their existence.

A thousand times she'd made this trek. With her mom, with Auryn, even with Jonah on occasion.

She envied all the Cyborgs who'd come before, Keir included, who'd had their memories wiped of the place. They didn't have to live with its burden. While she was haunted by it every single day.

She'd made her choice, and she hoped she hadn't made the wrong one.

It was up to Keir now and what he decided to do. If he wanted her, really wanted her, he would understand that duty and family came first, that their safety and security were paramount. And with all that had happened... Echo was done seeing those she loved struggle, even him.

If he did nothing, and never returned, she would pick up the pieces of her heart—like she always had—and move forward. There was an exodus in the works now, and the colony would need her help to prepare for it. Everything else—she glanced at her dad—she'd figure out. Keir didn't have to be involved. She didn't want him trapped like she was.

It was never her intention.

Echo wiped furiously at her eyes.

"Wait," she called out as they passed the nuclear reactor's enclave. "We should fix the reactor first before heading to the labs..."

"Agreed. It won't be safe until it's stable."

Auryn diverted from the path.

Ozone filled her nose, making it itch, as she followed him through the old security rigs. The doors had all been shut since she'd last passed through here, and she wondered if it was Keir's doing. She'd barely glanced at the room earlier when she'd rushed down and found her father detached from it. Now, she took in the burn streaks up the stone walls and charred labels on the walls.

Entering the space that held the reactor, her dad scowled. "Stay back. It's not leaking anymore but it was."

He strode to the reactor, where it hummed with energy. His attachments hung off from it, lying across the floor. She watched as he tested a metal piece that had been soldered onto the main machine.

Keir, again, helping her. From the beginning he'd been helping her.

Still scowling, Auryn turned from the newly soldered material and picked up one of the attachments off the floor.

She didn't stop him.

He tugged up his shirtsleeve, fitting it into his arm. His eyes brightened momentarily and his whole body trembled.

"Can you—" she licked her lips, feeling her own nanocells going to work again to keep her safe from the environment "—can *we* fix it?

"Not without stability," he murmured. "It would be unwise."

"You'll have to reattach yourself for that."

Auryn canted his head in her direction, and she tensed all over. It was a very Keir reaction, and it hurt to see. She saw Keir doing the very same thing—for her—just as how Auryn thought he was doing this for her mom.

He loved her. He raised me as his own... For her.

Peering down at her hands, she flipped them over, looking at her skin. She swallowed and slid her eyes back to her dad. He had another attachment tight in his grip.

He abruptly looked back at her and caught her gaze.

The light from the reactor dulled as he stared at her, and his face fell. There was a moment of clarity, true clarity and she took a step towards him. "Dad."

"Don't Echo, it's not safe. I'm barely keeping my system's aligned."

She stopped, and his hand clenched on the attachment, bringing it to his frame to fit it in.

"You don't have to." Tears fell down her cheeks. "You don't."

"Hanna's gone, isn't she?"

Pain gripped her chest. "Yes."

He nodded mutely. "I know all of this, I just don't want to accept it. I won't accept it. I love her."

"She—"

"She always loved Malin more."

Echo threw her arms around him and pressed her face to his arm. "I love you more." She wasn't her mother, nor had she been privy to her mother's choices and the events that shaped her and Auryn's lives, but she knew this. "I chose you. I *choose* you."

Maybe she had always known her mom wasn't in love with her dad. Maybe her mother couldn't. Now that Echo was aware that it was Auryn who had killed Malin and what that Cyborg had meant to her mom, she could understand why.

Her dad covered her hand and squeezed it. "You need to choose yourself. I've taught you better than that."

"You're sounding like Jonah. Stop."

Auryn groaned, and she smiled sadly through her tears.

"He's a good man," he said. "He'll keep you safe."

"I don't need him to keep me safe."

"That's my girl."

He lifted his free hand to caress her cheek with one metal finger and she pulled back.

"You look so much like her, Echo. I wish you were mine."

"I am yours," she breathed.

"No. You're not. You're his now," he nodded towards the soldered piece on the machine. "Help me with this, will you? Unless Volun now has the resources to build another reactor, I need to rechannel and control the energy before it finishes deteriorating, and rejoins the universe." He stated this like the last two days hadn't happened at all.

Echo wiped her eyes, trying to take his lead. "Are you sure?"

"When Keir returns, tell him to visit me."

She flinched. "He might not...return."

"He looked at you like how I looked at Hanna. I'd forgotten until I saw the picture... He'll be back."

Just then, the reactor released a rush of energy, blasting the air and amplifying her nanocells' power. The rush of energy that seized her felt like bliss—and destruction—all at once. She gasped from the sensation.

She and her dad faced the machine, and Auryn picked up another attachment. He stepped out of his pants and fitted it into his thigh.

"You don't have to do this."

He handed her an attachment and turned his back to her as his response.

With trembling hands, she lifted his shirt. Several plates in his spine opened up and created a hole. She pushed the end of the attachment in. Auryn plugged another into his side. His stance diminished.

"Dad..." she sucked in a shaky breath, knowing this was goodbye again. For how long? She refused to think about it. "Can I ask you something? Something that's been... bothering me?"

With the last attachment in his hand, he paused and waited for her to speak.

"I promise you," she vowed. "You won't be like this for much longer. I will fix this."

"What is your question?"

She shuddered and took the attachment from him. "How do you... How do you deal with immortality? I've stopped aging..."

He stared at her for a time before answering. "You learn how to say goodbye," he uttered, almost painfully, shuddering himself. Then he cupped her cheek. "And you learn to appreciate every moment you're given, and you give your life, this extra life that's been bestowed upon you, to those who need more of it."

"How?"

"By making the most of the time you have with those who matter."

She leaned her face into his hand. "I love you."

"I love you too."

Echo plugged the last attachment into his chest. He stepped away, and moved towards the reactor and leaned against it. With his eyes blazing, she looked his chest so she wasn't blinded. And it was easier, she realized.

Easier to let him go.

Because, what she'd failed to remember, was that he was immortal too.

And they would see each other again very soon.

THIRTY

THREE WEEKS HAD PASSED since she put her dad back onto the reactor and had sent Keir away. Those three weeks had felt like twenty years—far longer than the years after Ares's demise.

After she emerged from under her home and left the outpost, she realized time had moved on without her. She'd lost days. She never lost days.

Walking down from her deck, it had been a new beginning. The burnout was coming to an end, and the clouds had returned in their thick masses to cover the sky. Gone was Utha's giant mass, the crazy weather, and everyone she cared most about in the world.

The energy from the reactor was still rushing through her cells then, and she'd sat on her deck with a glass of water and watched the sky and listened to the forest, the breeze in the trees, the hum of the leaves ballooning, and the critters chittering, replaying the past several weeks through her head. She'd sat there for hours, trying to purge her body, and just letting herself rest.

She had thought about her life, her mom, Dad, Malin, and even Ares. She'd thought about bad coding, cybernetics, and the curse of power and its eventual fallout. She had thought about the war.

She'd taken a leap of faith, and now it was up to her to face the consequences, whether it turned out for the better or worse.

If Echo could go back in time, she would. She would've confronted her parents long ago, and perhaps, been able to save Ares's life, even her dad's. Echo wondered if she still could—if somewhere in the universe that technology had been developed.

The EPED was run by a Cyborg, one Keir was loyal to, and then there was Ghost City. And as far as she knew, neither was run by the military. If Keir could control himself, perhaps others of his kind would be able to also.

After she had finished her water, she retrieved her bike, fixed it, and returned to the compound to get back to work.

Gregory had met her at the front of his garage, where he and several others had begun to pack up the cots and fans, and return some of the more robust folks back to their homes. The oldest and more fragile had since been moved to the medical hall where Todd continued to watch over them.

Keir had kept his word and had taken Madeline, Linda,

and the baby off world for better medical treatment—Jonah and Sarah included.

Echo had spent those first days fielding questions and helping Todd pack up the elderly's belongings and bringing them down, keeping them and their items centralized. Without Madeline to do the work, Echo had slipped right into her position. The work helped keep her focused, giving her the distraction she sorely needed.

Jonah's tasks were split between her, Gregory, Todd, as well as several others.

Despite this, it was hard.

She knew everyone in the compound, some much better than others, but she knew everyone all the same. How could she not? She'd lived with them her entire life. Most of them had been here since birth themselves, and they had naturally formed a tribe—had become family. This place and each other were all they knew.

Now, everything was about to change. For her, for them, for everyone.

Watching them having grown old around her, all while she had remained the same, used to hurt, used to frighten her. And even though it was still hard, it was satisfying giving her life away to those who needed more of it. The hurt lessened, and she stopped taking every moment for granted.

Echo always thought, since she was physically able, she should be the one out in the world, providing from afar, never realizing that she was missing so much of her life doing just that, and losing precious time being with those she cared about. She'd always thought Madeline had made the easier choice, when in reality, she'd made the harder one.

Echo wiped the sweat off her brow and looked up at the sky.

After a week had passed, a new normal had set in. She stayed at Jonah's apartment each night, went through his personal systems, and worked on the exodus filing in the evening, compiling it so when the next commercial ship arrived, she would be ready, just in case something hadn't been finished, praying all the while Jonah had survived.

She hadn't seen him again after she'd left him in her living room and called Gregory for help. Echo had found out Sarah had dosed Jonah with radiation microbes, but with his years of smoking, he needed more than that to bring him back to health.

She only wished she could have gone with them...

Imagining never seeing Jonah again alive, and never being able to say goodbye, hurt too much to dwell upon. He'd been a dad to her too. She wasn't ready to see him go.

She wasn't ready. For how much change was happening around her, and not all of it was good.

Echo buried her face into her hands and wept. She had curled up in Jonah's bed and clutched his pillow, had breathed in the faded scent of his cigs, and prayed he would return alive with Keir.

Another week passed, and she stopped looking at the sky so much.

She'd begun going out and hunting again, and as one day morphed into the next, things became easier. The weather had returned to normal. People laughed around her, now excited for what was to come, and she couldn't help but be swept up in it. A new adventure was about to start, and for many of them, they were going to tackle it together.

Gregory prepared big meals each day with the meat she brought in, and everyone gathered in the evenings in the garage to plan and share stories.

Some had decided to seek out family that had left years prior, some argued where they should go, whether Gliese or Earth, but it was all with an air of interest that she wanted to be a part of, even if her own fate was up in the air.

It helped her forget, if only for a little while, and Echo sought out these hopeful moments wherever she could. She never missed any evening meal.

And when those moments came to an end, she thought about Keir, replaying the few memories she had of him.

Her worries fled, she'd gained perspective, and she'd realized—at some point—she no longer waited for his return, but *anticipated* it.

She talked to the sky when she was alone, pretending he was there, just out of sight, listening to her.

They had a conversation to finish.

So when she spotted a massive ship in the sky, she grinned. There were no deliveries planned this week or next, and there was only one outsider she was expecting...

Echo watched the sleek, silver battalion pierce through

the clouds and streak in the direction of the compound. Rising from where she hid in the bushes, she went to her bike, and threw on her helmet just as her wristcon buzzed with Gregory's name.

She was ready.

THIRTY-ONE

He ignored the unread comms flashing across his ship's panel.

Seeing Volun in the distance—a tiny orb in front of giant Utha—his flesh prickled. His thoughts had been scattered since he'd left. He had kept his promise to Echo, and got Madeline and Simon safely away. Now that he was done with her mission for him, his systems surged with electricity, his synthetic blood pumped, eager for his reward.

Every second away had been a trial.

He missed the way her hair kept slipping from her ponytail, the way her breath shortened and her lips parted whenever he closed in on her. He missed her smell, her innocent reactions when he pressed near, and the sound of her pulse ratcheting when she argued with him.

He even missed her stubbornness. She was loyal to a fault, even to those who didn't deserve her loyalty, just because they needed her. She was everything he had been made to be, but had never been able to step into. He wanted to be by Echo's side, and only her side.

She had gotten so far under his skin, that even when he'd repaired himself, she had remained. He felt her inside of him, but couldn't sense her nanocells as being amongst his.

Keir watched as the moon got closer. His AI slowed his ship to adjust for a landing as they neared. They were still hours away and yet, he could see the cloud mass covering the moon, and the landmasses that peeked through them. He focused his gaze solely on them, and ignored the other details around him.

If only he saw better, maybe then, he could spot Echo from space. Keir rubbed his face.

He'd gone crazy—illogical. He dropped his hands and glowered.

Had she worked things out with Auryn? Had she been able to get through to him?

He didn't know if she was okay, if she was being safe, and it didn't sit well with him. Even if she could be considered superhuman, to him, she was still just a human. She was his mate. Until she was back in his arms, and under the shelter of his wings, he wasn't going to be completely logical.

Like Auryn...

Keir pushed the thought from his mind.

Keir had hastily patched up the reactor when she'd sent

him away, but he didn't know if the patch would keep. These thoughts raked his mind, and he was ready to put them to bed.

Their time together had been too short, too volatile. If she tried to send him away again...

Keir gritted his teeth.

At some point in the last six weeks, he'd stopped caring about money and his sanctuary on Titan. The place he'd originally chosen to nest. And no matter how hard he tried, he couldn't make himself care again.

If it hadn't been for Madeline, who seemed to understand him and his predicament more than he wanted to admit—how could any normal human understand him?—he might have lost the rest of his mind and strangled Jonah.

She told him about Simon—her baby's father—at length, and Echo as well, sharing with Keir their childhood and how it was like being the only two little girls on Volun. How Echo wanted to be one of the 'men' while Madeline had preferred dolls. How she and Echo never had anything in common but were often together anyway. Until, one day, Echo began to avoid her.

Madeline even told him she would be returning to Volun to stay with Echo, regardless of an exodus or not, to wait for Simon's possible return.

To hell with that. Keir may have made mistakes when it came to Echo, but he wasn't going to make those same mistakes with Madeline and her baby.

He'd contacted Cypher and had him search for the man

based on the information Madeline gave him. Simon was easy to track down as he was still working as a crew hand for the same medical supplying company, EonMed, Madeline had met him from. Keir bought out Simon's contract and sent the man funds to travel to them, as well as an address to the suite Madeline and Linda would be staying in during their time at port.

After Keir imparted this information onto them, neither Madeline nor Linda were happy about it. But he'd made them understand and even assured them he would return at a later date.

Jonah, on the other hand... The man demanded to return home.

Jonah's throat had been burned from the fumes, but he hadn't been subject to them long enough for lasting damage. With some boosters and skin grafting, as well as a whole body flush and another dose of microbes, he was back on his feet, carrying around his drugs, and making life aboard the ship exhausting.

The fumes from Jonah's cigs now permeated everything, despite air purifiers constantly running. Keir had taken up smoking with the man, just to keep him from talking.

He was as eager to get back to Volun and Echo as Keir was. Jonah was able to discern how much Keir cared for her, despite Keir refusing to discuss the subject. It had only been a matter of time before Keir snapped and undocked his ship and started the journey home.

After several grueling days of waiting for his ship to be

refueled, and waiting for Cypher's response, Keir had done just that.

Leaving the last, and biggest problem left to be addressed...

The unread comm flashed behind Keir's eyes. He stared through it as he looked at the moon. He hadn't figured out how to respond yet. Nightheart was keeping track of him, and probably had been, for quite some time. The comm had come through the moment Keir disembarked from Volun.

What Nightheart wanted from the cybernetic's laboratory, Keir could only guess. And now that he knew what the laboratory held, he wasn't certain how to share the news to Nightheart, if he was going to tell him at all.

Echo wasn't going to let the half-made Cyborgs die, and neither was Auryn.

Neither was he. He didn't agree with more Cyborgs being created, but if there were still some, waiting for a life of their own, who was he to deny that?

The Trentian Cyborgs needed to be finished, but by whom?

And then there was Auryn, Ares, and Malin...

Threading his fingers together, he brought his hands to his lips and rested his elbows on his knees. Glowering at the comm, he leaned forward. He'd run out of time. Every minute Volun got a little closer.

Nightheart would catch a lie, Keir was certain of it.

And if Nightheart didn't, and found out later that Keir had lied, it would be...problematic. No one went against Nightheart, not anymore. The Cyborg held too much power, had too much influence. Nightheart's motivations had always been an enigma, except the most basic one among the shifters—the need for control. The only faction willing to stand up to *The Swarm* was those in Ghost City.

Keir had no allegiance to those in Ghost City. Bringing a dozen alien Cyborgs aboard the city ship would either get them killed or would at least create an enormous amount of friction for his brethren that ran the city.

He trusted Echo to be safe there, but not beings with alien blood running through their veins...enemy blood, Xanteaus knight's blood...

Volun's stormy mass grew as his ship neared. He sat back and buckled his straps and had his AI alert Sarah and Jonah to stop whatever they were doing and to buckle in for touchdown.

The EPED was on their way to Volun regardless of what he told Nightheart. Whether it would be truth or lies.

I promised her that everyone would be safe.

The bridge door opened behind him.

"About fucking time," Jonah grumbled. Keir closed his eyes as the man sat in one of the empty cockpit seats and strapped in.

Sarah walked in afterward and took the seat farthest from Jonah.

"You didn't have to join me for the descent," Keir scowled under his breath. "Every room has seats."

"And miss the landing where there's no view? I don't think so." Jonah settled in, folding his hands into his lap. "About damn time."

Keir cocked his head in Sarah's direction. "Are you good?"

"Just about."

He nodded and waited for the click of her buckles.

Settling back in his seat, Keir clenched and unclenched his hands.

THIRTY-TWO

SHE DROVE her bike right through the open gates and straight towards the airfield.

No matter how hard or how fast she drove, she wasn't able to beat Keir's ship to the compound. She'd tried at first, her heart pumping wildly, needing to see him, enjoying the adrenaline rush from the race, but only managed to over-excite herself instead.

Would be happy to see her? Or... had he changed his mind?

She slowed down as she had neared the compound. Her excitement had given way to doubt. So many things could change in a matter of weeks. She and Keir had spent more time away from each other than they had with one another.

Just because they had a fling while he'd been here didn't mean that fling would turn into something more. It felt like it was more than a fling at the time... But had she just been deluded from so much stress?

She wanted more. It had taken her a long time to admit it, but she had *always* wanted more.

But would he want that too, and with her? Would he share her burden?

She thought about what her life would be like if she left with him and joined him on Titan. She knew nothing about the war-ravaged world, only that Keir lived on it. She thought about taking on the wilds of a new land, a new life, and leaving everyone and everything she knew behind and to live an adventure.

Echo drove around the last of the outer buildings, kicking up plumes of dust all around her, and caught sight of Keir's ship at the center of the field. Dozens of people were gathered outside of it, and she parked her bike at the side of the last building.

Scanning the crowd, she yanked off her helmet and set it aside.

She spotted Keir immediately, standing over the others, his head cocked to the side. His back was turned to her, and he was talking to someone she couldn't see. He was dressed in a dark gray and black uniform, looking completely out of place amongst those around him. A commander and Cyborg to his bones, even if his title was fake.

She would follow him into battle.

His face turned to the side and his sharp, pale, hawkish features filled her vision. Even from a distance, it was all she could see.

He'd made a complete recovery. Echo swallowed thickly, straightening her shoulders. Her heart was pounding erratically. She was afraid he'd hear it from so far away.

If he'd moved on, left for Titan, she would know soon enough. Echo got off her bike and shifted on her feet.

Sarah and Todd were standing at the edge of the group, talking to a small crowd gathered around them. They seemed in good spirits. Echo spotted Gregory next. He was bellowing in laughter at something she couldn't hear. It brought a smile to her lips seeing him so happy.

And then she saw Jonah.

Echo left her hiding spot and went straight for him, her lashes already brimming with tears. Jonah spotted her just as several others did. He barely had time to open his arms before she plunged right into them.

"Missed you my girl," he grumbled, swallowing her up in his arms.

"I missed you too." Echo breathed him in, comforted by the smell of cigs on his flannel shirt. "I'm glad you're okay. I don't think I've cried so much over anyone in my life."

Fuck, she loved Jonah. He was her rock. He didn't have to love her, he never had to love her, but he always had anyways. He was just a man. They weren't related. And yet, in their many years, he was the only person who had remained by her side. He'd been around since the beginning, and he was here now.

"Hey, Echo's here," someone called.

She pressed her face harder into Jonah's chest, feeling like a little girl all over again. She missed him, a lot more than she ever thought she would. All while everything was settling around her, she'd feared for his life, and that she would never get a chance to say goodbye.

Jonah grumped. "Of course I'm okay. I've never been better. What's wrong with you?"

She squeezed him tighter, rubbing her face against his shirt and wiping her tears. "I was worried about you."

He patted her shoulder. "Yes, yes, I was worried about you too. I'm glad to see everyone survived without me. Fucking miracle that is."

Echo pulled away. She smiled. "It wasn't easy."

Gregory grunted in agreement, coming up to them. "We missed having you around, old man. This place isn't the same without you."

"Oh, stop. Both of you." Jonah's cheeks flushed red. "Don't you all get weak on me now. We have a lot of work left to do."

Echo wiped the last of her tears off. "You keep a shitty filing system. It took me days to go through all your correspondence and get it organized."

"You did what?"

A hush fell over the crowd and Gregory shifted to let someone by. Echo looked from Jonah just as a shadow fell over her. Keir stopped beside her, pinning her with his eyes.

"Now before—" Jonah started.

Gregory slapped his hand down on Jonah's shoulder. "Not right now, we have things to discuss. Let them be."

"We should go too," Todd announced. "Sarah's tired. I'm going to take her home."

One by one, the crowd departed around Keir and Echo,

and she couldn't do anything to stop it from happening. She couldn't look away from Keir either.

With pupils so dark, they sucked her in like a black hole, making the rest of the world fade away. Swirling silver, gray, and purple clouds ringed his eyes, a miasma of emotion and brewing intensity. Her reflection stared at her within them, mirroring her emotions back at her.

Her lips parted.

She tried to pretend to have courage, to pretend that he didn't have her heart cradled in his hands... Her heartbeat quickened anyway, giving her away.

Seeing him, seeing Jonah, even Sarah all well and happy, returned home, had broken whatever shell of a wall she had left to shield herself with. All that remained was her raw, vulnerable soul.

Her hands shook as she tried to find the right words to say.

There was so, so much to say.

What words would be perfect to tell him exactly how she felt? Echo didn't know them. And for as much as she prayed for this moment to come, she was terrified of it just as much.

"We live worlds apart," she whispered.

He reached up and tucked her hair behind her ear. "We do."

Echo could scarcely breathe, trapped under his gaze. For how heavy it was, she loved it upon her. She loved being watched by him. His fingers stayed by her ear to thread through her rebellious strands.

A shiver ran through her. "I don't..."

His neck tilted slightly. "You don't?"

"I don't want us to live worlds apart."

Why was the truth so hard? She could go her whole life caring for others, protecting others, but when it came to herself, she had no idea what to do.

Keir cupped her cheeks and brought his face to hers just as another tear freed from her lashes. He wiped it away with his thumb. "I don't want us to live worlds apart either."

"You don't?"

He pressed his brow to hers. "No, Echo, I don't."

She sucked in a breath. "I missed you."

"Not as much as I missed you."

His hands strained on her face as he slanted his head and devoured her lips. Echo clutched him back, grasping his uniform in her hands. She was defenseless against him. He made her weak. His kiss deepened as she pressed forward. His arm dropped and clamped around her back, holding her tight. Her feet were lifted off the ground as he hauled her up.

She hooked her legs around his waist and curled her arms around his neck, roughening the kiss. She squeezed her legs, pushing them into his sides, telling him without words to keep going.

She was desperate, aching—in agony. Echo strained for more.

She kissed his lips, his cheeks, his nose, brow, and eyes as his hands ran over her. She dotted kisses on his chin and ears all while he did the same. She didn't care who might be watching them, it didn't matter. Her lips brushed everywhere she could reach, afraid if she stopped now, he'd slip from her grasp and disappear.

How many kisses would it take to convey to him her love?

Keir's hold tightened and she was jolted up even further. A breeze pulled at her hair and swept over her limbs. Echo glimpsed Keir's wings as they soared into the sky, cutting through the air in a *woosh*.

"Don't stop kissing me," he demanded.

Clutching him harder, she gave him what he wanted. Her hair blew wildly, her clothes ruffled, and she repositioned downward to rub against his erection.

She didn't know where he was taking her but it wasn't to her home, and it wasn't somewhere in the compound. The land changed beneath them. The plains faded away until there were only mountains. Wherever they were going, it was far, far away. And it was the best thing she could have ever hoped for besides being back in his arms.

When they finally landed, it was at the edge of a forest and at the shores of the ocean. The ocean was several days of travel by foot from the compound. Keir released her and she slid down his body to stand on the grass. Echo shivered and dropped to her knees to touch the ground and feel the dirt.

She blushed, knowing he stood behind her, watching her every move. She looked at the ocean. It was calm and quiet. It wasn't the water pounding in her ears, it was her heart that was threatening to deafen her.

Keir captured her hand and she glanced up at him.

"I came here briefly on my first day," he told her.

She smiled. "I haven't been here in years."

"Good."

His response made her toes curl, and her smile turned into a smirk. "It's extremely dangerous. The creatures that live within it are... frightening."

He took a step toward her and closed the gap. "Even better."

"You'll want to stay near me for protection," she teased as one of his wings came forward to bend jaggedly around her. The sharp ends of his metal feathers glinted like the water; they were a fan of blades.

Nothing about Keir was soft, and that was okay because she wasn't soft either. Only he made her that way.

And babies, she realized. She liked babies. She liked Madeline's baby. She hadn't seen either amongst the group...

He arched a brow. "I've been warned."

"You have."

"I've completed my mission."

Echo stood and pressed her finger to Keir's lips, her chest constricting. "Please, not yet."

He curled his hand around hers. "I want my reward."

"Oh."

Oh.

She tilted her head and smiled again. "And what is it you want?"

Keir's gaze darkened, and his hand moved to cup the

back of her neck. He cocked his head to either side as he lowered toward her. Echo licked her lips.

He held her eyes as he pressed his mouth to hers again and ravaged them.

The next thing she knew, they were tearing at each other's clothes. Keir's clothes slid off easily, unthreading at will, but hers were a struggle. Echo yanked off her boots as he pulled down her pants and underwear until she was only in her undershirt.

Slipping his hands up her body, her curves, he lifted her shirt and leaned down to kiss her nipples, her navel, and lower still, stopping at the crux of her thighs. He knelt in front of her and looked up as she threaded her fingers through his dark, wind-tossed hair.

She stared down at him, taking him in. She took her time, trailing his predatory features to the muscles that made his body large, even frightening. She'd never had the chance to really study him the way she had wanted. Echo wasn't going to let this opportunity pass her by.

For how beautifully crafted and powerful as Keir was, his demeanor said otherwise. The way his fingers pressed into her skin, was the same way hers pressed into his—possessive, hungry, needy.

He was just as vulnerable as she was. Maybe even more so.

Behind him was the ocean.

His gaze was desperate now, taking her breath away. But he didn't move further, waiting for her cue.

Echo nodded.

Keir lifted her leg, and thrust his tongue inside her.

She cried out as he kissed her there like he'd devoured her lips, like he'd die if he didn't. It was too much, too fast and she came quickly, slumping in his arms. Quivering, he held her to his chest as she recovered.

He lowered her to the grass and spread her legs wide. He sank the blade-like tips of his wings into the ground on either side of her. Rising up and over her, Echo arched her back, and fanned her fingers over his chest.

With his face above hers, holding her gaze, he pushed his cock inside her, forcing her to take the burden of his body. Her knees bent, and she lifted them to press into his sides as he worked his way inside, stretching her with small shunts. His girth was wider than her, and she dug her nails into him, gritting her teeth.

And when he was all the way in, he roughly pulled right out and slammed back in.

Echo gasped and grazed her nails over his flesh. His eyes heated, darkened, keeping her soul transfixed as he thrust again and again. His fingers spread out and over her face, her hair, as if he was memorizing them.

"I love you." They were the only words he spoke.

She came and screamed when he rose back up above her, thrusting his hips in quick bursts.

"I love you." He growled it again.

She gasped and dug her heels into his backside.

"I love you."

Feeling her orgasm fade and another come on, she closed her eyes.

"You're my reward." He continued to fill her head with his delicious words. "You're mine now."

She cried out as he stretched her even further. His seed, fiery hot, flooded her womb, burning her from the inside out. Heat streaked through her limbs in waves.

This time, she gave into it.

"I love you too," she gasped, accepting his claim.

THIRTY-THREE

SHE AND KEIR rinsed their bodies in the ocean and then returned to the forest to dry off and dress. They had spent the day together, doing nothing more than being near one another, talking about senseless things. He also told her about Madeline, the baby, and Simon, and how, for the time being, they would remain at port, taking some of the pressure off of Echo's shoulders.

He'd also been insatiable.

Her body was warm from his fervency, and she had basked after every time he had seeded her. There was no pain, and any remaining aches she had, were quickly healed.

She knew little about the dynamics between Cyborgs outside her dad and Ares, and what her mom knew technically. Echo knew even less about herself and her position in the universe in regards to them. Keir told her there weren't many Cyborg women among the species as a whole, and those that were, had never paired with another of their kind. Their reason? He didn't know. There were no romantic Cyborg unions as far as he was aware.

Echo looked at her hand, flipping it over.

She hoped that was all going to change in the years to come.

She dropped her hand and gathered the rest of her clothes. To her right and several yards away, Keir was watching her. Echo took her time anyway and dressed.

It was evening now, and moving towards twilight. It was almost time for them to head back.

Keir joined her on the ground when she sat to tug on her boots.

"Ask it," he said, breaking the bubble they had erected around themselves today.

Her eyes slanted his way. "Have you told anyone?"

"Not yet."

Surprised, she faced him fully. "What about your mission?"

"I don't care about the mission anymore. I haven't in a while."

"What will happen if you don't turn it in... If you lie? If you leave it?"

Keir's face went grim. "I can't say for certain. I don't know Nightheart's motivations, I can only guess them. He's been searching for the lab that created him for as long as I have known him. Even if I lie and leave, he won't stop."

"And Titan?"

"Will always be there waiting, when it's time."

Echo's brow furrowed. "What do you mean?"

"I'm staying with you, wherever you are, that's what I mean."

"Oh..."

"The last few hours should've convinced you of that."

She blushed. "Yeah."

He cocked a brow at her. "Yeah?"

She blushed harder. "I had to ask."

"We'll go there eventually, maybe. Titan is like Earth, but better, bigger, greener, and has far less humans."

"I like humans. I'm human."

Keir sighed dramatically and some of his dark hair fell into his face. "Don't remind me."

She pushed at his arm. "And my dad? The Cyborgs? We need to do something about them." Her amusement faded. "I'm worried. I don't know who to trust."

"Me."

Her heart jumped. She was going to have to get used to it.

Then she hoped she would never get used to it.

"I figured out how your boss might have figured out that the lab he was searching for was here," she said quickly, not wanting to feel so vulnerable anymore from his words. There was only so much she could take at a time.

"Oh?"

"When I was going through Jonah's correspondence, I read through everything between him and the EPED. He mentioned the lab, not outright, only that it had an unstable, unconnected reactor. It was part of a list of safety concerns he was forced to put together for the application." She watched Keir's face as she said it. "It's just a guess though. Although it does explain the coincidence of you showing up when you did."

"It does," he agreed. "It could be. Nightheart has gone on less. He made no mention to me about a reactor, about any of that."

"Is that... odd?"

"It's not completely unlike him. He holds his cards close."

It was freeing, finally being able to talk to Keir like this.

She didn't have to hide from him. Emboldened, she climbed into his lap and straddled him. His neck bent as he eyed her curiously, putting his hands on her hips. He hardened and pressed against her as she got comfortable.

He'd been inside her multiple times, was still inside her now in some capacity, and the knots in her stomach whenever it came to touching or being near him, had yet to go away.

"If the EPED is already on its way, if they know about the lab in some capacity, will they trust you if you tell them otherwise? Knowing Nightheart will hear this?"

"I'm a famed commander, with a face more people and aliens know than I'd ever care for. They would have no choice but to believe me."

She studied him, plucking strands of his hair off of his face. "Would you be okay with that?"

"Yes."

"I don't want to lie anymore."

He cocked his head.

She continued, "My whole life I've been dealing in lies and it hasn't solved anything. It's only made things worse. Doing something has to be better than doing nothing."

"What are you saying?"

Echo chewed on her lip. "The last time I made a choice for someone else, I... ended a life. I don't want to make the next choice alone. Not for you, not for anyone. I'm afraid." Around them the shadows lengthened. The forest and shore hummed with whispers.

He rolled his shoulders and ran his hands up and down her back. "You're not making any choices right now but the ones you're making with me. What do you want to do?"

"I—" She pressed her lips together briefly before forcing the words out. "I want to be selfish. I want to be with you."

His hands strained on her, and he closed his eyes like her words were bliss. It made her want to borrow against him and never let him go. It made the selfish ball growing inside her get bigger.

"No more lies," he rasped, keeping his eyes closed.

"No more lies," she agreed.

His eyes snapped open. "No more running?"

"No more running. I promise."

She kissed him.

"Then it's settled," he said.

She remained like that as he flew her back to the compound and landed them outside Gregory's open garage, where she had to begrudgingly let him go. It was dark out but the lights from within the garage brightened everything around it. Inside, people were gathered in groups eating and drinking. Todd strummed a guitar as Jonah complained boisterously about how everything was out of order. The smell of good food made her stomach growl.

Feeling more hopeful than she had in years, Echo stepped towards them.

Keir didn't follow.

She turned back and grabbed his hand. "You're not an outsider anymore. You're with me."

He gave her a horrified look. "If I must."

"You must." She smiled reassuringly. "I'll help you. You don't have to pretend anymore either. I've got your back."

Keir pulled her to him and clutched her hard, squeezing the air from her lungs.

When he released her, she led the way.

EPILOGUE

KEIR WATCHED the EPED ships come down from the sky. There were three in all, alike in every way, and larger than his own ship. They were sleek in design, though their tubular bodies tapering to points at their fronts, didn't appeal to him.

They landed in succession in the same airfield he had landed on several months prior. Since then, he had moved his ship outside Echo's outpost.

After he and Echo had returned to the compound, they had gotten to work.

The first thing he did in the weeks following was clear the land outside her home for his ship, all while she'd emptied the outpost of her things and moved them to the compound. When they were done, they'd tore down the outpost itself. The only thing that remained was the back entrance to the lab. They'd worked tirelessly, stripping his ship of parts to re-stabilize the broken reactor below, and released Auryn from his self-imprisonment.

The Cyborg had attacked him again, but he'd been ready for it this time.

Keir—with the help of Echo and his ship's AI—recreated Hanna's voice for Auryn to listen to. Keir's AI did the rest, taking old pictures of Hanna and recreating her appearance. He and Echo managed to bring Auryn aboard with the ruse, and Keir repaired what he could of Auryn's mind and body while Auryn had been transfixed. Keir had given what boosters and spare parts he could, grafted Auryn's synthetic skin back on, and got him physically corrected. Auryn's nanocells did the rest.

Auryn's mind, and the other systems that had been irreparably damaged from being attached to a nuclear source for an extended period of time, would have to wait for more qualified hands than Keir's. Rewiring nanocells and replacing their code wasn't his forte. Auryn needed a functioning cybernetics laboratory and skilled scientists to make a complete recovery.

All of which Keir planned to pay for and find with his own resources. Even if Auryn wasn't Echo's father, Keir would've helped him. His dislike was with his creators, not their creations. Keir would've at least gotten Auryn to Ghost City where there were Cyborgs filling positions humans used to have dominion over.

Despite his broken pieces, at the end of the day, Auryn was still a logical being at his very core. It had helped him knowing that the other Cyborg's still down in the lab would be fine without him. Auryn was weak, unfinished, and he knew it, just as Keir knew he'd been made into a pawn to recruit people for war.

They all had their problems.

Auryn, more than most.

Spending time with the Cyborg made Keir appreciate— if only a little bit—his functioning self and systems. His sense of degradation was nothing compared to what had befallen Auryn. Keir could've just as easily been made into him, as Auryn could've been made into a shifter.

They had spoken at length.

Auryn had made his intentions clear—that if Keir failed Echo, Auryn would be there, and there would be consequences. Keir threw Auryn's words right back at him.

In the end, they had come to an understanding. Both of them wanted to be in Echo's life, and part of her future, and to do that, they had to work together.

Only, Auryn wasn't strange like Keir was. This male didn't have an animalistic side. What with his boyish features and charming demeanor, he could blend right in with humanity—when he was working properly. Auryn looked like Echo's brother, not dad, and it made Keir uncomfortable. Seeing them interact with such familiarity tightened his throat and made his jaw hurt from being clenched so much. He wasn't certain if it was envy he felt, or jealousy.

He rarely left Echo's side because of it, feeling like he needed to stake his claim as her mate, her only mate, constantly—if only to reassure himself—and have Echo reassure him.

He and Auryn still had a lot to work on.

Heavy footsteps crunched the gravel and grass behind him. Jonah stopped at Keir's side and lit a cig, offering Keir first draw. Keir accepted the cig, took a drag, and handed it back. Together they watched the ships finish their descent in silence.

It was the middle of the night, and they were the only two awake.

Jonah hadn't wanted to make a big deal of the EPED's arrival. As the day had drawn nearer, many of the colonists had grown anxious, and those who were still demanding to remain had only gotten harder to deal with. The honeymoon phase had come and gone. Jonah didn't want anyone running for the plains at the last minute.

"I guess this is almost the end," Jonah said. "Been here all my life. It's hard to comprehend that everything is about to change."

Keir cocked his head.

The ships landed. Wind blasted the two of them, knocking Jonah's cig from his hand and making the man curse. Jonah went to stomp the cig out as Keir stepped towards the ships.

He seeded outward, searching for Nightheart.

He wasn't there.

Keir turned away and left. As he walked off the airfield, he heard the first ship's hatch open and saw Gregory striding towards him from the garages. They nodded at each other.

When Keir was out of sight, he extended his wings, flew back to his ship, and checked on Echo in his captain's quarters. She was still asleep, her hair fanned out across the pillows. He gazed at her for a moment before heading for the bridge. Now that he knew Nightheart hadn't journeyed here, he finally answered the Swarm's comm. Several minutes went by before Nightheart's voice entered Keir's head.

"I'm sure you have a reason for not connecting sooner," Nightheart began, his voice dry, stilted. Numb? "I'm aware my ship's have landed."

"They have," Keir said. "I came out to see if you were among them."

"I see. Did you think I would be?"

"No, but I wanted to be certain."

There was a pause before Nightheart responded. "What have you found out?"

"The cybernetics laboratory you've been searching for is here."

"And?"

"It's no longer being operated. The lab is severely damaged and the energy source powering it is unstable from decades of mismanagement. The laboratory hasn't been fully functional since the war, before the government pulled out of Volun."

"I know. Anything else you want to tell me?"

Keir paused. "You know?"

His systems seeded outward, scattering in tendrils across the land. He searched for Nightheart's signal but didn't find it anywhere.

Something whipped past his head, and Keir was on the other side of the bridge, gun in hand, talons out a moment later. His eyes caught hold of the object as it flew around the room before landing on his ship's systems panel.

A tiny metal wasp turned and faced him, its gleaming silver wings twitching.

"I thought I found all of them," Keir hissed, lowering his gun. He seeded outward again and was unable to connect to the wasp. It was like it didn't even exist signal-wise.

"Only the ones I let you find. I've been here the whole time."

Keir's jaw ticked. He stormed to the wasp and grabbed it.

It shot away faster than his hand could move. Keir pivoted to keep the bug in sight.

"Why?" Keir gritted. "Why send me at all if you could've infiltrated yourself?" Anger stirred in his chest as the wasp landed on the wall and crawled across it to his left. The other wasps he had discovered hiding on his ship had all been dormant.

"Do you really think I have the time for that?" Night-heart asked.

"Then why not fucking tell me?"

"You seem to think just because I hired you, and we've worked together these past decades, that I wouldn't keep an eye on you? I keep an eye on everyone. For the very reason you've proven to me these past months, *Commander* Keir," Nightheart stated coldly. "I hired you to do a job, one you have failed to complete."

Keir bristled. "How much do you know?"

"Enough."

There was a distant rush of air that filled Keir's audio systems from outside his ship. The ground trembled beneath his feet, shaking his entire ship. Keir stormed to the window at the front of his bridge and looked out. The trees shook viciously as if being blown over by heavy gusts of wind. There were flashing lights in the sky.

His head snapped to the door and down his ship's hallway and towards his hatch. With his gun at the ready, he left the bridge and walked out just in time to see another ship landing on the gravel road, scattering dirt, rocks, and leaves everywhere. It broke and crushed the trees around it.

"You should have told me." Nightheart's cold voice filled Keir's head. "Cyborg's made with the enemy's DNA?" Nightheart tsked. "I never expected *you* to fall for a human. They've clouded your judgment."

Dread—an emotion Keir rarely felt—seized his systems. His talons strained and outstretched as he released the wings from his back.

Far, far in the distance, sirens sounded in the direction of the compound.

The ship finished its landing, making the forest dark and quiet.

"What do you want?" Keir growled.

"Everything."

Someone grabbed Keir's hand, and he turned to see Echo standing beside him, her expression unreadable as she gazed out at the ship before them. Her hair blew around her face from a breeze coming down from the mountain. Keir withdrew his talons and curled his fingers around hers.

She looked up at him, and he shook his head slowly. She squeezed his hand harder.

"Todd commed me," she said, her chest rising and falling heavily. She stared at the ship ahead of them. "Androids have stormed the compound. Everyone is being gathered and taken to the airfield. They're waking them from their beds, not letting them dress."

The hatch of the ship across from them disengaged and began to lower. Keir shifted to throw his wing around Echo, shielding her on all three sides.

"What's happening?" she asked.

"Nightheart knows everything."

"Everything?"

"Yes."

She closed her eyes and inhaled slowly. When she opened them, she faced him and they were full of doubt and uncertainty. It hurt more seeing her this way than any wound he had ever suffered.

Keir closed the remaining distance between them and cupped her face. "I made a promise to you. Remember?"

She nodded shallowly.

He brought her hand to his lips and kissed her fingers. "It will be alright." He leaned down and pressed his face to Echo's belly—where his child stirred within.

Whatever Nightheart had in store for Volun and its residents, Keir would be there to defend them. They were his to protect.

Volun was his home now, and he would do whatever it took to protect it and keep it safe, no matter who came. Even if it was the *Swarm* himself.

A man he thought he could trust...

Keir pressed Echo closer to him.

Figures appeared at the top of the hatch and Keir pulled away. He and Echo straightened and faced them. A single, white light casted the figures into view from the ship's interior light behind them, darkening their features. He squinted. Several were androids bearing weapons, the rest were humans. Keir seeded to connect with them, finding their processors encrypted with codes he had never seen before. He downloaded them into his database and ran diagnostics.

"Stand behind me," he commanded, shifting his wing forward to shield Echo again as the beings walked down the ramp. They followed a being at the front, a human with several cybernetic modifications inside of them. Keir sensed their electrical signatures.

The voice stopped and called out. "Echo? Is that you?"

Echo startled then went still. "Mom?"

Keir furrowed his brow and shifted his wing.

"Mom, is that you?" Echo said with disbelief.

"Echo don't." Keir snatched her wrist before she stepped forward.

"It's me," the woman responded with relief in her voice.

With the androids flanking her, the woman continued walking towards them only to stop again several yards away. She lifted her head to the light pouring from his ship and her features came into view.

Hanna looked exactly like Echo, only much older. Her hair was cropped short around her ears and she had a cane in her hand, a cane she wasn't using.

Beside him, Echo shook as she and Hanna stared at each other.

Echo tried to release his hand. "What are... What are you doing here?"

Keir gripped her tighter.

"I missed you," Hanna breathed, "So, so much. I've come back for you."

Hanna glanced at Keir, and her face hardened.

Echo moved into his side and under the shelter of his wing. She leaned against him but positioned herself forward, as if she was giving him her protection too.

"I'm here to save you," Hanna answered, studying the two of them sharply, eyeing him with suspicion. "I've finally figured out how."

Keir's other wing snapped outward, cutting Nightheart's wasp in two as it flew out from his ship. The bisected wasp dropped to the ground with a ping; one of its metal wings fell over the side of his ramp to be lost in the shadowy brush below. Nightheart's connection fell from Keir's head as both women flinched.

They watched the metal bug until it stopped.

Hanna outstretched her hand towards Echo. "Come here, Echo."

Everything went quiet. Echo remained rooted at his side.

"Echo? Come here." Hanna's frown deepened, and she took a step back as her eyes widened. "Auryn... is that you? You're... You're off the reactor." Hanna suddenly looked around, taking in Keir's ship where the outpost used to be.

The other Cyborg joined Keir and Echo to stand at their side. "Hanna." His voice was stern adoration. "I knew you wouldn't leave me."

A legion of androids rushed from the ship behind her as Auryn stepped towards Hanna.

Keir yanked Echo hard against him and hauled her into his ship, closing the hatch behind him just as the androids flooded the area. They ran to the bridge to watch the androids head straight for the passage leading down into the laboratories. On Keir's security feed, Hanna remained standing in the darkness, staring where he and Echo had just been, as Auryn made his way towards her. She turned for the passage, but Auryn stepped into her path. They stared at each other as the androids swarmed around them.

Echo shakily exhaled beside. "What are we going to do now?"

He already had an answer for her.

"We call in backup," he said.

She looked at him, her lips parting.

Keir closed his eyes and commed Ghost City.

ABOUT THE AUTHOR

Thank you for reading *Wings and Teeth, Cyborg Shifters book 9*. It is the second to last book in the Cyborg Shifters series. The last book will be Nightheart's. Will he be able to accomplish his endgame when his most trusted assistant walks out on him? Stay tuned.

If you liked the story or have a comment, please leave a rating or review!

Wondering when *Cyborg Shifters book 10* is coming? Join my newsletter!

And if you love cyborgs, aliens, anti-heroes, and adventure, follow me on Facebook or through my blog online for information on new releases and updates.

-Naomi Lucas

Turn the page for a sneak peek at Viper, Naga Brides Book 1... A sexy, dystopian SciFi romance with cunning alpha aliens who hunt down their human brides!

VIPER (NAGA BRIDES)
THE PACT

Vruksha

"Our truce ends after they release the females," I growl, peering at the males around me. The King Cobra's mane flutters, the Boomslang nods. Others react; some don't respond at all. I take their silence as agreement.

We're the strongest of our kind. The oldest. The deadliest. We saw the humans' ship breach our sky and land within our forest.

We're also competitors. The fact that we've all come together for this—*for them*—is a miracle. It shows how much we want *them*, how desperate we are to have *them,* and that we would risk our lives to make a deal with *their* keepers.

Their puny males.

Males who do not deserve the warmth of a female. They don't realize how lucky they are to have females, so we will take their females and covet them, mate them, make them queens to the lands we rule. As is how it should be.

There are many wrongs that need to be righted, and many mistakes in our past that need to be fixed.

My fingers tighten around my spear as I scrutinize the nagas gathered today, sizing them up. Some of us won't survive.

Humans are different from us, at least from what I've seen, and it's more than the way they look.

We thought them long gone. A species that had been eradicated when we were born on this Earth. Neither me nor the other naga males around me have ever seen a living one, not once, until recently.

They flew down from the sky in a large metal machine. Machines like the ones here, but not overgrown with weeds, roots, and vines. Not ruined the way Earth was ruined.

No, this machine—this ship of theirs—came to us clean of the forest and landed outside the old ruins of a civilization long gone, deep in the mountains. Other smaller machines came out with weapons and cleared the ruins. They erected a barrier and cut down the trees.

The humans restored the ruins into what it once was: a military facility.

Meanwhile, I watched the robots from afar, from the shadows of the trees, and soon found other nagas watching them too. We didn't know why they were here, or what they wanted, but we are determined to keep our secrets...secret.

At first, there were only machines to watch. We didn't realize there were humans on the ship. The robots poured from their vessel in droves, destroying the terrain we once knew. The terrain *I* once knew. A growl tears from my throat at the thought. The robots left us alone, though, having one singular purpose, a purpose we nagas did not know until several weeks after their landing.

They were making the facility ready for human inhabitants.

When the humans first stepped out of the ship, I stared in awe, thinking it was only machines that had flown down from the sky, nothing else, nothing so exciting as *women*.

Thinking back on that day quickens my heart.

Her red hair. My fingers twitch. I can imagine the softness of it running between my fingers. I've never seen such a shade of red like my own tail...

Zaku, the King Cobra, went to the humans when we realized they had females among them. He made our presence known. He wanted to meet them, court them, mate with one... We were bigger, stronger, larger than their males, and thought that because of it, they should be ours.

I did too.

Perhaps we could offer our help in return? Who knows?

Zaku came back to us enraged. The humans turned their weapons on him, refusing his request. They told him this land was theirs, as it has always been, and as long as he —we—abided by that, they would not kill us.

Hah. I would like to see them try.

They have no idea what they're up against when it comes to us.

I know now that if I want my red-headed beauty, I'll

have to fight for her, kill for her. And I'm willing to do more than that, but I do not want her hurt. And fighting? I've seen enough death to know accidents happen.

It wasn't that long ago. Days, maybe? Seems like an eternity. The other nagas came together after word spread of what happened to Zaku.

It wasn't hard to win me over. I would do anything for *her*.

When I first saw her, everything changed.

Gone was the bloodlust, the anger. Real lust took its place. Red hot desire, with a wild mane of red hair to match. Transfixed, I stared that first day as she descended from the ramp, realizing something more miraculous than machines had fallen from the heavens. She stared at her surroundings with wonder and curiosity.

She had gazed at the sky and the clouds above. She had touched the grass at her feet. Her tongue poked out to swipe at her lips.

Her eyes had found mine, even as I hid beyond her barrier, in the shadows of the forest. From that moment, she was mine.

A human female, wondrous in her rarity, who with one look ruined me.

My female.

The way her eyes widened. The way her lips parted...

The fear on her face hadn't bothered me at all.

She was mine. I expected her to face her fear and come to me then, but instead, she turned away and rushed into the shadows of the facility, leaving me bereft, lusty, and angry.

But she had looked at me, had met my gaze. She saw me, and that was all that mattered. Now I know I am in her head. She will always remember the first time she saw me. For I am a strong male, a vicious one, and refused to be forgotten.

It would be dangerous to forget me.

My anger had returned after I lost sight of her, and my agitation at these human interlopers built. My need for this female stole my mind. Reclaiming the facility and this land meant nothing if I couldn't have her. I wanted both but only cared about the latter.

I saw her first.

She saw me first.

She was in *my* head. No other naga's head mattered unless they were hanging from a rope off my belt or lobbed off and impaled on my spear, decorating the entrance to my den.

But as whispers of human females spread through the forest—the mountains—the other nagas had similar thoughts. My female wasn't the only one, and nagas from far afield, males I have not seen in years, returned to see them, to steal them, to mate with them, and hoard them away in our respective nests.

The need to mate overcame us all like a storm. To conquer. These females came from the skies to be ours. We became very aware of our diminishing numbers, and with the threat of invaders from the skies on our minds...our biology altered against us, clouding our minds.

I wasn't the only one changed, nor the only one desperate to nest. A piece within us unlocked, and it can't be undone. Some nagas feared the change—this need to conquer—and fled, hoping the change would reverse.

Less to die by my hands. I hiss out a breath of air.

Azsote, a Boomslang, snaps his tail. "And if they don't release them?"

"We invade with our weapons and strike them down. They need to know this land is not theirs, not without a price," Zaku snarls. Some of the other males snarl with him. The King Cobra is out for blood, one way or another. A king, even though Zaku wasn't one, doesn't like being told what to do.

Zaku's only king in name, and he holds no more sway or dominion than the rest of us.

"They will pay for it with females," I say.

Azsote snaps his tail again. "Yesss."

"They want our technology, our land... We will give them a little for a lot more," Zaku agrees.

I eye the facility far, far in the distance, through the trees and across the shattered landscape, hoping to see her. A splash of red among the green. But she's nowhere to be found from our vantage point way up on the cliffs.

I haven't seen her in many days. Venom leaks from my fangs. I need to see her soon or I may do something crazed, like storm the humans' barrier and take on their robots for just a glimpse.

She is the same color as me. I never thought such a female existed besides my sisters. One with Viper in her blood.

No creature in all the verdant lands or the oceans of sandy waste has ever been the same color as me. She is mine because of this. Even if I haven't memorized her face, even if I don't know the sound of her voice, or her name, she is mine.

My hands tremble with the need to comb my fingers through her hair. My nose itches to burrow into her neck and languish in its warmth, in the scent of her skin.

"We give them nothing, and they won't be the wiser," I hiss, "while they give usss everything in return."

The other males beat their chests and hoot in agreement. The coming hunt excites us. I feel it in my veins, the way my blood pumps heavy. My member rises to the occasion. I slam my fist against my chest and hoot with them.

"How many females are there?" Vagan asks when we settle. "Not enough, last I checked." His blue scales and long, slender body are like mine, except he is blue where I am red. Vagan is of the Blue Coral clan, a ruler of the dangerous waterways. He may be brightly colored like me, but to face him near water was certain death.

Of all the nagas gathered, Vagan is the one I watch the most. Him and the Death Adder.

But Zhallaix, the Death Adder, is not here. He would rather kill us than work with us. An enemy to us all. He has no honor, nor allegiance. Ruthless and wild, he is probably fucking a mossy rock and spitting venom somewhere off in the hills. I have not seen Zhallaix since the ship first appeared.

"I have only seen three," Zaku answers. The King Cobra is fearsome, but I do not watch him like Vagan and some of the others. One bite and the Cobra could take out any one of us, but he has honor in his cold veins.

Honor I do not know if I have. But Zaku isn't just honorable, he's pompous and hard-headed. Everything is beneath him, and it shows in his inability to help anyone but himself, even in this. If Zaku could steal a female human for himself, he wouldn't have gathered us. Sometimes I think he's not honorable at all, just overzealous.

I keep an eye on him anyway. If Zaku doesn't win one of the females today, he's going to destroy the world. Or die trying.

As for everyone else? They watch me.

I tighten my grip on my spear, meeting their eyes.

"Three? Three is not enough!" Vagan shouts. "There are at least seven of us here, and more yet in these woods. How will three brides appease us all?"

"They won't," I say. "We will fight for them when they are handed over."

Some growl, some hiss in agreement. We size each other up, considering who we could off now before the humans arrive.

The Boomslang with the shimmery green scales slips to the ledge, his voice lowering. "Why not fight now? Until there are only three of us left?" Azsote suggests, waving his hand.

"Why not let the females choose who they want to mate with?" another offers. I look at the naga and bare my fangs. It's the Copperhead. He is a quiet one. I'm surprised to hear him speak at all.

"No," I snap.

"That won't work," Zaku says at the same time.

"We will not honor their choices," I add. If my female chooses another over me, I would kill him and take her.

I am not honorable, after all.

The Copperhead nods. He knows what I say is true. The females can't have the luxury to choose, not now that their very presence has created a strange fervor.

Our members have filled up with unspent spill, causing pressure, bringing us pain. When I first saw my human, my shaft flooded with seed, seed that has been dormant for years, and I have had to milk my prick nightly to relieve the pressure.

If I'm suffering, the other nagas are too.

"Three females is a problem," says Zaku. "But I have an idea. If we fight for mating rights to them, there is a chance they will run while we battle. It is paramount that the females do not come to any harm. Especially by us or our ways. They may be all there is, and we can't lose them. We must keep them safe."

We mumble in agreement. I love the red of my female's hair, but it is the only red I wish to see upon her. I do not want to witness her blood outside her moon cycle.

Zaku continues, "If they run, the animals could kill them, the pigsss. They could get hurt—"

"So what's your suggestion?" Vagan interrupts.

"I suggest we spread out when the human males hand them over. So we do not fight. I suggest they run, we follow, and we hunt them down. Whoever catches the females first wins nesting rights to them."

Silence hangs over us as we ponder Zaku's words. It is a good suggestion but not the greatest. My redhead is already mine. But the other male nagas will want proof, and a hunt —because I know I will catch her—is a good way to prove it.

"I like this idea," Boomslang speaks up first.

"Of course you do," Vagan snaps. "You are a hunter of the forest."

Azsote shrugs. "I am. That does not change that this is a good suggestion."

"And what about me? What about Syasku? We fare best in the water. A hunt over land cripples us."

Nobody cares about Vagan or Syasku, but I don't say that aloud. "There is water nearby, a lot of water. If the females head for it, then you have an advantage."

"And if they don't?"

I turn back to the facility, not caring enough to answer.

"I will accept a hunt," says Syasku of the Cottonmouth clan. *Good.* If the other water naga accepts a hunt, then Vagan has no grounds to argue it.

Vagan scowls.

"It is settled then," Zaku declares. "We will hunt for nesting rights to the females."

Another wave of shouts soar in the air. I lift my spear

and release a bolt of electricity to the sky. I like this. I will win. I have destiny on my side. Vicious, red destiny.

The other males pound their chests, and some release their well-hung and hard members from their scales. Tails coil and thump the ground. For a frenzied moment, excitement and real camaraderie return to us. It is a rare thing. We are deadly as a group.

We are deadly alone, but together... The world would tremble with fear.

But the excitement does not last. I turn back once again to see if my bride is outside, if she's being gathered with the other females to be handed over.

And for a second, I see her. My heart stops.

She's being led to one of the flying transport machines. Another female is fighting, kicking, and screaming behind her. She's lifted off the ground and hauled to the machine.

My female goes calmly.

She knows her fate. Knows who awaits her

Me.

Venom fills my mouth. My heart revs back up.

The others have gone silent, and I know they are watching as well.

"She is the one I want," Azsote rumbles. My eyes flick to the Boomslang watching my female, and I slam my spear into his side.

I attack him, striking out with my tail, knocking him over. He evades my speartip, rolling away before I can plunge it into his gut.

"She is mine!" I roar, fury surging through me. "Mine!"

How dare he want her. How dare he even look at her! Azsote strikes back, hitting me with his fist, slicing me with his claws across my bicep. The sting of pain erupts, but I barely notice, needing to see his blood splattered across the ground.

Hands grab us, pulling us apart.

"Enough!" Zaku shouts.

Fighting his hold, I spit venom in Azsote's direction. He pushes his capturer away and shrieks a battle cry. Furious, only his blood on the ground and his spine in my hand will appease me now.

"I sssaid enough! They're coming! Do not let them see us fighting." Zaku shoves me away, getting between us. Growling, I rise to fight the King Cobra as well, but he's facing the horizon.

Behind him, the humans' transport vehicle is heading our way. It glides soundlessly through the air.

All thoughts of Azsote and the others fall from my mind. My female is heading for me.

In mere moments, I will see her up close for the first time. My body tenses to not only fight, but to fuck as well.

"Present the technology," Zaku orders.

Vagan hands Zaku a small metal box. A data collection. An ancient thing left here by aliens. Both this technology and the humans once shaped this world, but for countless years, both have been ours. Times have changed and now the technology is wanted by these humans that have returned from the sky.

I don't care about the technology. I have my den, my

weapon, and enough resources to last me into old age. These trinkets that we are giving the humans is nothing compared to what we keep hidden.

The transport flies past us to land on the clearing behind. Some of the males scatter, readying themselves for the coming hunt.

When the transport opens, the only ones left are me, Zaku, and Vagan.

I will not lose this chance to finally see my female up close.

My fangs drip. A male dressed in a powersuit steps out.

My spine stiffens when another man follows after.

Where are you, little female?

My hands clench.

Then I see her, and my mind blanks.

Want more? Click here!

ALSO BY NAOMI LUCAS

Naga Brides

Viper

King Cobra

Blue Coral

Death Adder (Coming Soon!)

Cyborg Shifters

Wild Blood

Storm Surge

Shark Bite

Mutt

Ashes and Metal

Chaos Croc

Ursa Major

Dark Hysteria

Wings and Teeth

The Bestial Tribe

Minotaur: Blooded

Minotaur: Prayer

Stranded in the Stars

Last Call

Collector of Souls

Star Navigator

Venys Needs Men

To Touch a Dragon

To Mate a Dragon

To Wake a Dragon

Naga (Haime and Iskursu)

Valos of Sonhadra

Radiant

Standalones

Six Months with Cerberus

Printed in Great Britain
by Amazon